# GAME THEORY

# ALSO BY BARRY JONSBERG

# BARRY JONSBERG

# GAME THEORY

**ALLEN&UNWIN**
SYDNEY·MELBOURNE·AUCKLAND·LONDON

First published by Allen & Unwin in 2016

Allen & Unwin – Australia
83 Alexander Street, Crows Nest NSW 2065, Australia
Phone: (61 2) 8425 0100
Email: info@allenandunwin.com
Web: www.allenandunwin.com

Allen & Unwin – UK
Ormond House, 26–27 Boswell Street,
London WC1N 3JZ, UK

A Cataloguing-in-Publication entry is available
from the National Library of Australia www.trove.nla.gov.au.
A catalogue record for this book is available from the British Library.

ISBN (AUS) 978 1 76029 015 3
ISBN (UK) 978 1 74336 876 3

Teachers' notes available from www.allenandunwin.com

Cover & text design by Ruth Grüner
Cover images by R-J-Seymour (iStockphoto), jaroon (iStockphoto),
duncan1890 (iStockphoto), Meplezii_Ck (iStockphoto)
Set in 10.8 pt Minion Regular by Ruth Grüner
Printed in Australia by McPherson's Printing Group

1 3 5 7 9 10 8 6 4 2

For Sonja and Kate Jonsberg

# PROLOGUE

**Clouds part and moonlight steals through my curtains, a silver intruder.**

I sit upright in bed and the gun is clasped in my right hand. I have been in the same position all night; the pillow is rucked against my back and there is a pain in my neck. My hand aches from gripping the gun's handle too hard. I have not slept, though I tried at first.

Killing someone with a gun is not easy. I know this from the research I've done. There are two elements to consider – the physical and the psychological. The psychological poses the most obvious problem. It's one thing to fire at targets on shooting ranges, quite another to point a gun at something built of flesh, blood and mind. This is well known. Even those who hunt animals – people who *enjoy* snuffing the life from a pig or a kangaroo – find it's very different shooting a human being. Look someone in the eyes, point the gun, apply even pressure to the trigger, knowing there is a point when the hammer punches a cap

1

that explodes a charge that propels a bullet that tears and bores through air. Less than a second. Much less than a second, from the finger's tipping-point to the violation of body, metal tunnelling through flesh, destroying all it touches. Everything is cause and effect. But this effect is monumental, far out of proportion to the physical cause. The tiniest of pressures, gentler than a caress. Life ended.

I have never fired a loaded gun. Until today.

Then there is the practicality of death by gunfire, the physics involved. Most people don't consider this because television makes it seem so easy. Television makes everything seem easy. I will admit that a rifle with a scope would be different. So too would an automatic weapon. Press the trigger and bullets stream out. Provided you are holding the weapon somewhere near the target you are bound to do damage. This is why it is the weapon of choice for psychopaths whose demons lead them to school buildings and shopping malls.

I have a hand gun. They are notoriously inaccurate, even if they are of good quality. I suspect mine isn't.

A hand gun kicks, which moves the barrel, which alters the bullet's trajectory. It is very easy to miss. In fact, without practice, it is much easier to miss than hit. I have had no practice. I will have to be close. Close enough to see the widening eyes, to smell the fear. Up close and personal. Many of my hours throughout the night have been occupied with these thoughts. They circle in my head, buzzing like insects.

I swing my legs out of bed and place the gun next to me. My hand is stiff. I hold it up before my eyes and work the fingers, loosening the muscles. It feels like a claw, looks like a claw. Then I stand and walk carefully to the window, draw the curtains. I know my bedroom, know where the boards creak, so I do not make a noise. I look out. Dawn is an hour away. There is the thinnest smear of orange on the horizon. Above, one cloud squats, its white edges dissolving into the blackness of night. It is time to go. It's not the time for my appointment. That is over three hours away. But it's time for me to go.

Before I went to bed I set my clothes out. Dark jeans and a black T-shirt. Black runners. I feel like a cliché but I get dressed anyway. Pulling on the T-shirt, I smell myself and it is sharp, unpleasant. I am tempted to tuck the gun into the waistband of my jeans, in the small of my back, but I settle for pushing the barrel as far down into my right pocket as I can. I check that the safety is on. For the hundredth time. That was another image. The gun going off and shooting me in the leg. It's absurd enough to happen.

It used to be that Summerlee – my older sister – would come home at three or four in the morning and stumble up the stairs, crashing into things, and Mum and Dad would never wake. She would laugh about that. *I was so shitfaced I could barely crawl, and they slept through the whole thing.* Now Dad cannot sleep. If I were to open my door at night, he would be there, eyes wide with fear and looking like death. His hair is grey and thinning by the hour. I imagine him in bed, propped up like I have been all night, staring into nothing and weaving nightmares from it, one hand twitching at the bedcovers. I cannot leave by the door. Not just because of Dad but also because there are two police officers camped in our front room. This is why I left the window open all night; one reason – not the *main* reason – why I didn't sleep.

The backpack is under my bed, the rope attached to its handle. It is heavy and my muscles cramp as I lower it to the ground. Once I feel the weight ease, I drop the rope after it. Then I throw one leg over the sill and reach for the drainpipe with my left hand. I put the other leg out, so I am sitting on my window ledge. The gun is bunched up in my pocket and its heavy bulk is uncomfortable. My bedroom is on the first floor, hence the drainpipe. I am not athletic. It is not in my nature to shin down pipes but I manage without falling. I am relieved I have made it so far without waking anyone.

I stand on the lawn and look around. Bushes and trees crowd me with thick shadows and everything is unfamiliar. I detach the rope from the backpack, which I ease onto my shoulders. I take the gun out of my pocket and tuck it now in the back of my jeans. It is time to go but I am reluctant. It is like the tipping-point of a finger on a trigger. Once I move away from my house, take that first step on the journey, then I will set in motion a train of events leading to one conclusion or another. Cause and effect. I shiver but I am not cold. Somewhere an owl hoots. The sound is mournful and thin. I take the first step and the second is easier, the third easier still. My body moves and my mind is subservient, still and cowardly, happy to let the rhythm of muscles take charge and move me, second by second, to whatever destination awaits.

I walk into the road and turn right. I keep to the track of broken lines in the middle of the street. Everywhere is dark. Everywhere is quiet, except for the soft kiss of rubber soles on tarmac.

Game theory has brought me to this point and I must follow where it leads.

Even though this is not a game.

# PART ONE

Five months earlier...

# CHAPTER 1

'Tell me again.'

'I've told you ten gazillion times.'

'Ten gazillion and sixty.'

'So why do you want to hear it again?'

'To make it ten gazillion and sixty-one.'

'That's not a reason.'

'It is too.'

'Not.'

'Is.'

Phoebe wore the pyjamas I'd bought for her sixth birthday, nearly two years before. They had mathematical equations all over them. $E=mc^2$. The Drake theorem. I'd gone crazy. I had a Fourier series: $f(x) = a_0 + \sum_{n-1}^{\infty}(a_n\cos\frac{n\pi x}{L} + b_n\sin\frac{n\pi x}{L})$ and quadratics: $x = \frac{-b\pm\sqrt{b^2-4ac}}{2a}$. She had no idea what most of them were. Seven years old, okay? But she loved them. I'd bought some plain PJs and taken them to a custom print company, the kind that does corporate logos on work shirts. Each equation was done in a different colour. They'd cost a fortune, but I didn't care. Now she refused to wear anything else at bedtime. Mum had to wash and dry them during the day, so she never missed a night. Phoebe had grown and the material had shrunk, so the sleeves were only just below the elbows and the legs halfway down her calves. It looked like she was preparing for a flood. Some of the equations had faded and the material was pilled, but she still didn't care. Phoebe wasn't interested in mathematics. She liked stories. But she *was* interested in me, her brother, which was why she loved the pyjamas.

She knelt on the bed, her skinny butt on her ankles, and bounced up and down. I loved it when she did that.

'There's this gorgeous princess and her name is Phoebe.'

'Why is she gorgeous?'

'Because she has long, straight hair all down her back.'

'None on her head, just all down her back.'

She liked to beat me to the punchline.

'Am I telling this, princess, or are you?'

'You are.'

'You bet your skinny butt I am.'

'Go on, then.'

'She is so drop-dead gorgeous, so fantastically pulchritud-inous, so "oh-my-god-I-can't-believe-she-is-not-bursting-into-flames-she-is-so-hot" that suitors come from far and wide to beg for her hand.'

'It must be a great hand.'

'It is a fabulous hand, but they want her other bits as well.'

'But mainly the hand.'

'Indeed.' I really wanted to tickle her in the side until she curled into a foetal position and begged for mercy, but I couldn't until I'd finished the story. Phoebe had standards and she had rules. Tickling came later. I folded my legs into a lotus position and rested my chin on interlocked fingers. 'The suitors are reduced to three. Their names are...'

'Luke, Alex and Corey.'

The names changed according to Phoebe's whims. Corey was always there because he was Phoebe's best friend in Grade Three – a strange looking kid with thin hair and a big nose; but there's no accounting for taste. Luke sometimes made an appearance, but Alex was new to me. He must have been nasty to Phoebe at school recently. I filed the information away.

'They decide they'll have a fight and the winner will win Phoebe's hand.'

'And her other bits.'

'Indeed. So they choose their weapons...'

'Rats.'

'What?'

'Rats.'

Phoebe changed the weapons when she felt like it, as well. We'd had guns, bows and arrows, even purses filled with explosives. But rats were new. She wanted a pet for her eighth birthday, which was a couple of months off, so she had become a little obsessed. Mum wasn't keen on the idea, on the reasonable grounds that she didn't want to share the house with a rodent whose sole notion of social skills was to run around a wheel while shitting prodigiously. Phoebe thought this was an entirely *un*reasonable position to take, and often made her views plain.

'Ninja rats,' I agreed. 'When you threw them they latched onto the jugulars of their targets and bit them to death. The thing was, Luke was an expert ninja-rat thrower. He never missed. If he threw a rat three times, it hit three times. Alex was pretty good as well. He hit...'

'Two times out of three.'

'Correct. But poor old Corey. Well, he wasn't great at rat-chucking. He only hit one time out of three. So, the suitors stand at the points of an imaginary equilateral triangle, rats in hand. They are, as a result, an equal distance from each other. Fair's fair. And then Princess Phoebe...'

'The gorgeous Princess Phoebe.'

'The exceptionally gorgeous Princess Phoebe says: "In order to be *really* fair, the suitors must take turns in throwing their rats until only one person remains standing. But they *have* to throw in turn. And, what's more, it's only fair that the worst ninja-rat chucker gets first go."'

'That *is* fair.'

'Indeed. So Corey will go first, followed by Alex, followed by

Luke. If there are still two standing, then they will continue to take turns in that order until only one suitor remains to claim Princess Phoebe's hand. And her other bits.'

'So who should Corey aim at first?'

'That, dear sis, is the question.'

Phoebe bounced up and down on her bed and ran her hands through her hair. This was so cute, I didn't know whether to shit or pick my nose. I didn't do either, just fixed my eyes on hers. She scrunched up her brow in concentration.

'For his first go he should aim at Luke because Luke never ever misses, so if he could get rid of him then that would be brilliant and give him the best chance of claiming the gorgeous Phoebe's hand.'

Phoebe knew the answer because we had been over this on ten gazillion and sixty occasions, but we had to go through the same routine every time.

'Wrong, bozo,' I said. 'Spectacularly wrong. Corey has only one chance in three of killing Luke. Even if he gets super lucky, that leaves Alex to go next and he only has Corey to target. And that means there's a two in three chance of Corey being cactus.'

'I know, I know.' She bounced up and down on the bed again. 'He should aim at Alex.'

'Even worse, bozo,' I said. 'Super spectacularly wrong. If he is really lucky, then Alex is dead and that leaves Luke's turn and he never misses. So Corey is *definitely* cactus.'

'This is dumb.'

'You're dumb.'

'Not.'

'Are too.'

'Tell me.'

'I've just told you. You're dumb.'

'No. Tell me the answer.'

'Okay.' I made as if I was going to shift my position on the bed, but then grabbed her under the armpits and flipped her onto her back. She squealed and tried to kick out at me but I was too quick. I bounced on top of her so she was pinned, my knees in the crook of her elbows, my butt on her scrawny legs. I put my head down so my fringe tickled her face. She thrashed her head from side to side, but she was laughing so hard stringy bits were coming from her nose. 'Yeeuk, gross,' I said. 'You are so gross. You are a gross, dumb bozo.' She was screaming by now but trying to talk at the same time. It came out all strangled.

'But I'm ... also ... gorgeous.'

'Granted,' I said. 'A gorgeous, gross, dumb, bozo princess. Listen up, poo for brains. This is game theory and that means you don't just think about what *you* are going to do, but what *others* will do. That's the point of it. If it was Alex's turn first, who would he shoot at?'

'Luke.'

'Correct, bozo. Because if he doesn't, he's dead. Luke knows that Alex is his biggest threat, so he will shoot him first. If Alex kills Luke then Corey gets the next go and he stands a chance. So what Corey should do is shoot his gun in the air.'

'HIS RAT, poo for brains.'

'Right,' I said. 'His rat. By deliberately missing, he's guaranteeing one of the others will die because they will target each other. Either Luke or Alex is dead and it's Corey's turn next. So he will get the first shot in a duel. It is statistically his best option of getting the hand of the gorgeous Phoebe, not to mention her other bits.'

'And does he?'

'Does he what?'

'Win.'

'I don't know. That's not the point. It's game theory, bozo, not a fairy story.'

'And you call me dumb! You don't even know how the story ends.'

I hopped off and pulled the bedclothes over her. She instantly snuggled down so that just her nose peeped over the blanket. There was a broad, slimy patch on the material where her nasal discharge had found a glistening home. I ruffled her hair and made for the door. I was halfway through when I turned back.

'Okay. Corey *does* win. He wins the gorgeous Phoebe but after a week he finds out that she is a dumb bozo with poo for brains, so he throws his own rat at his own neck. That's how bad she is.'

'He'll miss two times out of three.'

I laughed so hard I nearly got my own nasal discharge.

'I love you, Jamie,' she said as I went to close the door.

'Course you do,' I said. 'You might be dumb but you're not insane.'

# CHAPTER 2

**Summerlee, Jamie and Phoebe.** Maybe it was a private joke between my parents. Maybe they just liked names that ended in the -ee sound. Whatever the reason, it sucked but there's nothing you can do about it.

Phoebe loves Mum and Dad. I tolerate them. Summerlee despises them. Does it always work that way? Someone once said that you start by loving your parents, then you judge them, and rarely, if ever, do you forgive them. It's clever enough to be true. But it's also sad. I don't want Phoebe to grow up and away from them. Up and away from me, too, I guess. Not because of Mum and Dad's feelings or even mine, but because there's something pure and innocent in her love. It doesn't make conditions and it doesn't expect disappointments. At some point we grow into that and I don't know why.

I am a mathematician and I am not comfortable with stories. I'm at a loss for how to tell this tale because words are not what

I'm best at. And you have to use so many of them just to express a simple truth. Maths isn't like that. Take $E=mc^2$, the most famous equation in the world. Five symbols, but they tell a story of the universe and the laws that govern it that would take – *have* taken – volumes and volumes of writing just to scratch its surface. Energy, mass, the speed of light and the relationship between them. It is the story of everything. In five symbols. How concise, how *beautiful*, is that?

There are no symbols to tell Summerlee's story, so I'll have to make do with the clunkiness of words. She is my other sister, eighteen years old. She used to be a stunner, when she was between the ages of about thirteen and sixteen, but in the last couple of years that's changed. She's dyed her hair, for example. It used to be dark and when it caught the sun it would explode with flashes and gleams. Now it is a dull blonde, leached of life. Like straw. Her eyes are like that, too. Not blonde, obviously, but a pale blue that seems to get paler as time passes. Sometimes I think she's being dissolved as a person – all that vibrancy, personality and joy in life has been exposed to some kind of element that's stripped everything away until all that is left is hard, yet brittle. Pale. It is like watching something baking in the sun and dying by degrees.

I can't recall when she changed. It appears a sudden transformation in my memory, but I guess it must have been gradual. I *do* remember one incident that made me realise the sister I knew was somehow lost. She was in Year Ten, about fifteen. I was in Year Eight at the same school. It was breakfast time and I was chowing down on a bowl of cereal, while Mum was getting Phoebe ready for kindy. It was a routine. Dad had normally gone off to work by then. He sorts out people's mortgages which, apparently, involves long hours at an office desk. So Mum was left with three kids to feed, clothe, make presentable and then take to their respective educational institutions. I guess it was a ritual played out across the entire nation. And I also suppose it was a stressful time for Mum. But I was in Year Eight, when other people's stresses, particularly your parents', fly way below your radar.

Phoebe was putting things into her little school bag – God knows what you need for kindy, but she was taking it all very seriously. I had my face in the cereal bowl. Mum was rushing around, as normal.

'Where's your sister?' she asked me. I shrugged. Not my responsibility.

'Still in bed, probably,' I said.

'God damn it,' she muttered. 'Give her a yell, will you?'

'I'm eating breakfast,' I pointed out. I think I even gestured towards my cereal bowl as if presenting incontrovertible evidence. Mum stopped rushing about for a second and looked at me, balancing decisions. Go off at me and create further conflict? Too hard; take the line of least resistance. 'Watch the toast then, Jamie. Will you do that for me?'

'Sure.' Watching didn't expend much energy.

Mum ran to the foot of the stairs and bellowed up them.

'Summerlee! Out of bed. Now. You are going to be late.'

Mum reappeared just as the toast pinged up, which was fine by me. One job less. I returned to my cereal while Mum started spreading marg. She did it with practised efficiency. I took a leisurely spoonful of cornflakes. Phoebe unpacked her bag and started re-packing it. She'd always been fussy, basically as soon as she got out of the womb. Everything had to be just so. I finished breakfast and stuck my bowl into the sink. Mum had tried to get me to wash up as soon as I was done, but I skirted the chore whenever possible.

Mum made sandwiches for all of us. She had to do different batches because we all had different fads. Phoebe was into Vegemite, providing it was the thinnest smear. Sometimes it was difficult to tell there was any on the bread. Waving the pot above the sandwich was probably the way to go. Let a few molecules drift down. I liked cheese and tomato. Well, I told Mum I liked cheese and tomato, but I'd normally dump the sandwich into a bin at school and buy myself a hot dog from the canteen whenever I could afford it. I feel guilty about that now. I didn't then. Summerlee had to have something with meat, preferably salami. Mum sliced, filled and cling-wrapped.

She placed the food into three separate lunch boxes, added a muesli bar each and an apple. I *always* dumped the apple. Then she rushed back to the stairs.

'Summerlee, for God's sake. We are leaving in ten minutes. Get down here now!'

There was some kind of muffled response from upstairs,

followed by considerable thumping and the sound of glass breaking.

'Summerlee!' Mum yelled.

What happened next was not pretty. In fact, it was one of the ugliest things I've ever witnessed, and I have witnessed a few. The thumping sound increased, resolved itself into a girl coming down the stairs. *Forcefully* coming down the stairs. Phoebe stopped packing her bag. I stopped doing whatever I was doing – probably nothing at all. We watched the door to the kitchen. Some kind of energy was approaching. I could feel it on my skin and the sensation was hypnotic.

At some point around the age of thirteen, Summerlee discovered the power of the F-word. In that she was not alone. Where she differed from the rest of us was in understanding that sanctions against the word were essentially worthless. Or rather, most of us knew that swearing was antisocial, that it upset people and was therefore best limited to your mates. I swore constantly around my friends. It was a badge of courage, a ticket into an exclusive club, some kind of passport to adulthood I was experimenting with. But I would never have dreamed of using it to a teacher, for example. Or my parents. Not because of any physical punishment. What could they do to you? But because I wanted to protect their sensibilities, as well as their good opinion of me, which was, still *is*, important. Summerlee didn't recognise that limit on her behaviour. She simply didn't care. So when she appeared at the kitchen door, hair mussed up, in a stupid nightdress pretending to be lingerie, she was something elemental. There was an aura of hostility surrounding her.

'I am fucking sick,' she screamed. 'Why don't you fucking leave me alone?'

Mum had heard the swearing before. She didn't like it, but nothing she'd said or done had made the slightest difference. Dad simply ignored it, like he ignored most things that might lead to conflict. Mortgages didn't shout and he was comfortable with that. Now Mum tried to ignore the swearing as well, as if, in doing so, it would go away on its own. As a tactic, it was doomed.

'You are not sick, Summerlee,' she replied. 'And you *are* going to school.'

One of the reasons I stopped swearing so much around my mates was that after a while it became boring. Worse, it seemed not so much an imitation of adulthood as a permanent emblem of childhood. So I won't record exactly what Summerlee said next, because the language would become tiresome. Suffice it to say she did not utter one sentence, often not one phrase, that didn't contain an expletive. She told Mum that school was a waste of time, that she wasn't going. She also informed my mother that those times when she *had* gone to the front gates, she'd skipped off anyway. The curriculum was dumb, pointless and had nothing to do with the real world. Who needs to know about Australian history or stupid short stories or algebra? The teachers were all losers. The school itself sucked. She was leaving and there was nothing anyone could do about it. No one could force her to stay.

I'm conscious that this listing of points does not sound, in itself, dramatic. I'd made many of them myself over the years. But it was the *manner* in which she made them. Even without the swearing, there was no mistaking the venom of her remarks, like she was tapping into a vast reservoir of bile. And, once tapped, there was no stemming the source. It flowed from her, an incoherent outpouring of hatred. It battered against us.

Phoebe left the room after a minute. I saw tears in her eyes. Like Dad, she hated conflict and ran from it whenever possible. I should have done the same, but I was paralysed. Only later did I think that standing there and listening to Summerlee's rant was a further diminishment of my mother, that it must have been painful for her to know her son had witnessed her impotence in all its heartbreaking detail. But a train wreck is difficult to walk away from. And this *was* a train wreck.

When Summer had spent her rage, she stormed back up the stairs. I watched Mum in the aftermath of the tempest. She hadn't been given the chance to say a word. She wiped her brow and turned back to the chopping board. Took Summerlee's lunch box and put it in the fridge. I swear it was the saddest thing I ever saw her do. Then she hustled me and Phoebe into the car. She drove in silence to kindy, ushered Phoebe through the door, kissed her goodbye. Then it was off to my school. She knew better than to kiss me, so she waved through the car window as I joined my mates in the yard. I waved back, in that self-conscious way that characterises a Year Eight student, before I turned away from her.

One of the kids wanted to show me something, though I've no idea now what it was. I forgot about Mum, didn't see her drive off to whatever world she inhabited. I had my own world and it demanded all my attention.

Looking back now, I know what I should have done. I should have talked, I should have put my arm around her, told her I loved her and that everything would be okay. Even if it wasn't going to be okay. Mum and Dad had been fine with childhood. They did all the right things, read us stories at bedtime, mopped our brows when we got sick, were fiercely protective and wrapped us in unconditional love. The problems arrived with adolescence, when their sweet children underwent a metamorphosis and emerged as strangers. And one of those strangers was hateful. The other was simply distant. Dad retreated, bunkered down at work. Mum was confused, hurt and powerless. I might have helped her. I didn't.

Summerlee never went back to school, not properly. She turned up to some classes in a fitful way, got into trouble because of her attitude, was suspended on numerous occasions. This struck me as monumentally stupid since her attendance was running at about twenty per cent anyway, so it obviously wasn't a punishment. Eventually, she got a job at a local supermarket, stacking shelves. Naturally, she hated it and thought it beneath her. Her immediate boss, it transpired, was a moron.

Then she met Spider and her troubles really started.

# CHAPTER 3

**Here's the thing.**

Picking up highlights, or lowlights, of Summerlee's behaviour tells a story, but it doesn't tell the *whole* story. Three or four years out of eighteen cannot be truly representative of who she is. You see, beneath the facial piercing, the one visible tattoo, the dyed hair and the uncompromising make-up, there is a kernel of the kid she was and the adult she can still be. She is all style, Summerlee, but the style is something she occasionally hides behind; a mask, not always worn convincingly.

So here's another story, this time only six months back, and maybe it will redress a balance.

Phoebe was involved in a dance performance at primary school. It was part of a broader show that the school was putting on to mark their twenty-fifth anniversary. Parents and local dignitaries were invited one Friday afternoon for drinks, nibbles and a demonstration of the school's talent. It was a big deal, and Phoebe was heavily into big deals. She was almost sick with anticipation. Every time we sat down to dinner we were regaled with stories about rehearsals, what the teacher had said about the routine, the mistakes that the troupe were desperately trying to correct. Beneath all the nervous chatter was a sense of terror at the ordeal ahead. Phoebe did not want to screw up, but was terrified she would. So she did what she always did when she was nervous. She worked and worked and worked. It was her belief that disasters could be averted, provided you expended enough sweat.

I used to believe that myself. I know better now.

Part of Phoebe's frantic determination to avoid crashing and burning involved constant private rehearsal, normally in our front room after dinner and after she had finished her home-work. Sometimes I would watch and offer the occasional murmur of praise. But you can't fool some kids and you could *never* fool Phoebe. She understood that what I was offering was emotional support, but she wanted more than that. She needed help.

Summerlee gave it to her.

She spent hours watching Phoebe, and she didn't just tell her she was good when she wasn't. I'd do that all the time, partic-ularly since, even to my inexpert eye, Phoebe *wasn't* any good. She had no sense of timing, for one thing. She would put the music on – Phoebe had got Mum to buy the dance music the school would be using – and then she would go through the routine, time after time. I tried telling her that she needed the other kids there, that doing it by yourself wasn't ideal because she couldn't follow leads. Phoebe understood and acknowledged the point, but it was herself she was most concerned about. She worried she would let the rest of the troupe down and any work she could do in advance would help avoid that embarrassment. I couldn't see the plan working. Phoebe *didn't* get any better, despite her best efforts. I've got two left feet myself, so I understood. If you're just naturally shit at something, no amount of practice will make you significantly better. Phoebe tried to *force* her body to make the right moves, rather than relying upon a natural timing she simply didn't possess. When all was said and done, Phoebe was just crap at dancing.

'You're not doing that side shuffle properly,' said Summerlee. 'You need to take two steps, like this.' She showed her. Summer *did* have natural rhythm. 'See? Go with the beat. At the moment, you are *off* the beat. Listen to the music, mouse, and let your body react to it.'

Phoebe tried again. I couldn't see any improvement, but Summer nodded.

'Yeah, better,' she said. 'Do it once more time and remember your arms. You're concentrating so much upon what your feet are doing, you're forgetting everything else.'

I left them to it. To be honest I wasn't that interested and I felt like a fifth wheel, anyway. But *they* didn't give up. When I came down from my bedroom an hour and a half later, I heard them through the door. Summer was saying, 'Don't forget your arms, mouse. Think about your arms and listen to the music…' She showed patience to her sister that had never been extended to me.

The day of the show arrived and Phoebe was up at some ludicrous hour. I'm not sure she'd slept at all. When I came down for breakfast, she was trying on her costume in the kitchen.

'Yo, poo for brains,' I said. 'The big day, huh?'

Phoebe frowned.

'Does my bum look big in this, Jamie?' she asked. 'I want the truth.'

It was just as well I'd had a pee as soon as I woke, because I might've pissed myself on the spot. But I knew better than to laugh. Phoebe would have disembowelled me with one stare. There's a gene in our family responsible for that, but it's limited to the female side. So I put a finger to my lips and looked her up and down, all serious.

'Turn around,' I said.

The costume was like a fist in a black eye. She had on a tight top, a bit like a singlet, but made of something similar to spandex. It was bright green and covered in glittery specks. In fact, *all* of the costume was covered in glittery specks. A little gold flouncy skirt and red tights completed the outfit. I have no idea what it was meant to represent, but it was in appalling taste. Phoebe gave me a small twirl. She was stick thin, like so many kids her age, chest a narrow tube, legs resembling bamboo poles. It was difficult to spot her bum, it was that small.

'Nah, all good,' I said, after a suitable pause. 'You look hot as.'

'Thanks,' she said. 'I'm just going into the front room to have one last practice.'

'Do *not* put the music on loud,' I said. 'You wake Summer and she's going to make you regret it for the rest of your life.'

'Okay.'

I ate breakfast to the muted sound of bad dance music. I was a little worried. This performance was so important to her and I had a niggling suspicion it was all going to turn out disastrously.

**Dad could not get any time off work, though he said he tried.** But Summer had rearranged her shift at the supermarket and Mum picked me up directly after my last lesson of the day, so we all met up at Phoebe's school. The place was buzzing. There were hundreds of parents there, obviously, but they'd also dragged out various dignitaries, including the mayor and a selection of local members of parliament and even a past student who had made the final of *Australia's Got Talent* a couple of years back. She'd been eliminated early on, but she was the closest we had to a celebrity in the area. Some of the little kids were scrambling around her trying to get an autograph. They had no idea who she was, but there was a kind of hysteria going on.

Tiny tackers in school uniform ushered all the guests into the auditorium and we took our seats. First up was the *Talent* finalist, who sang the national anthem. Badly. Then there was an address by the school principal, who told us how proud she was of the students, and threw in an appeal for volunteers for School

Council. This was followed by a brief but enthusiastic opening of ceremonies by the mayor, who gave way to the local MP, the shadow minister for education. He droned on about something forever, while people in the audience shuffled in their seats and muttered. The pollie stopped when it became clear we were on the verge of storming the podium and possibly running him out of town, tarred and feathered on a pole.

Finally, the show got under way. Five hundred camcorders started to whir and there was so much flash photography it was like we were caught in a violent electrical storm.

Phoebe's routine was second, after a discordant warm-up by a bunch of kids on recorders. I remembered playing the recorder when I was in primary. I couldn't get anything other than a screech either. Then the oh-so-familiar dance music started up and seven or eight kids filed onto stage. Phoebe was second from the right. I glanced over at Mum. She had her hand to her mouth and there were creases around her eyes. I saw my own fears reflected in her face. It is so hard watching someone you love on the brink, possibly, of showing her arse to the world. An arse that would be recorded by countless camcorders and frozen forever in dozens of digital hard drives. Summer, on the other hand, was smiling and relaxed. I watched her nod encouragement at her sister, despite there being no chance Phoebe could see it. *Please God*, I thought. *Let this go well. If this goes well, I might even start believing in you.*

Well, there is no God, apparently.

It wasn't that Phoebe was any worse than the rest of them. As far as I could tell, there was only one kid who knew what she was doing and six or seven who were making it up as they went along. It was great, actually. I mean, who needs flawless choreography in a primary school dance? It's just kids leaping around and having fun. Except that Phoebe wasn't having fun. I could tell. She kept glancing at her fellow dancers and trying to match their steps. Unfortunately, their steps were all over the place as well, so it kind of degenerated into an aimless thrashing about (apart from the one kid who was keeping time. I bet *her* parents had their camcorder focused entirely on her. Maybe they edited out the rest of the group later). The more Phoebe's rhythm, which was almost non-existent to start with, went awry, the more her body stiffened and the worse it got. But it was the ending that really fell apart. Literally.

The way it *should* have gone, I imagined, was that all of the kids finished on one knee, in a line, left hand raised towards the audience at the moment the last chord sounded. There was never any chance of that. The final note sounded and the one dancer in the group slid gracefully into position. The rest followed, at their own pace. Two had their right hands raised, three their left and Phoebe had apparently forgotten that part entirely. Because of the mingling around, intentional or otherwise, Phoebe was now on the extreme right of the line. She teetered on one skinny knee, lost her balance and lurched to her right. It was almost like those scenes in the movies where it all happens in slow-mo. If she'd gone to her left, it might have turned out okay. But she hit the kid next to her, who in turn lurched and knocked the next in line. The dominoes tumbled. I heard a gasp from Mum and general laughter from the audience. It wasn't nasty laughter. I could tell. It was laughter that expressed a kind of joy at the gaucheness of kids. It was affectionate.

But Phoebe didn't see it like that. She glanced along the row of fallen soldiers, a look of horror spreading across her features. Then she scrambled to her feet and ran from the stage, face buried in her hands. There was wild applause from the audience, but Mum and I were too stunned to clap.

Summer pushed past me.

'C'mon, Jamie,' she said. I got to my feet instinctively and followed as she moved down the side aisle towards stage. Mum stayed in her seat.

'Where are we going?' I asked.

'To mend a broken heart,' she said over her shoulder. 'So you shut the fuck up and leave the talking to me.'

It wasn't difficult getting backstage. A teacher pointed out Phoebe, sitting by herself in the furthest corner and sobbing. I have to admit, my heart clenched. There is almost nothing worse in this world than the unhappiness of children. Summer made a beeline towards her, and got down on her haunches.

'Hey, mouse,' she said. 'What's with the tears?'

Phoebe took her hands away from her face. Her eyes were puffy and her mouth twisted in a strange, distorted shape. She wore her misery for everyone to see. She tried to say something but all that came out was a mangled wail. Summer rubbed her back, brushed away a strand of her hair and waited.

'I messed up,' said Phoebe finally.

'No,' replied Summerlee. There was sternness in her voice. 'That is *not* true, Phoebe. You *fucked* up. Right royally.' Phoebe's face twisted again. 'But it was *brilliant* and no one noticed. Only me and that was because I knew how it was supposed to finish. Did you hear that applause at the end? Did you?'

Phoebe stopped crying long enough to register confusion.

'What do you mean?'

Summer took her hand, held it in a firm grip.

'What do I mean, mouse? What do I mean? I mean that the planned ending sucked big time. It was boring. All that on-one-knee shit, with the stupid hand in the air. *Yawn*. What you did – and I know you didn't mean it – was turn it into something fantastic. With all of you lying in a row across the stage. *That* was the ending the routine needed. Just like in a ballet. And *you* did it, mouse. You did it. It was great. Wasn't it great, Jamie?'

'Absolutely,' I said. 'Artistically, it was...perfect.'

'Really?' said Phoebe. I almost cried then. Maybe you *can* fool kids, even Phoebe, when the incentive for believing a lie is strong enough. 'Cross your heart and hope to die?'

'Swear!' said Summerlee. She put a hand on her heart. 'I am so proud of you, mouse. That applause. The audience loved it. They loved *you*.'

Phoebe turned to me. Tears were drying on her face, leaving pale track marks.

'Do you swear as well, Jamie?'

I followed Summerlee's example and put a hand over my heart.

'You were fantastic, poo for brains,' I said. 'I'm bursting with pride. True.'

And when Phoebe smiled I knew Summer had done what she'd set out to do. She'd mended her sister's broken heart and I loved her for it.

What a pity she was a total twat the rest of the time.

# CHAPTER 4

**My best friend is Gutless Geraghty.** It's not his real name, obviously, but it's what everyone calls him. His proper first name is Sean, but I only know that because he's my mate.

Most people assume the name 'Gutless' is a cruel and ironic joke, since he is anything but. It hangs over his pants and encircles his waist, a huge and wobbly doughnut of fat. Gutless is a gamer. He spends nearly all his leisure time on the computer, firing at endless ranks of disturbingly Asian-looking soldiers with vast supplies of similarly disturbing weapons. Occasionally, he takes time out from cyber-slaughter and stuffs thick-crust pizza into his mouth, washed down with Coke. Most times, he does both simultaneously. He is a walking cliché. But, according to Gutless, this is not how he came by his nickname. He told me the story once.

It seems Gutless was a large boy from the get-go. In primary school he was an imposing figure, teased because of his size but feared for the same reason. His parents, worried he was turning into a human blimp, tried to impose enforced exercise and en-rolled him in a junior rugby team. The coach, understanding that Gutless was unlikely to display an impressive turn of speed, placed him in defence where his physical stature would inspire fear and trepidation in the opposition. It was a sound strategy, but unfort-unately there was one flaw. Gutless was a coward. He hated – he *still* hates – physical conflict, which is ironic since he dishes out so much of it on the computer screen. In the first training session, a whippet-like ten-year-old ran through the pack and bore down on the try line. Gutless, understanding *something* was expected of him in this situation, lumbered over to the touchline and made like an immovable object. The boy, to his credit, did not turn to jelly at the prospect of colliding with something the size and consistency of a brick shithouse, but straight-armed Gutless, who fell to the ground with a wail and had to be carried from the field. It took four of his teammates to achieve this.

'You're gutless, Geraghty,' said the coach in the dressing room afterwards. 'Totally gutless.' This was probably not the most politically sensitive remark to make (or, indeed, brilliantly motivational), but the name stuck. According to Gutless, he took his belly in both hands and jiggled it, to the considerable amuse-ment of the assembled players.

'And you're blind, coach,' he said.

I have my doubts about the accuracy of the last bit. It sounds like something you *wish* you'd said. But, anyway, Gutless's parents accepted defeat and didn't try to get him to do sports again. For which Gutless was grateful. But the name stayed, even when the story that inspired it had faded from memory.

In fact, most teachers called him Gutless.

**I mention this because I want to throw the preparation for Summerlee's eighteenth birthday party into sharp relief.** I said Gutless was my best friend. I neglected to mention that this is because he's my *only* friend. Oh, I know plenty of kids at school and get along fine with them. We chat and laugh and hang out at recess and lunchtime. It's not like I'm reclusive or that there's anything seriously wrong with me. But I don't spend any time with them *after* school. I just don't see the point.

Women are different. They make loads of friends and each one, apparently, would lay down their life for you at the drop of a hat. They hug, they wail, they chat, they gossip, they cry, they bitch, they pour out the deepest secrets of their emotional lives to each other. *All* the time. Hell, Phoebe does it and she's not even eight yet. I talk to Gutless about video games and mathematics. He'd shut down if I tried to bring up feelings. Maybe bring up an Error 404 message. And I wouldn't blame him.

Summerlee spent two months preparing for her eighteenth birthday party and it cost Mum and Dad a fortune. They'd offered to pay as a part of their present, but I didn't think they had anticipated Summer wanting something a Hollywood actor might consider excessive. She booked a club in the city and Dad put a thousand bucks on the bar – just for wine and beer.

The guests would have to buy their own spirits. But that was only the tip of the iceberg. There was a DJ to pay for and decorations and flowers to arrange. Mum was for doing that part of it herself, but Summer insisted on employing an event organiser who stinted on nothing, especially her own fee. As the bills came in, Dad's face got gloomier, but there was nothing he could do apart from get out the chequebook and eye the bank balance nervously on the internet.

Summerlee invited two hundred friends. I heard later that Dad's thousand-buck bar tab lasted all of fifteen minutes. She didn't invite me. She didn't even invite Mum and Dad on the grounds that she was eighteen and it would be desperately sad to have your parents at a party. They were a bit depressed at her decision, not because they wouldn't see how their money was being spent, but because she was their daughter and they wanted to share her big day, if only for an hour or two. Summer vetoed it.

Spider was going to play at the club with his band. He even had the nerve to charge Mum and Dad two hundred bucks for the gig. He told them *he'd* be happy to do it for nothing, but the other band members needed to pay bills, so they stumped up.

Spider. What a dick! He had a wispy, pathetic moustache and a face pocked with old acne scars. I never found out his real name. Probably Brian or something. But what kind of wanker would choose the name 'Spider'? Well, Spider, it seems, was exactly that kind of wanker.

He'd been Summer's boyfriend for two years. It was as if

she'd deliberately gone out to find a partner who would piss off her parents, not to mention her brother. He was unemployed, obviously. Well, he *said* he was employed as a musician (a bass player in a band that never got bookings because they were shit. I'd heard them practising and they were woeful). But this alleged employment apparently didn't stop him claiming the dole, which he spent on cannabis and whatever other drugs he could get his hands on. I rarely saw him when he wasn't stoned. Actually, I rarely saw him, which suited me down to the ground.

Two days before Summer's birthday she came into the front room. I was sitting in Dad's big leather recliner chair, reading a maths book. She harrumphed and I peered at her over the pages.

'Come to tell me you've changed your mind, Summer?' I said. 'That I am now officially invited to your eighteenth as the guest of honour?'

'Get real, Jamie,' she said. 'You'd hate it.'

She was right, but I would have liked to have been asked, anyway. There's nothing worse than being denied the opportunity to decline on your own terms.

'So to what do I owe the pleasure?' I said.

'I need your advice.'

I was surprised. I was more than surprised. I was stunned. Summerlee hadn't asked my advice for years. Actually, I don't think she had *ever* asked my advice. Normally our only interaction was me smiling at her and her grimacing like I was something unpleasant she had just stepped in.

'Sure.'

'I'm buying tickets for the lotto on my birthday. It's a rollover jackpot and I'll be eighteen, so I thought what the hell. So what are good lotto numbers to get? I thought you might know, being the hot-shit mathematician and all.'

'Are you serious?'

'Do I look like I'm joking?'

She didn't. Summerlee never looked like she was joking, not anymore. It was one aspect of her tragedy.

'It's random, Summer,' I said. To my credit I did not sigh. At least I think I didn't. 'There are no "good" numbers to get. Do what everyone else does. Birthdays, favourite numbers, whatever. Your odds are the same whatever you choose. Better still, get the computer to do it for you. What are they called? Lucky picks?'

She shifted her weight, cocked her hip, put one hand on it and gazed at me through impossibly long and dark eyelashes. They were impossible because they were fake. Contempt oozed from every pore. She made as if to leave and I suspected that would be it as far as sibling communication was concerned for the foreseeable future.

'I can tell you what numbers *not* to choose, though,' I added. That stopped her.

'Whaddya mean?'

I settled back into my chair. There weren't many occasions when she was keen to hear what I said – hell, there weren't *any* occasions – and I was enjoying myself.

'Game theory,' I said after a suitable pause. 'What other people do must affect what you do.'

'Meaning?'

'Let's say the jackpot is fifty million and your numbers come up. Fantastic. But then you have to share that money with whoever else has come up with the same numbers.'

'Yeah. So?'

'So let's say there are fifty winners in total. That leaves you with one mill as your share. Not bad, but not as good as fifty. Nothing like as good.'

She twirled her hand, encouraging me to get to the point.

'So what some people do,' I continued, 'is choose numbers that no one else in their right minds would choose, numbers that are outrageously unlikely to come up, even though statistics tell us that every combination is as likely as any other.'

'Fuck's sake, Jamie. Get to the point.'

'So they choose something like 1, 2, 3, 4, 5 and 6. They work on the principle that if those numbers come up, then they won't have to share the jackpot with anyone, because who would think of 1, 2, 3, 4, 5 and 6? Instead of a measly one mill, they snag the whole pot.'

Summerlee raised her extravagant eyebrows.

'What dumb fuck would choose those numbers? There's no chance of them coming up.'

'Wrong. They have exactly the same chance of coming up as 10, 13, 27, 28, 39 and 41. Or any other combination. It's all about not sharing what you win.'

'And so that's a good idea, is it?'

'No. It's a really bad idea,' I said. 'It's a spectacularly bad idea.'

She did the hand-twirling bit again.

'At any given time there are probably a couple of hundred people in the country who choose 1, 2, 3, 4, 5 and 6 precisely because they think no one else will choose them. I tellya. I would love it if those numbers *did* come up because those greedy bastards would only get a quarter of a million, rather than the fifty mill they'd be expecting. Can you imagine how pissed off they'd be?'

'So what're you saying? Don't choose 1 to 6?'

'That's exactly what I'm saying.'

'Well, thanks for nothing, Jamie, 'cos I wasn't going to choose them anyway. You'd have to be a dumb fuck.'

'Yeah, but at least you now know *why* you'd be a dumb fuck.'

'For someone who's supposed to be so smart, you really are a dick, you know?'

'I aim to please.'

I didn't try to stop her when she made to go this time. But she stopped at the door, anyway.

'What were those other numbers you said?'

'Which?'

'When you were telling me not to pick the dumb fuck numbers. 10, 13, whatever.'

'It was just an example.'

'Yeah, but they sounded good. Write 'em down for me, willya?'

I sighed. This time I sighed. But I took a piece of paper anyway and wrote them down: 10, 13, 27, 28, 39, 41. Was that it? I couldn't remember, but it didn't make any difference. I gave her the paper and she slipped it into her jeans' pocket.

'Good luck,' I said, but she left without replying.

# CHAPTER 5

Gutless invited me round to his place on the Saturday of Summerlee's birthday. I had nothing else to do. He wanted to show me a new video game he'd bought. Gamers never say 'computer games'. They say 'video games'. It must be cool to be retro in the world of hardcore gamers. To be honest, I'm not the slightest bit interested in computer games. I tried to be. Throughout the early years of high school, you didn't really have a social life in the playground unless you were. But I never got into them. They were okay to while away a few hours, but then I got bored. I found it difficult to understand how someone like Gutless could spend days, *weeks* on the damn things with virtually no breaks. He told me there were others worse than him. He knew someone in Canada (Gutless knows lots of people around the world. Well, he knows them in a *virtual* sense) who wouldn't even leave his computer to take a piss. He had his mother collect all these bottles and he would piss in them and leave them around his bedroom, just so he didn't have to walk down the corridor and be away from his screen. And the really great thing was that his mother *would* collect the bottles and empty them for him. And bring them back, presumably, so he could start it all over again. I asked Gutless what his friend did when he needed a shit, but Gutless didn't know. Just as well. I don't think I *wanted* to know.

Gutless invited me to stay for dinner and that was fine by me. His mum was a good cook and, being well aware of her son's waistline, dished up huge quantities. We ate in Gutless's bedroom, of course, on the grounds that time around a dinner table, eating with the family, was time wasted when you could be blowing things up. I didn't mind that too much, even though Gutless's bedroom smelled of mouldy pizza, festering underwear and old farts. I didn't mind because his dad was a bit of a dick and would try to get my opinions on politics and current affairs. Gutless didn't expect anything from me and I was cool with that.

'Don't you ever make your bed, Gutless?' I asked, looking around the darkened wasteland. He never opened his curtains but even in the murk I could make out rumpled bedclothes, an assortment of dirty dishes and a small collection of Coke cans scattered on the carpet.

'What's the point? I'm sleeping in it later on.'

'Fair enough.' At least he stopped gaming to sleep. Did he dream about crosshairs and exploding heads?

I tried to find a place on the bed to stretch out while Gutless booted up his computer. I shifted a dinner plate from where a pillow might have rested if it hadn't fallen onto the floor. Something brown and congealed was smeared on the plate. God knows what it had been, but there were tinges of green around the edges. I wondered how long it had laid there. We might have been talking weeks. Life was thriving in Gutless's bedroom. It just wasn't the kind of life I'd be happy sharing *my* pit with.

The big G himself plopped down in his computer chair and stuck on his headphones, leaving one ear exposed, the better, I imagined, to gather my responses to his gaming wisdom. That was fine by me. I didn't normally listen to him anyway, but just grunted at regular intervals. What I'd do is watch the huge flatscreen TV that he had permanently turned on in the corner of his room. That is one thing about Gutless. He doesn't stint when it comes to electronic gadgetry. He has more stuff than an average JB Hi-Fi store. State-of-the-art computer gear, five-hundred-dollar earphones, a gaming mouse he proudly told me cost nearly three hundred bucks, as well as console machines, TVs and other things that wouldn't have looked out of place in NASA headquarters. Well, assuming NASA had no problems with dinner plates that were growing their own bacterial cultures and bedding that hadn't been washed in living memory.

I avoided the centre of the bed. I couldn't see clearly and I sure as hell didn't want to look, but I reckoned the odds were good that I'd be lying in some stain or other. Then I'd start to wonder where the stain came from and it's a short step from that to asking if I could take a hot shower. So I lay along the edge where

I could see the TV over Gutless's right shoulder. There was some desperately sad game show on. The sound was turned down, but that didn't matter to me. Those kinds of shows are much better when they are muted.

'Dude,' he said. 'You have got to check out the size of the maps on this video game. They're at least half as big again as *Insurgency Max*, or *District 19, The Revenge*. We are talking fucking huge. Shit-hot graphics, as you'd expect, and up-to-date weapons shit. Based on some of the latest developed in the States. Hey, some of these guns aren't even used in the actual military yet. Plus, a bigger range of vehicles. Look, I've messed around with that capture-the-flag shit, but the real good stuff is in the death matches. Now, I know what you're going to say…'

I was glad he knew, because I had no idea. On the TV screen some guy with impossibly white teeth and exceptionally bad hair was charming the hell out of an old woman with brown teeth and equally bad hair. She looked like just being in the game show host's presence was a validation of her existence. *Take me now, Lord, at the pinnacle of my happiness.* I hate television, but it can be entertaining. Especially when the sound is muted.

'…it all depends on the quality of your team. Shit, man. I got myself into this team of complete fucking noobs last night. I made this head shot and they're all like, whoa, that was fucking great, man, and I'm like, yeah, it would be to you bunch of dicks 'cos you have no fucking idea what you're doin'…'

I let his voice drone on. It's better that way. Sometimes I fall

**47**

asleep for fifteen minutes or so and Gutless never notices. I wake up and he's still talking. I'm like that dinner plate. I could be there in three weeks and going green around the edges and he probably still wouldn't notice. I love Gutless. If he didn't exist I'd have to invent him.

The game show ended and there was a news report. Some blonde chick only about four years older than me was staring at the cameras and looking all serious. She was probably talking about the latest crisis in the Middle East and giving the impression she'd been studying this shit for years and was some kind of expert. Seriously. About twenty. I know a number of twenty year olds. They couldn't find their own arseholes with a torch, let alone the Middle East on a world map.

Watching the news with the sound off is much better than listening to it. I like to work out when the fun human-interest stories come on. The face of the presenter normally changes from this-is-serious-shit-so-I've-got-a-serious-expression-on to a broad smile. Occasionally, I get it wrong. She smiles and then a picture comes up in the background of people dying in some third-world country. What can I say? I've got to play some kind of game while Gutless is occupied with his.

I almost didn't notice the lotto numbers on the bottom of the screen. But it must have been the mathematician in me, picking up on patterns. They seemed familiar, which was weird. Just as I was *really* paying attention, the numbers disappeared and I didn't catch the last three. Something came up instead about

**48**

oil futures, whatever they are. I tried to put it out of my mind. It always seems to happen with lotto numbers. When they come up, they appear an obvious winning combination. 12, 18, 37, 38, 39, 45. *Of course. What else could they be?* But I couldn't rid myself of a nagging thought.

'Gutless?' I said, interrupting him in full flow.

'What?'

'Are you on the internet?'

'Duh, dude. It's an online game.'

'Okay. Could you check the lotto numbers for me, please?' I could have used my phone but it's pre-paid and I was low on credit.

Gutless took his eyes away from the screen and gave me an incredulous look.

'I'm in the middle of a death match, man. Can't it wait?'

'I guess,' I said. 'How long?'

'Well, shit...' His screen exploded with flashes of light and the sound of panicked voices dribbled from one headphone earpiece. Gutless turned back to his computer and the barrel of a machine gun loomed up in the screen's foreground. I waited while he did whatever needed to be done. This appeared to involve crawling through a realistic swamp, bursts of gunfire, considerable swearing and even more smoke. At one stage, the machine gun dipped out of sight and a hand grenade appeared briefly. A flash of light and an explosion followed. It was incredibly loud and I was getting only half the sound effects. God knows how

Gutless's ears were dealing with the strain, but I reckoned he'd be stone deaf by the age of thirty.

Anyway, I returned my eyes to the television and tried to get the numbers up again in my mind: 10, 13 and 27. I was sure of those. And now I knew why they seemed so familiar. The numbers I'd given Summerlee. I'd just made them up on the spot, but I thought they were the first three.

Eventually, Gutless must have succeeded in wiping out sufficient of the enemy because the noise abated and he half-turned in his chair.

'Lotto, man? You serious?' I nodded. He turned back to the screen and brought up a small Google window, though the game continued in the background. He typed a few letters, selected from the drop-down options and within twenty seconds, the numbers were on the screen. I sat on the side of his bed and peered over his shoulder.

10, 13, 27, 28, 39, 41. Supplementary numbers 7, 21.

I couldn't remember. Not exactly. But I was pretty damn sure she had most of those. If she had bothered to get the ticket at all, of course. She hadn't mentioned it to me again. I pulled out my mobile phone and excused myself from Gutless's bedroom. I don't think he heard or noticed me leaving. His bedroom is close to the back door, so I slipped out into the garden. The last thing I wanted to do was run into his old man. He'd probably want my opinion on Syria, and unfortunately I didn't have one.

Summer's number is in my phone, even though I never call her and she never calls me. I pressed to connect. Her phone rang for what seemed like ages and I was sure it would divert to message bank, but then she picked up.

'Hello?'

The noise was horrendous. Of course. Summer's eighteenth birthday do was never going to be a quiet affair. I wondered if her two hundred mates had drunk themselves into oblivion and spread wall-to-wall vomit around the public conveniences. How can anyone have two hundred mates? I've got one, Gutless, and he probably doesn't even count. It will be a sad occasion, my eighteenth birthday. Me and Gutless in a pizza place, him talking about video games and me wondering where my life had gone wrong.

'Summer?'

'Who the fuck's this?' She was bellowing into the phone, competing with a song in the background that could loosen your fillings. At least it wasn't Spider's band. This had a semblance of harmony.

'It's me. Jamie.'

'Who?'

'JAMIE.'

'Jamie?'

'Yes.'

I was glad I hadn't been invited. If this was the quality of conversation you could expect on Summer's big day, then I was better off talking to Gutless. At least I could hear him, even though I didn't want to.

'Whaddya want?'

'Did you get lotto tickets for tonight's draw?'

'WHAT?'

'Lotto tickets. Did you get them?'

'I can't hear you.'

'Never mind.'

'WHAT?'

What a waste of the little credit I had. I hung up. She had them or she didn't. It was unlikely she'd have them on her person, anyway, even if she *had* bought them. When she'd left home with Spider, she'd been wearing something tiny, tight and flimsy. Lotto tickets had nowhere to hide.

I went back into Gutless's bedroom. I was right. He hadn't noticed I'd gone. I lay down on the bed again and closed my eyes. Those numbers. They rang bells. They rang very loud bells.

# CHAPTER 6

**Sunday.** Normally, Summer would have to work but she'd had a word with the supervisor and rearranged her shift. This was undoubtedly wise. I hadn't heard her come in, but I guessed it wouldn't have been much before three or four. When Summer parties, she parties hard. And she'd have a hangover with a long half-life. I guessed it would be late afternoon before anyone would see her.

Phoebe had had her breakfast hours before I made my appearance downstairs. She gets up at sparrow fart, while I like to have some kind of sleep-in on the weekend. She was in the front room doing homework. I think Phoebe does homework even when it hasn't been set.

'Yo, poo for brains,' I said. 'How are you?'

She lifted her head from the exercise book and gazed at me blankly for a moment or two. She gets so into homework that returning to the real world can take a moment or two.

'What?'

'Did you sleep well, or did you make a few mistakes?' I said.

'I slept great until Summerlee came in.'

'What time was that?'

'Dunno. Really, really late. Or really, really early.'

'Made a lot of noise, huh?'

'No, but she *stinks* when she's been drinking. I mean, she *stinks*. She's all sweaty and then she sleeps with her mouth open and everything and that just spreads the stink further. It takes like about two seconds for our bedroom to get filled up with this smell of sweat and booze and it just stinks.'

Her little mouth was set in a thin line. I could see what she'd be like in ten years' time and, boy, you wouldn't want to be on the receiving end of her disapproval. I felt sorry in advance for her boyfriend, the poor bastard.

'I think you're trying to tell me something, Phoebe,' I replied. 'Reading the subtext, I think you are trying to suggest Summerlee stinks.'

'It's not funny, Jamie.'

'No. You're right.'

'So why are you laughing?'

'I'm not.'

'You are.'

'Only a bit.'

Phoebe returned to her exercise book. She printed something carefully, methodically, onto the pages, the tip of her tongue peeking from the corner of her mouth. 'She snores as well,' she added.

I cracked up then, which didn't please Phoebe at all. She made me leave, so I went to my bedroom and started up my computer. It's a bit of a sad machine when you compare it to Gutless's. It doesn't have a clear case and flashing lights within. It doesn't have the design style of something taken from the flight deck of the starship *Enterprise*. It's dark and box-like, but it works, which is the only thing I care about. I checked the lotto website, just to confirm the numbers. The site had been updated and showed the number of winners: four division-one winners, each receiving seven million, five hundred thousand dollars. Division two was way down at eleven grand because there were so many winners, but still, let's be honest, better than a poke in the eye with a burnt stick. I confess I was a little excited. Summer was going to get something. Shit, four numbers paid sixty bucks and I was pretty damn sure she had four. Assuming she'd bought the tickets. I closed the site and shut down the computer. I had homework of my own. English and maths. Hmmm. Tricky decision. I got out my maths textbook and turned to a section on deductive geometry.

**Summer surfaced at four in the afternoon.** She edged her way down the stairs as if every step was torture. Turned out it was. When she got down she stood for a minute or so, holding the banister for support, then oozed into the kitchen and sat at the table. A small moan issued from her mouth and she put her face into her hands.

'Afternoon, Summer,' I said. 'Good night, was it?'

She moaned again. It was music to my ears and I adopted an even cheerier tone.

'Sounded like good times when I rang you,' I added. 'The place must have been hopping.'

'Stop shouting, Jamie,' she whispered through her fingers. 'Please?'

'I'm not shouting, sis,' I said, though I confess my decibel count might have been slightly higher than normal. 'Drank a bit too much, huh?'

'Shitfaced,' she groaned.

'Alcohol,' I said. 'The work of the cursing class.'

'Stop shouting. Please.'

I'd been looking forward to tormenting her, but it wasn't as satisfying as I'd anticipated. She *did* look like hell. Her hair was knotted and lank at the same time. When she lifted her face from her hands I would, under normal circumstances, have pissed myself. It was obvious she hadn't removed her make-up before collapsing into bed. She'd probably been *incapable* of removing her make-up. Mascara was spread all around her eyes and down her right cheek. She'd lost her false lashes on one eye, which gave her a lopsided look. It was a situation ripe for ridicule, but I couldn't bring myself to do it. She was so vulnerable. The night before had kicked her senseless and I didn't have the heart to add my own boot-print. Instead, I got up and went to the fridge. I poured a glass of orange juice and then took two paracetamol from the kitchen cabinet. I placed them on the table.

'You need some vitamin C, sis,' I said. 'And pain relief.'

She groaned, but took the tablets and washed them down with the OJ. She grimaced and I suspected her mouth must have had the texture and consistency of the bottom of a bird cage.

'Thanks,' she said. Then she lay her arms across the table and rested her head on them.

'Did you ever buy those lotto tickets, Summer?' I asked.

'What?' She didn't move her head.

'The lotto tickets. You were going to get some for your birthday.'

'Oh. Yeah.' The synapses were clearly not firing. They'd probably been drowned or pickled. Maybe both.

'Did you use the numbers I gave you?'

'What?'

Having a conversation with Summer was, at best, like pulling teeth. This was almost impossible.

'Do you know where the tickets are?'

'What?'

Jesus Christ, I was talking to a vegetable. I almost gave up, but decided to give it one last go.

'Do you know where the tickets are?' I enunciated each word carefully and slowly as if communicating with a moron. Which wasn't far from the truth.

'Handbag...bedroom...I think.'

'Can I check?'

She moaned, which I took as agreement. It was much more likely that she hadn't heard me, since under normal circumstances Summer would never let me go anywhere near her personal possessions. But I was curious and she was brain dead. I skipped up the stairs before she had a chance to process the request, understand it and stop me.

Phoebe was spot on. The bedroom stank. It was a sour smell, a heady cocktail of sweat, vodka, vomit and cigarette smoke. I felt sorry for the little tacker, having to sleep in that miasma. No wonder she got up at sparrow fart. Summer's bed was a dump and so was her bedside table, shit littered across the top and dribbling down onto the floor. Literally dribbling. A half-used tube of some kind of cream. I couldn't find her bag. In the end I got down on my hands and knees and looked under her bed. It was on its side about half a metre in and I fished it out, removing a couple of rather unpleasantly damp tissues that had stuck themselves to it. I sat on the bed and opened it.

I fossicked carefully. There were bound to be tampons and associated gear that I *really* didn't want to see, let alone touch. I found the ticket in a side compartment. It was all scrunched up and I had to use Phoebe's desk to flatten it out and make it readable. She'd bought herself about ten or twelve entries. I nearly crapped myself laughing when I saw the first set. 1, 2, 3, 4, 5 and 6. What a dick. But it was the second line that almost caused my heart to stop. I read it twice. Then I read it a third and a fourth time. I even took Phoebe's ruler and laid it under the line to make sure I wasn't transferring a number from the string of numbers below. I checked the date. I checked the line again.

Then I stumbled down the stairs, the ticket in my hand. The noise of blood pumping in my ears was loud and everything seemed strangely distant.

'**Summer**,' **I said**. 'You've won the lotto.'

She didn't stir. She must have fallen asleep again, there at the kitchen table. I prodded her arm with a finger and she grunted in annoyance, twitched her hand and settled her head further into her arms. I shook her shoulder. That produced a response. She lifted her head up and fixed me with spectacularly bloodshot eyes.

'Will you just FUCK OFF, Jamie?' she said. Then she grimaced, probably at the volume of her own voice. 'Leave me alone, willya?'

'You've won the lotto.'

'What?' Her eyes hadn't cleared, but at least I had her attention and some connections were being made in her alcohol-soaked brain. 'Whaddya on about?'

'The lotto. Drawn last night. You won.'

She sat up then and wiped a strand of hair away from her face. 'How many numbers I get?'

'All of them,' I said. 'Well, not the supplementaries, obviously. That's not possible, not if you got the six. Which you did.'

'I got all six?'

'Yes.'

The enormity of the news had not struck her yet. I had had

a few minutes to let it sink in. Plus, I knew the pool prize. She had no idea. Summerlee took a long swig of her orange juice and grimaced again.

'You're telling me I won the lotto?'

'C'mon, Summer. This is not a difficult concept. Well, actually it is, in a way. You got all six numbers in last night's lotto draw.'

'You're bullshitting me.' She gave a half-grin of triumph. 'And how would you know, anyway, since you don't know what numbers I bought? You're winding me up, Jamie, and it's not going to work.'

I held the ticket up.

'That's how I know, Summer. Your winning ticket, where you said it would be. In your bag.'

'You've been in my bag?' Her eyes narrowed.

I was tempted to rip the fucker up at this stage. Here I was, telling her the biggest news of her life and she was about to go off at me because I'd been in her bag when she'd said I *could* go in her bag. Well, she'd grunted, which is definitely not a refusal.

In retrospect, I wish I had ripped it up.

'You said I could,' I lied. 'Anyway, that's not important. You've won. Check for yourself, if you like.'

She took the ticket and peered at it through bleary eyes. I indicated the winning lines.

'Those numbers I wrote down for you, remember?' I said. '10, 13, 27, 28, 39, 41. That's the winning combination.' I took out my mobile phone, logged onto wi-fi, and did a quick search on the internet while she was trying to focus on the ticket. I got the result up and held the phone's screen to her face. 'Look,' I said. 'Check it out. The winning numbers. You've won the lotto, Summer.'

I think that was when she started to truly believe. She looked from the screen to her ticket and then back again. She still looked dazed.

'That's the good news,' I said. 'The bad news is three other people got them as well. That means you only got a quarter of the division-one prize.'

'How much?' she said.

I paused. I really wanted to draw this out, but in the end I couldn't bring myself to do it.

'Seven million, five hundred thousand,' I said.

'Fuck me,' she said. 'I've won a quarter of seven million dollars?'

'No,' I replied. 'The pool was thirty mill. Seven and a half million is your share.'

# CHAPTER 7

**There are many reported cures for hangovers.** Raw eggs with a dash of Worcestershire sauce. Stacks of painkillers, obviously. Some say three litres of tap water will do the trick. In my admittedly limited experience, winning seven and a half million dollars on the lotto is the most dramatic remedy.

Summerlee jumped to her feet, the ticket clutched in her hand. I don't think you could have prised it loose with a crowbar. She took the phone from me and scrutinised it again. Held it up to the ticket, compared the numbers. Then she went to the computer where Phoebe was compiling a PowerPoint presentation, wrestled the mouse from her hand and shoved her out of the computer chair.

'Hey,' said Phoebe. 'I'm doing my homework.'

'Never mind, mouse,' said Summer. 'This is important.'

'So is my homework.'

'No, it isn't. Not at the best of times and certainly not now.'

Summer closed the presentation without saving it. It was something to do with Egypt, because most of the images contained pyramids. I also caught sight of a camel before it vanished into the ether. Phoebe wailed.

'I've spent hours on that,' she said.

'You should save your work,' Summerlee replied. 'Your fault, mouse.'

'But *you* could have saved it,' wailed Phoebe. 'It came up with a "save changes" option and you...'

'Too bad, so sad,' said Summer. Her hands raced over the keyboard, bringing up the Google search box. I watched in silence. I could understand that she would need independent confirmation. In her position I would have been doing exactly the same. 'Anyway,' Summer continued. 'If all of this is for real, I'll buy you a fucking pyramid, all right?'

'Watch your language,' said Phoebe. She'd stopped grizzling by now, though her mouth was set into one of those formidable lines.

Summer found the site, brought up the numbers. They were still the same, for the very good reason that it was the identical site I'd got on my phone. She went over it again. And again. Checked the pool prize. Examined the numbers again. Finally, not even Summerlee could fail to accept the truth. She was a millionaire. She slumped back into the chair.

'Fucking hell,' she said. 'I've won.'

'Watch your language,' said Phoebe. 'What have you won?'

There was silence for a good thirty seconds.

'What have you won?' said Phoebe. 'What?'

Summer leaped up from the chair and grabbed Phoebe by the hands. She twirled her round and round, an old-fashioned barn dance routine or something from one of those period dramas where everyone is in frock coats or massive flouncy dresses. Phoebe leaned back, her hair flying, and for the first time a smile cracked the veneer of her annoyance. I smiled. They swirled around the front room, faster and faster, shrieking. Finally, they came to a halt. Phoebe staggered a few steps and plopped herself down on the sofa. Summer fell to the floor, her arms outstretched, a huge smile on her face.

'I've won the lotto, mouse,' she said. 'I've only gone and won the fucking lotto.'

'Watch your language,' said Phoebe. 'How much?'

'Seven and a half million dollars. That's how much. Seven point five million big ones. What do you think about that, Phoebes the rodent?'

Phoebe put a hand to her mouth. Her eyes were huge. No one said anything for ten seconds or so.

'Fuck me,' said Phoebe.

Summer and I cracked up. We laughed until our sides hurt and tears ran down our faces. I think it was the last time either of us was truly happy.

**Summer insisted I go with her to the shop where she'd bought the tickets.** It was a Sunday and I thought it was unlikely they would be able to scoop seven and a half million from the cash drawer and redeem her winning entry. But I was curious about how all this worked, so I was happy to tag along. Phoebe came with us as well. She was so excited I don't think we could have stopped her anyway.

'Do you want me to put the ticket in my wallet, Summer?' I asked. 'Keep it safe.'

'I'm not letting it out of my sight,' she replied. Or her grasp, as it turned out. She held it tightly scrunched in her hand. Even when we got to the shop she was reluctant to release the vice-like grip of her fingers.

'Can I help you?' said the guy behind the counter, in a tone that suggested he wasn't the slightest bit interested in following through on the question. He was about my age and had asymmetrical hair. For some reason I've always distrusted people with asymmetrical hair.

'I've won something on the lotto,' said Summer. She offered up the ticket but her fingers were white around the knuckles and she didn't let it go. The guy took hold of the small amount of ticket not buried in Summer's fist, but even then she didn't release it. He glanced at my sister and raised an eyebrow. For a couple of seconds I thought they would remain locked in a completely pointless tug of war, but finally Summer relinquished it. It clearly took a monumental effort of will. The guy, exuding an aura of practised boredom, scanned the ticket into a machine on the counter. I guess he was expecting to pay out twenty bucks, maybe a hundred. *Been there, done that. Ho, hum, life is tedious.* But what the machine told him caused his eyes to bug out. He shook his head as if clearing it of hallucinations and his asymmetrical hair swung in an annoying fashion. He moved his head closer to the machine, then took a pace back. Then he brought his eyes right up to the display. They bulged even further.

'My God,' he said. 'You're a division-one winner.' His voice was hushed and awestruck.

'I know,' said Summer.

'You've won seven and a half million dollars,' he said.

'I know,' said Summer.

If anything, the guy was more excited than Summerlee. After he got over the initial shock, he insisted on having his picture taken with her. I had to operate his mobile and take countless snaps of him with his arm around Summer's shoulder, my sister brandishing the ticket, which she'd reclaimed with indecent haste. He called over his fellow employees and they had their photographs taken as well. It quickly became a carnival atmosphere in the store. A few customers joined in, laughing and whooping. 'I've never sold a division-one ticket,' the guy kept repeating in reverential tones. 'It's amazing.' I thought this was a strange reaction. I mean, it wasn't as if *he* was going to be seeing any of the money, but apparently that didn't dampen his enthusiasm. He appeared positively orgasmic to be in the presence of someone who, in an instant, was worth far more than he could ever hope to earn in his lifetime. He *admired* Summerlee. It was like he was in the presence of an A-list celebrity.

Maybe I shouldn't have been surprised at his reaction. After all, he had asymmetrical hair.

Eventually, we found out that Summer would have to wait a few weeks before the money came through. An employee rang the lotto company, confirmed the winning ticket and then took down Summer's bank details. She wasn't impressed with the apparent delay in getting the money. I guess Summer was still hoping there might be the odd seven and a half mill floating around in the cash register. We finally left the store, staff and customers patting her on the back and all of us grinning like lunatics. The ticket was back in Summer's hand and her knuckles were white again.

'What are Mum and Dad going to say?' Phoebe piped up. Our parents had left the house early in the morning to visit our grandma at her residential home a few hours' drive away. We never went with them on these monthly trips. Grandma had long since forgotten who we were. She didn't even recognise Mum or Dad, so it was pretty pointless.

'They are going to shit themselves,' predicted Summer. 'They are going to poop their parental pants, mouse.'

Phoebe laughed.

'I'm so glad my numbers came up, Summer,' I said.

'Whaddya on about?'

'The winning numbers. Remember? I wrote them down for

you. 10, 13, 27, 28, 39 and 41. You said they sounded good and boy, you were right.'

'I don't know what you mean, Jamie,' she said. 'I just picked all the numbers at random.' I noticed she didn't meet my eye.

'Whoa, hang on, Summer,' I said. I couldn't let her get away with this. I wasn't expecting a share of the winnings – well, maybe a gift for services rendered wouldn't be out of the ball park, but it wasn't like I was going to sue her for half, or anything. This was a matter of principle. I *had* given her those numbers. What I wanted was acknowledgement, nothing more. It was only fair and it wasn't going to cost her anything. 'You had 1 through to 6, as well. The very numbers I said were a really bad idea, according to game theory. You can't tell me you've forgotten that.'

'No,' said Summer. 'I remember you mentioning them so I put them down as a joke. But the winning numbers – they were mine.'

I stopped in the street. This could get nasty. I felt a knot of resentment building in my throat. Summer didn't stop, however. She kept on walking. Phoebe halted somewhere between the two of us, looking back and forth. In the end I forced myself to catch up with my sister. I started to work through possible explanations. Maybe Summerlee had simply forgotten that I'd provided the numbers. She'd entered them and another ten others and simply couldn't recall where they came from. But I knew it wasn't that. She damn well knew they were my numbers. Even now, she couldn't give me anything, not even a small glow of satisfaction.

'I don't want any money, if that's what you're thinking,' I said to her back. 'But I know those numbers were mine. And *you* know it. Why can't you just say thanks? Why do you have to be such a bitch about it?'

She stopped then and turned to face me, hands on hips. The ticket was still clutched in her right hand.

'Fuck off, Jamie,' she said. 'This is where it all begins, isn't it? I've won some money and now you're trying to weasel in on it. I tellya. I've read about shit like this. Family and friends turn against you. Everyone wants a piece of the action. Don't worry, brother dear. I dare say you'll get what's coming to you. But I will not hear that, basically, *you* won the fucking lotto. I did it. *I* did and don't you forget it.'

She took off again. Phoebe looked from me to Summerlee, torn. Then she trotted after her sister, took her by the hand. Summer's left hand. I watched them disappear down the street, the sound of drumming blood loud in my ears. I was brimming with rage. It seeped from my skin, like sweat. They *were* my numbers. She could keep the money. I didn't want a cent. But I'm a mathematician and they were my numbers. Eventually, I calmed down sufficiently to drag myself home. I couldn't bear to look at my older sister and she wasn't interested in seeing me either. She and Phoebe played Monopoly. Great joke. I went to my room to brood.

I'd read about situations like this, as well. And I knew that lotto winners were often destined to crash and burn, and that families and friends were nearly always casualties. Wealth changes people, normally for the worst.

Trouble was, Summerlee was starting from a pretty low benchmark to begin with.

**Phoebe reported back to me later about Mum and Dad's reaction.** I couldn't bring myself to come down the stairs when I heard the crunch of tyres on gravel. Seems there was the normal euphoria as the news sank in, but then it rapidly turned pear-shaped.

Mum did all the stuff about avoiding publicity, warning her daughter that there were nasty people out there who would try to take advantage. Dad weighed in with suggestions about financial advisors, even proposing that she put the money into a trust fund where she couldn't touch the capital until she was twenty-five. He did some quick calculations on his computer and told her that the interest alone on seven and a half million would bring her hundreds of thousands of dollars a year. More than the Prime Minister earned. Dad likes numbers, too.

Summer's reaction was predictable. It was her money and she wouldn't be told what to do with it. As for putting the cash into a trust fund – were they mad? You only live once, she told them. She was going to have fun while she was young enough to enjoy it. And beneath her sad, predictable bluster there was that underlying element of suspicion. Phoebe didn't pick up on it, but I sensed it even through her reporting. Mum and Dad had an agenda. Suddenly, Summerlee was a target for other people's greed and she wasn't going to stand for it. The walls she had so carefully built around her would become reinforced.

Eventually, none of us would ever find a way in and she would languish in a fortress of her own making, convinced she was under siege.

Summerlee left home that evening. Spider picked her up and they booked into a swish hotel in the city. She still had some savings from her job at the supermarket and her credit card wasn't quite maxed out.

She never came home again.

# CHAPTER 8

**This is true.** There was a rock concert way back in the nineteen-sixties, at a place called Woodstock in America, and all the big bands and artists of the time were playing. They did it in this farmer's field, and it wasn't a buy-the-tickets-in-advance deal. You just rocked up. So the organisers had no idea how many people would show. In fact, no one knows even now. Some say there were a couple of hundred thousand, others well over half a million. What's *not* in doubt is that the concert was so freaking brilliant it took on legendary status.

Here's the point.

Half a million may have been there. But, *after the event*, maybe twenty million *claimed* to be there. Woodstock was so awe-inspiring, millions of people lied just to bask in reflected glory.

I would love to lie and say I was there when Summerlee gave up her job at the supermarket. Maybe in a few years I will. Perhaps there will be thousands of us, sitting at dinner tables, or in shady corners of bars, saying, *Hell yes, I was there when Summerlee Delaware gave up her job. I remember it like it was yesterday...*

Gutless *was* there. By some cool cosmic coincidence, he happened to be doing a little shopping when Summerlee breezed into the supermarket on Monday afternoon. Even more remarkable, he was close enough to the customer service desk to catch the whole exchange. Gutless is already a legend in my book. This just confirmed his status. This is what he told me:

'I was browsing the stationery section, looking for a cheap calculator, if you must know, when I happened to glance up as Summerlee entered the store. She caught my eye and I waved but she cut me dead, like always. She was wearing her uniform. You know, that pink thing with red beading and that crap logo on the back and on the front pocket. Makes you look like you're wearing a fucking condom. Anyway, she walks past me and picks up a bottle of Coke from one of those refrigerated displays close to the checkouts. They put those things there, so when you get bored queuing, you think you might as well have a drink, so you buy one. Same with the chocolate bars and the women's magazines and...'

'Yeah, Gutless,' I said. 'I'm aware of chainstores' marketing strategies. You were saying?'

'Oh, yeah. Well, I thought then that there was something different about your sister. Nothing I could put my finger on, but her eyes were kinda hard, you know, and her mouth this thin slit. I mean, I'd seen her working there before and she always looked monumentally pissed off, but this was different. Like she had a purpose. So, I get back to browsing 'cause it's not like there was anything *dramatic* going on, you know? Just picking up a bottle of Coke, that's all I'm saying.'

'Gutless, have you been rehearsing this?'

'Whaddya mean?'

'It's like you're doing the slow build-up thing, man. It's a cheap narrative ploy.'

'Yeah well, fuck you, Jamie. You wanna hear this or not?'

I made a circular motion with my hand and smiled. Of course I wanted to hear it. But I also wanted Gutless to know that *I* knew he was stringing me along.

Gutless gave me a hard stare, but continued. 'So she goes to the customer service area where the supervisor is flickin' through this ledger and looking mega important. I have to say, she *does* seem like a real bitch. She's got a mouth like a cat's ringpiece, for one thing. All puckered, like a smile would split her face in two.'

'You talking about the supervisor or Summerlee?'

'Yeah, well, both, come to think about it. But I mean the supervisor. And Summerlee kinda slinks up, you know? Sort of embarrassed and worried. And the supervisor, she keeps on flickin' through the ledger, ignoring your sister, letting her hang. So Summerlee coughs and *still* the supervisor ignores her. Eventually, she closes the book and gives your sister the long, hard glare routine as if she's a pile of dog shit someone's just stuck under her nose. Her mouth gets even more puckered. I thought her face might turn itself inside out, the way she was going.'

I laughed. I liked the idea of someone's face turning inside out. Gutless is pretty crap at English. He's not interested. But with observations like that, he could do okay if he just made more effort. I sounded like a teacher, so I put the idea to one side. Gutless was in full flow, anyway.

'And then she says, all snotty, "Good of you to join us, Summerlee. And only…", she glances at her watch, "…twenty minutes late for your shift." And Summerlee keeps her head down. She's swishing the Coke bottle in her hand and looking all…sheep-like'

'Sheepish.'

'What?'

'The word you're looking for is "sheepish".'

Gutless frowned. 'What-fuckin-ever, man,' he said. 'So. The supervisor glances around, checking she's got an audience, you know? And then she lets rip. Tells Summer she's on thin ice, that if she doesn't want the job she can leave, there's plenty of people who can replace her, she's unprofessional and the store values customer service and Summerlee is lousy at customer service and they've had complaints and this is her last chance. Tellya. Rips her a new arsehole. And the supervisor's enjoying herself. You can tell. I mean, what a turd. Customers had stopped to listen and then the supervisor finishes with, "So what have you got to say for yourself, young lady?" and Summer looks up. Her hands are behind her back, swishing that Coke bottle back and forth.'

I thought I knew how this was going to end. I mean, I know my sister. And it's not a good idea to keep on smacking a live hand grenade with a sledgehammer. The end result is guaranteed to be ugly.

'And Summer mumbles something. "What did you say?" says the supervisor. So your sister speaks louder. "I said fuck you, Miss Abbott." There's this stunned silence. "What?" says the supervisor. "Sorry, you deaf bitch," says Summer. She really raises her voice now. She's yelling. "I said, fuck you and the horse you rode in on. You can take your job and shove it up your arse. You can…"' Gutless waved his hand around. 'Hell, man, I can't remember all she said. But she didn't repeat herself once and it was awesome. Some of the things she told her to do were…oh, man. But the best thing was the supervisor's face. Stunned mullet. *This can't be happening.* By this time the whole store's frozen. There's not even any canned music going on. Just Summer's voice getting louder and louder and the supervisor's face getting redder and redder. It was beautiful, man. When she finally finished, a couple of us started to clap, it was that good. Turns out your sister wasn't finished. She unscrews the cap of the Coke bottle.' Gutless smiled. He was reliving the scene and bathing in its glory. 'And all this Coke comes bursting out. She'd been shaking it for ages, so it was like a bomb waiting to go off. Goes all over the supervisor. Drenches her, man. Hair is dripping with the shit. And still the Coke keeps coming. Tellya, man. I nearly pissed myself laughing.'

I laughed myself. This is not behaviour I normally approve of, but sometimes you don't have any choice but to immerse your-self in the moment. I could see Summerlee, loaded with the bullet of information that she was a multi-millionaire and therefore immune to anyone's crap. Emancipated, her finger on the trigger and without a care in the world. Payback. Hell, I don't have any-one I hate, but if I was loaded I'd probably start looking for someone to fit the bill. Summerlee. What a flawed masterpiece.

'So, this woman is, like, standing there with Coke and shit dripping from her hair and face and Summerlee holds out her hand, slaps some coins down on the counter. "Four dollars," she says. "For the Coke. On the grounds I've quit this shitty job, I'll forget about the employee discount. But you really should get someone to mop up this mess, you know." And she walks out.'

'Wish I'd been there,' I said.

'Yeah,' said Gutless. 'She sorta ruined it though, right at the end. She's out the store and then she turns back. "Fuck the lot of youse," she yells. Tellya, man. I wish she hadn't done that. It sort of fucked up everything that had gone before.'

'Yeah,' I replied. 'That's Summerlee for you. She can take something perfect and then screw it up at the last moment.'

Gutless nodded sagely. I meant it, though. Summerlee was destructive. It was embedded in her nature. Nonetheless, I couldn't help but admire what she'd achieved.

There was no doubt about it. Nothing became her in her job like the leaving of it.

None of us in the family saw or heard from Summerlee that entire week. She didn't pick up her phone and we had no idea whether that was because she recognised our numbers and ignored the calls or because she was too trashed to be able to speak.

But we heard *of* her.

The television news was splashing her story around and she was being interviewed right, left and centre. The local paper made her the front page headline. Mum and Dad heard her on local radio. It was clear Summer was loving the attention, and maybe a psychologist would have found the reasons obvious. It was equally clear she hadn't just ignored Mum's advice about avoiding publicity, she was actively courting it. We watched a news report on the Thursday evening and maybe the viewers would mistake that slightly glazed look in her eyes as stunned excitement. I could tell she was stoned out of her gourd.

After the report finished – Summer even implied she was thinking about charitable works, for Christ's sake – Mum pressed the remote and the screen went black. We sat in silence for a moment.

'I've got a very bad feeling about all this,' said Mum. 'She is simply not mature enough to deal with such a huge amount of money. I worry about what it will do to her.'

'I'd love to disagree,' said Dad. 'But I'm with you. I think there are troubles ahead.'

I was surprised. Mum and Dad never normally criticised any of us if a sibling was around.

Dad turned out to be right on the money about troubles. None of us, however, had the slightest hint just how devastating those troubles would turn out to be.

# CHAPTER 9

**Mum shook me awake.** It had been so long since anyone had had to do that, that I jerked upright, my heart hammering.

'What the hell?' I croaked. I was completely disorientated. My bedroom was in full darkness, for one thing, and Mum was nothing more than a looming bulk against the black. All those buried tales of monsters coming to get you in the night momentarily resurfaced. For a second I was five years old again. I sat up further. My eyes were sticky and I was conscious I was naked beneath the sheets. I pulled them up instinctively, rubbed my eyes with one distracted hand.

'Wake up,' said Mum.

'I'm awake,' I muttered, though that was not entirely true. 'What is it?'

'It's your sister.'

I thought at first she meant Phoebe. That she was ill, had to be rushed to the hospital or something. I reached over to my bedside lamp. The green numerals on my alarm clock flashed over to three-thirty. Saturday morning at three-thirty. I turned on the light and ran a hand through my hair, kept the sheets firmly in place with the other. Mum resolved from monster-in-the-cupboard to Mum, hair akimbo and face taut with anxiety. A different kind of monster.

'What is it?' I repeated.

'She's been arrested.'

Even then it took a second or two to make the connection. Phoebe had been arrested? What had she done, stolen another kid's peanut-butter sandwich? My brain started working again. Summerlee.

'What's she done?'

'God knows,' said Mum. 'We've just had a call from the police station. We need to get down there now, so get dressed.' She stomped out of my room, not exactly slamming the door behind her, but not being too gentle either. I swung my legs out of bed and searched for my clothes on the floor. I brought my T-shirt up to my nose and took a sniff. A bit smelly, but it would do.

Dad was standing by his bedroom door when I came out. He clutched the belt of his dressing gown, nervously tightening and untightening it. Maybe it was a substitute for Summerlee's neck. I tried a smile and so did he. Neither came out well.

'Summer, huh?' I said and shrugged in a kind of 'what-can-you-do?' way. No one could ever accuse me of being at my verbal best at gone three in the morning.

'I just hope it's drunkenness,' said Dad. 'Drunk and disorderly, something like that.'

I nodded. Was it my imagination or was his hair turning greyer and thinner by the day? Can a daughter do that to you, like a virus sapping your strength, eating away unseen?

'We'll bring her home, Dad,' I said and this time *he* nodded.

I turned to the stairs and remembered that time when Mum had put Summerlee's lunch box back in the fridge, the day when Summer blew up and refused to go to school. I experienced that profound sense of sadness all over again. And it occurred to me that maybe, over the years, Mum had been given no option other than to be strong, that all the women in my family were tough and Dad and I were content to let it be that way. I shook my head and padded down the stairs.

Mum was pacing, jingling car keys in her hand. I thought about asking if I had time for a piece of toast, but the expression on her face convinced me it wouldn't be wise. I grabbed my runners from beside the front door and stuck my feet into them, but didn't bother tying the laces. Within two minutes of my rude awakening I was in the passenger seat of the car, barrelling through the night and encased in threatening silence. I kneaded my eye sockets with the balls of my palms and blinked furiously.

'You've got no idea what she's done?' I asked. The silence was too brooding. It demanded I break it.

'Arrested, that's all I know,' replied Mum. 'The police officer gave no details. I suppose we'll find out when we get there.'

Maybe it wasn't surprising that my brain was not at its sharpest. Being woken at three-thirty in the morning probably does that to you. But it was only now that an obvious question occurred to me.

'Mum?'

She adjusted the rear-view mirror slightly.

'What am I doing here?' I continued. 'Don't get me wrong, I'm happy to keep you company. But...I'm just not sure what good you think I'll be.'

'She's your sister.'

It wasn't an answer. It was a statement of fact. And then, suddenly, I realised. Mum didn't want me there to offer assistance. She wanted me to witness. *This is what happens when you screw up, Jamie. There are consequences to your actions and those consequences can be terrible. A prison cell. Humiliation. Pain and suffering for your family. Watch all this carefully. Learn. And never, never do to me what your sister has done.* It was unfair, but understandable. In a way, I was being punished for Summer's crimes, whatever they were. Like finding a pile of crap in the kitchen and rubbing a dog's nose in it. Any dog, not necessarily the culprit. This is what transgression smells like. This is the odour of judgement. Inhale. And be scared.

Then again, I was nothing like Summerlee and Mum knew I would never deliberately get in trouble with the law. So maybe it was a different kind of punishment. Maybe I was being forced to think about all those occasions when I could have helped Mum out, but didn't. *This is the world I've always had to deal with, Jamie. Now you know how it feels.* If that was the case, then I wasn't the only person who should have been in the car. Dad also abdicated responsibility; how many times had he put up sandbags against a rising tide of troubles and let Mum do the baling when it all spilled over?

The beauty of game theory is that it makes you constantly examine how other people might react to situations, but it's also a pain in the arse for the same reason. It was the middle of the night, I was tired and these thoughts buzzed round in my head, offering possibilities but skirting insight.

I wound down the car window and let the cool night air bathe me. It smelled of rain.

Mum found a parking space outside the cop shop. The station was brightly lit, curiously welcoming in a way. *Come on in. It's nice and warm and safe in here.* Mum walked quickly, purpose in her paces, and I trailed a couple of metres behind. I hadn't tied my shoelaces in the car and I worried I'd trip myself up. The waiting area was spartan: a few straight-backed chairs against the walls, a reception desk that was deserted. Someone had made an effort to brighten up the walls by fixing posters at intervals. Helplines. Something about Neighbourhood Watch. There weren't even any magazines to while away the time, but I guess a police station is not a doctor's waiting room. Car thieves reading *Motoring Weekly*. Mum went straight to the desk and pinged one of those old-fashioned bells that have a button on the top. The sound echoed through the building, but no one came. *You could steal these chairs*, I thought, *and make a clean getaway*. Mum muttered and jingled the car keys again. Summerlee was somewhere here, and that was a strange, disturbing thought. It was difficult to imagine cells behind those neat doors, places with bars and the taste of hopelessness. Much easier to imagine neat cubicles where people peered at computer screens and ate takeaway sandwiches at their desks.

Mum was about to ring the bell again when a burly officer in uniform appeared as if from nowhere. He was wiping his face with the side of a hand, possibly brushing crumbs away. He had a cardboard cup of what looked like coffee in his other hand.

'Good morning, ma'am,' he said to Mum. 'How can I help you?'

'I'm Janet Delaware. I believe you have my daughter, Summerlee, here.'

'Ah, yes,' said the cop. 'We certainly do. Please take a seat, Ms Delaware. The arresting officer will be right with you.' He picked up a phone on the desk and pressed a button. Mum stood for a moment as if unsure whether to follow the instruction or attempt to listen in to the conversation. In the end, she turned away and sat down beneath a poster publicising a twenty-four-hour drug support line. Almost immediately she started jingling her car keys. It made an annoying sound. I sat next to her and took the opportunity to tie my laces. I wondered if someone had taken

Summerlee's away, assuming she had any. Didn't they do that so you couldn't hang yourself in your cell? I sat forward, forearms on my thighs, and inspected the grouting between the floor tiles. It had once been grey, but now it was black.

They kept me and Mum waiting for forty-five minutes. I suppose it's not unreasonable. Perhaps the guy was off somewhere interrogating a suspect or filling out forms. Wasn't that the way it was in TV shows, the endless form-filling a barrier to catching the baddies? But I couldn't help concluding it was insensitive. Summer was eighteen. Yeah, an adult. But still eighteen. And her mum was there, not knowing whether she had dropped litter in the street or caved someone's head in with a hammer. Forty-five minutes of agonising speculation was excessive. Mum never stopped the key jingling, but she didn't say a word.

Finally, a door to the reception area opened and a man in a suit put his head around. His tie was undone, the knot hanging way below his chin.

'Ms Delaware?' he said. Mum stood.

'Yes.'

'Come this way, please.' We both followed him through the door and along a corridor to a small office. The cop didn't ask who I was and I didn't volunteer the information. I was half expecting Summerlee to be in there, but the room was empty. The man motioned to a chair and then sat behind a desk. There was only one chair so Mum took it. The place was pretty much like the cubicles I had imagined out there in the waiting room.

The only thing missing was the takeaway sandwich. The man picked up a thin manila folder and examined a page. He glanced up at Mum.

'At one-thirty this morning we received a call from the night manager at the Hyatt Hotel in the city. He reported that there was a disturbance in one of the rooms and asked for assistance. A patrol car was sent out and, as a result, your daughter and two other people were arrested.'

Mum sighed. It could have been worse, I suppose. A disturbance was better than an assault. Then again, the word 'disturbance' covered a multitude of possibilities.

'What has she done?' Mum asked.

The cop turned back to the folder.

'At present, the charge sheet reads affray, possession of illicit substances, resisting arrest and assaulting a police officer,' he said. It turned out the disturbance *was* an assault. He put the sheet down. 'In addition, Ms Delaware, your daughter trashed the hotel room. That was the reason the police were called in the first place. Apparently, she and her guests made a real mess. Smashed the television, destroyed the bed, tipped up the bar fridge, broke tiles in the bathroom...' He picked up the sheet again, clearly thought about listing more of the damage, changed his mind and put the sheet back. 'Let's just say that there wasn't much in that hotel room that *could* be broken that wasn't. I imagine the Hyatt will be hitting your daughter with a substantial bill for damages.'

'She can afford it,' said Mum. I didn't know if the police officer would pick up the irony, the weary resignation, in her words or interpret the remark as dismissive.

'Yes,' said the cop. 'Summerlee Delaware, multi-millionaire.' Did he intend the rhyme? I almost laughed. 'I read all about it. Saw the news. But that doesn't give her the right to destroy other people's property or assault police officers.'

'I know that,' said Mum. 'Believe me, I know.'

The cop stared at her for a few moments. I was really tempted to break my silence. The guy was looking at Mum as if she was a shit parent. Just another one in a long line of shit parents he had had to deal with in his career. *Your daughter didn't just turn out this way. You made her. How about taking some responsibility?* But Mum *had* tried. She was the only one who had. She'd fucked up, sure, with all of us, but which parent doesn't? In the end, she didn't deserve this. This was Summerlee's crime and it was painful to watch Mum being invited to share it.

'Anyway,' the cop continued. 'Your daughter is an adult and will be charged as one. We are prepared to release her tonight. But she is still very drunk and I require the presence of a sober adult to take responsibility for her.'

'Keep her in a cell overnight,' said Mum. 'Might do her some good.' I could only imagine the despair that led to that suggestion. It wasn't like Mum at all.

'No. We want to be rid of her. Though it's interesting you should say that. Your daughter also didn't want to be released to you and suggested the same thing. But, frankly, no one here has the time or energy to clean up her vomit or watch her constantly to make sure she doesn't choke on it. To be honest, Ms Delaware, we are tired of her. Take her home.'

Mum nodded. She seemed so worn down, shoulders sagging as if in some way she welcomed the burden. Or, at least, recognised the inevitability of carrying it.

'Come with me,' said the cop.

This time we were led to a room that *did* contain Summerlee. She sat on a bench, her head dangling between her knees, and she looked up as we entered. I have seen Summer in various states of drunkenness and most times she looked like shit, but she had outdone herself this time. Her top was torn and dirty and she didn't even have the energy to hitch it up to conceal grimy bra straps. The rest of her clothes, such as they were – Summer never considered herself decently dressed if she was decent – were in a similar state. Not dragged through a hedge backwards, but repeatedly forced through it on considerable occasions. But it was her face that shocked me more than anything. Cuts and scratches, make-up smeared, hair in a disastrous tangle. And her eyes. They seemed dead somehow, a window to misery. I actually wanted to go over and hug her, but I didn't have the guts. She would have recoiled anyway. Her gaze took us in, but it was uninterested, and she turned her eyes back to the floor. I noticed that they *had* taken her shoes.

Mum, to her credit, didn't launch into anything resembling a sermon. Just as well, because Summer might have found herself facing further charges. Instead, she jangled the car keys again.

'Time to go home, Summerlee,' she said.

Summer stood and walked past both of us, staggering slightly and banging her hip against the door frame. The cop led the way to the front desk and Summer was given back her possessions. Shoes, mobile phone, handbag, twenty-six dollars and twenty cents in cash. Summer counted it out carefully.

'I had more than this,' she said. 'I had at least fifty bucks.'

'You didn't,' said the guy in the suit. He had never given us his name. That was okay. I wasn't particularly interested. 'You had exactly what it says on that sheet. Twenty-six dollars and twenty cents. You signed. Here.' He pointed out Summer's scrawl at the bottom of the form.

'Yeah, well, I was pissed,' she replied. 'I woulda signed anything. I had more than a lousy twenty-six bucks.'

'Are you accusing us of theft?' said the guy. 'If so, there is another form that you will need to fill out.'

'Oh, sure,' said Summer. 'That's gonna work, isn't it? How fuckin' dumb do you think I am?'

For a moment I thought the cop was going to accept the invitation and spell it out for her, but he didn't. He kept his mouth shut and his eyes hard.

Maybe it would have been better to let Summer talk herself back into jail, but in the end we got her out of the station. You could feel the mood of the constabulary lifting as we went through the door. It was distinctly possible they would have had a whip-round to raise the twenty-four dollars to bring her cash up to the fifty she claimed. That would have been a blast. Giving twenty-four bucks to someone who was worth seven and a half million.

Summerlee shivered in the cool night air and wrapped her arms around her front. I couldn't imagine that would provide much warmth, but there was nothing to be done about it. She looked up at the night sky, teeth chattering gently. Mum opened the rear door of the car.

'Despite everything, Summerlee,' she said. 'I'm glad you got the police to call me.'

'I didn't,' she replied. She didn't even glance at Mum. 'They got your number from my phone. Isn't there some law against that? You can't just go searching through someone's mobile. That's invasion of privacy. I should sue the fuckers. Maybe I will.'

Mum sighed. I realised she was bone weary and not just because of the lateness – the earliness – of the hour. It was five-fifteen and the sky had taken on that quality that said night's dominance was ending. Stars were fading on the horizon. So too, closer to home, was Mum's resilience.

'Get in the car, Summer,' I said. 'You must be cold.'

'Nah, I'm right.' She pulled out her phone from that ridiculously small bag and punched in a number. 'I'll get a taxi.'

'Where to?' said Mum.

'There are other hotels.'

'Come home,' said Mum. 'You can sleep properly. I'll cook you breakfast. You can have a hot shower.'

'Maybe we could sing a song together in the car,' said Summer. 'Play happy families. Speaking of happy families, Dad couldn't make it, I see.'

'One of us had to stay and look after your sister.'

'Yeah. He's good at that, is Dad. Doing fuck all.'

Mum's hand clenched against the car keys. I saw the blood drain from her knuckles.

'Come home, Summer,' she said again.

'Nah, I'm right.' Summerlee turned her head away from us. 'Yeah, I need a taxi right away. I'm outside the police station in Gordon Street. Going to the city…Summerlee Delaware…ten minutes? Right.' She hung up.

'Summerlee…'

'Leave it, Mum,' I said. I took her by the arm. 'You're not going to get anywhere. Let's go.'

'But…' There was a puzzled expression in her eyes. *I can't just leave my daughter alone in the street at five in the morning. It's dangerous and I have to protect her. It was only yesterday that she would giggle when I tickled her and hug me and give me a big sloppy kiss on my cheek and draw me pictures, outrageously bad pictures, that I would proudly stick up on the fridge, and she'd get so wound up on Christmas Eve that she could never sleep but would sometimes make herself sick with excitement, and her first day of school...I can't leave her. It's what being a parent is about. It's hard-wired.* 'Please, Summerlee,' she added.

I felt anger at the abject pleading and a profound sadness at the same time. It was a curious emotional mixture.

'Nah, I'm right,' said Summer.

I grabbed my sister by the arm, and when she tried to wrench herself free, I tightened my grip, hissed close to her ear.

'You're a fucking bitch, Summer,' I said. 'Dad is worried, Mum has driven here to pick you up and all you can do is spit in her face. You don't even have the decency to say thanks.' She managed to finally free herself and her face was contorted in anger.

'"Thanks"?' she said. 'For what? I didn't ask you guys to come here, so you can fuck off if you want gratitude. This was about making yourselves feel good. All that family-sticks-together, blood-is-thicker-than-water horseshit. Mum's neediness, Dad's gutlessness, your overwhelming sense of fucking superiority. Well, I've had it, Jamie.' Her mouth twisted and suddenly she was ugly. Not the kind of ugly that can be fixed with mascara or a brush through the hair. This ugliness was stamped in the flesh. 'Or is it all about protecting the family interests, huh?'

'What are you on about?'

'Seven and a half million reasons to be nice to me.'

'Fuck you, Summerlee.' I didn't try to hide my disgust. I *couldn't* hide my disgust.

'Yeah? Right back at you, little brother.'

Even then, Mum insisted on waiting until the taxi arrived.

I was for getting the hell out right there and then, probably because I didn't have her hard-wiring. Summer got in the taxi without another word and we watched as she disappeared into the gathering dawn. Mum closed the rear door of our car.

'That could have gone better,' she said. I could see her fighting back tears.

'You did your best, Mum,' I said. 'Forget her. She's screwed up and it's not your fault.'

'It's always the parents' fault,' she said, though her voice was little more than a whisper.

'That's not true,' I replied. But she looked at me as if I knew nothing at all. Maybe I didn't.

We drove home in silence.


The money came through with a fanfare of publicity from the lotto people. We read about it in the papers.

Summer bought a mansion in the city for nearly two million dollars. Spider bought a car. We weren't invited to see either of them. There was sporadic contact. Summer had taken to answering our calls occasionally, though they were invariably unsatisfactory. We were polite enough, but the conversations only served as reminders of the distance between us, the gap none of us, to be honest, struggled too hard to bridge. Apart from Mum, that is. She kept trying, but from my perspective at least, it was like attempting CPR on a body that was way past resuscitation.

Summer, from the age of thirteen, had always been moving away from us, slowly and inexorably. The lotto win accelerated the process. We had become a family polarised. It wasn't just the money. In fact, it was mainly to do with personalities.

But, shit, the money didn't help.

# PART TWO

# CHAPTER 10

**This is what happened.** This is when the real terror began.

**I had a free, last lesson of the day, so I went to see Mr Monkhouse, my maths teacher.** He'd set me additional homework a week ago (no one else got this – apparently, it was to keep my brain 'fit') and I reckoned I'd nailed it.

Mr M was in his classroom marking assignments, and judging by the speed with which he pushed them to one side, he was pitifully grateful for my interruption.

'Mr Delaware,' he said. 'To what do I owe the honour?'

Mr Monkhouse was a brute of a man, about two metres tall and with a barrel chest. He kept his head shaved and his features were proportionately large and coarse. If you were designing a nightclub bouncer from scratch, Mr Monkhouse would make a perfect template. And yet his brain was beautiful. It often seemed to me that he taught not because it paid the mortgage, but because it allowed him to think about mathematics, and he could imagine nothing better to do with his time than turn symbols and ideas around in his mind, basking in their perfection.

'The homework, Mr Monkhouse,' I said. 'Cracked it.'

He smiled and spread his hands. 'Remind me.'

'The spaghetti problem.' I could tell Mr M had been pleased with this when he'd set it. *Jamie, you drop a single straight strand of uncooked spaghetti onto your kitchen floor and it breaks randomly into three pieces. What's the probability you could form a triangle from those pieces?*

'Ah, yes,' he said. 'Often called the broken-stick problem.' He pointed a finger at me. 'You didn't look it up on the internet did you?' I cocked my head. 'Of course you didn't,' he continued. 'I apologise. So. Amaze and delight me.'

'Quick version,' I said. 'If you want the full proof I can do it.' I picked up a whiteboard marker and drew an equilateral triangle on the board. I referenced the altitude theorem, added another equilateral triangle within the first and showed how, of the resultant four congruent triangles, it was only in the medial that the sum of the lengths of any two pieces exceeded the length of the third piece. 'Therefore,' I said, 'the probability of forming a triangle from the three pieces of spaghetti must be one in four.'

Mr Monkhouse laughed. 'One way of doing it,' he said.

'One way?'

'All right, Jamie. It's a *good* way. How about something more challenging? Never mind your spaghetti breaking into three.

Now – impossibly, I might add – it's broken up at $n - 1$ random points along its length, resulting in $n$ pieces, obviously, where $n$ is greater than or equal to 3. What's the probability that there exist three of the $n$ pieces that can form a triangle?'

This time *I* laughed. 'You're shitting me.'

'Would I shit you?'

I thought.

'Does the answer involve Fibonacci numbers?'

Mr Monkhouse smiled. 'Maybe. You tell me.'

'Has anyone ever told you that you're the most annoying teacher in the school, Mr M? Possibly the world?'

'I've heard the proposition before,' he said. 'But no one has yet provided the proof.' He stood, stretched and rubbed at his eyes. 'Mr D, I spend most of my time *telling* students how to solve problems, but you have a mind. Use it. Go think. It's what you were put on this earth to do.'

'It's to do with Fibonacci numbers,' I said.

'How's that older sister of yours doing, Jamie?'

Summerlee had been in Monkhouse's class a few years back. Well, probably not often, come to think about it. God knows how he would have coped with someone like Summer, who had zero interest in anything academic. It's what teachers do, I guess. Part of the job.

'Ah, you know Summer, Mr M,' I said. 'Same old.'

'I've read about her in the papers.' Everyone had read about Summerlee, it seems. It made me a kind of celebrity at school for a few days, before interest waned. Mr Monkhouse sighed. 'Seven and a half million dollars, wasn't it?'

I nodded.

'That's not far off what a teacher would make in a hundred years,' he said, but it was like he was saying it to himself.

There was silence and it was kinda embarrassing. I didn't really know what to say, but thought I should say *something*.

'Life's not fair, I guess.'

Monkhouse smiled and got to his feet. He picked up the pile of assignments and then tossed them back on the desk.

'That's pretty much the philosophy of my mortgage lender,' he said. This was getting even more embarrassing. I didn't know if I was expected to apologise for Summerlee, or say something about how much I appreciated what teachers did. Instead I shuffled a few paces towards the door.

'I'd better get going, Mr M,' I said. 'Picking up my younger sister from school, doing some food shopping for Mum.' I didn't need to go this early, but for some reason I wanted to get out into the fresh air.

'Of course, Jamie. I think I'll go home myself.' He pointed a finger at me. 'Remember, $n$ pieces of spaghetti. Don't make a meal of it.'

Even the best teachers think they're comedians.

It was a glorious day. The sky was a pale blue, dusted like a bird's egg, and a few lazy wisps of cloud nestled against it. The air was fresh, tinged with the scent of cut grass. I would be early, but I walked to Phoebe's school anyway. This is my job, picking her up after school, but it's not really a job. It was a ten-minute walk and by the time I got there I still had forty minutes to wait. Sometimes, on days when I had a free last period, I'd go into reception and wait there. The staff knew me and there was one girl in particular – well, not a girl, a woman probably in her early twenties – who had wicked green eyes and a way of biting on her bottom lip when she was concentrating. There are worse ways of spending time, sitting in a warm reception area and reading faces when no one knows you are watching. But I didn't feel like it today. I sat on a small swing in the school playground and tried not to look like a paedophile. I pushed against the ground with my legs, which wasn't difficult since the swing was designed for someone half my height.

I tried to remember what it was like to be in primary school, but I couldn't. This made me sad. I had been to Phoebe's school, for Chrissake, only a few years back, but now it was mainly lost to me. I could remember Mrs Griffin, who had a bad hip and bad teeth and a good sense of humour. God knows how many hours I spent in her company, but all that was left were fragments of memory and a few thin feelings. The past is like that. It dissolves and leaves you with a vague sense of loss.

It was no good. I still felt like a pervert, so I got up from the swing and circled the block. I passed a woman who was taking her blue heeler for a walk. Neither seemed to be enjoying it.

The dog was straining at the leash and the woman was straining against the dog. As I approached, it veered towards me, a low growl coming from deep within. The woman kept muttering 'good boy' to it, but that was fooling no one, least of all the dog. I stepped off the footpath onto the road but it tried to follow me. There were a few glistening threads of drool coming from its lips and the woman's arms were bunched with the strain of keeping it in check. I told her g'day, but she didn't bother replying. I hate it when that happens.

I did two laps of the school and settled down to wait outside the main entrance. Parents had gathered by then, mainly women but a few men as well. The majority were parked in LandCruisers, Pajeros and other four wheel drives. It's a prosperous neighbourhood. The women chatted among themselves. I guess if you see the same people five days a week, you're bound to find common ground. I kept to myself, though I'd often thought about joining the discussion. That would be cool, to chat with women twice my age about…well, whatever they were chatting about. The weather, how great their kids were, the preposterousness of men. I could do that, but somehow I'd never found the courage. That was a pity. Game theory is all about understanding how other players think, so it would've been…educational.

To be honest, the thing I loved most about picking Phoebe up was not so much seeing her come out – though that did give me a blast – but watching the other kids. Some dorky, some gorgeous and confident. Boys who wrestled each other because they were boys and couldn't hug; girls who hugged because they were girls and that was okay. But mainly the backpacks. Is it just me, or is there nothing better in the world than seeing a small scrap of a human being with a canvas bag as big as them on their backs? Some of the kids were like pack mules. I could see their bags were leaden with whatever was in them. Bricks? Anvils? Others had bags that were shrivelled and loose, presumably because there was nothing in them apart from a lunch box containing Pringle crumbs and a shrivelled apple. But the bags were still huge. It's really great.

Phoebe came out with Corey, as always. She was talking to him and it seemed, from a distance, an earnest conversation. He had his face turned towards her and his nose was enormous in profile. I was reminded of a wading bird, particularly since he has stick-thin legs made more prominent by extra-short shorts. He is going to be an accountant when he grows up. I would put money on it. Phoebe is one of the anvil-in-the-backpack brigade. I have no idea what she keeps in there but it is really heavy. I've toted it a couple of times. Maybe it's a piano. Corey was nodding. Phoebe was punctuating her words with extravagant wafting of her boater, which she carried in her right hand. Women talk, men listen. We learn this game at an early age and that's okay by me.

'How's it hanging, Corey?' I said when they reached me.

'Yeah,' he said. He always said 'Yeah' to me, regardless of my comment. That always cracked me up as well, but I didn't let it show. 'Later,' he added to Phoebe, and walked off to where his mum was waiting for him. She also had a beak of impressive proportions. Their car was a Mercedes. Maybe she's an accountant.

'Wassup small beast,' I said to Phoebe. 'How's school?'

'Okay.'

'What did you do today?'

'Nothing much.'

Mum used to complain about my responses to those questions, which were exactly the same as Phoebe's responses. Hell, she *still* complains. School is a private thing, though, even when there's nothing to be private about. I respect that, but I still ask the questions. If nobody asked, you wouldn't get the chance to stonewall.

'Is Corey going to be an accountant when he grows up?' I asked.

'No. An astronaut.'

'An astronaut?'

'Yeah. He wants to go into space. He's interested in space.'

I considered this for a few moments.

'Probably a wise career choice, then. Bet he ends up as an accountant, though. Astronaut. Accountant. They have a lot of letters in common.'

'You're dumb.'

'Takes one to know one.'

Phoebe took me by the hand. Many other kids of her age don't do stuff like that. They find it embarrassing, I guess. But she doesn't care. She's very tactile. Her hands were cool and dry. Mine weren't, probably as a result of that close encounter with the dog and a brisk two laps of the school

'We going shopping?'

'Yeah. Mum needs some things for dinner.'

This was another of my jobs. Mum worked as an assistant in a child-care centre and she often wouldn't get the chance. She stayed way behind normal school hours, looking after tackers whose parents were out at work until five or later. I don't mind shopping. And Phoebe loves it.

'What are we getting?'

'I can't tell you that, poo face. It's on a need-to-know basis. I *could* tell you, but then I'd have to kill you.'

'You're dumb.'

'So you say.'

We walked in silence for another five minutes. I kept glancing down at Phoebe at my side for no other reason than I liked to watch her when she wasn't watching me. I liked the way she put one foot in front of the other, lost in her own thoughts, like a proper human being, rather than someone in training for it. It never fooled her, though. She always knew when I was examining her. She glanced up.

'What?' she said.

'I nearly got savaged by a blue heeler today,' I replied. 'It wanted a piece of me, so I killed it.'

'You did not.'

'No. I didn't. You're right. I lied. Sorry.'

'So it didn't try to savage you?'

'Well, it would have done if there hadn't been a woman attached to it. My life flashed before my eyes. It was just as boring the second time around.'

There's a large shopping mall about fifteen minutes' walk from our house and we normally go there for groceries. Phoebe liked the supermarket best – the very supermarket that Summerlee used to work at – even though there were other shops that you'd think a kid of seven going on eight would prefer. She was a whiz with the fruit and veg. She'd squeeze avocados, sniff melons and inspect broccoli heads for signs of insect damage. I was always prepared to take my chances, but Phoebe wasn't. How did we, in our own ways, become gender stereotypes? It's a mystery. One area where she broke that, though, was in steering the shopping trolley. She wouldn't let me do that and it had been years since she'd actually sat in one. I remember one time when we were doing the shopping after school and I got in the trolley instead. I couldn't get my legs through the gaps and let them dangle, which was a shame. That would have been a blast. So I sat in the trolley and Phoebe wheeled me around, all solemn. Squeezing avocados and sniffing melons, while I stuck my thumb in my mouth and occasionally pleaded for a lolly. Eventually, an assistant made me get out for reasons she couldn't articulate. Summer was doing a shift that day and she gave her colleague shit for it. Pointed out that we weren't doing any harm and Phoebe was a really good driver. It didn't do any good, though. Sometimes people just don't like watching other people having fun. I don't know why.

'Do we need anything from the deli?' she asked after we had found a trolley and entered through the little swing gates that remind me of batwing saloon doors in old westerns. The deli was Phoebe's favourite and she insisted on doing the ordering. Sometimes the assistant had to crane over the big curved glass frontage to see her. I normally stood a distance off and watched. I didn't this time.

'Four salmon fillets,' I replied.

'Risotto,' said Phoebe.

I nodded. It was one of Mum's staple recipes. Risotto with mushrooms, dill and peas, topped off by grilled salmon steaks. Phoebe would be in charge of grilling the fish, a task she took very seriously. Mum would do the risotto, since it took a lot of stirring and constant attention to get it just right. I was never required in this process but I would sometimes watch Phoebe and the salmon. She'd check about every ten seconds, turning the salmon with tongs to make sure the fillets were cooked evenly, her tongue poking slightly out of the corner of her mouth, totally absorbed in the task. She *was* the salmon. In the zone.

'I'll get the herbs and the mushrooms,' I said. We had peas at home and there was plenty of arborio rice. 'Meet you at the chocolate section.' Occasionally I would buy Phoebe a Mars bar or something. Not always, because she was an addict and you can't feed addicts, but I was in the mood this time. I left her with the trolley, mainly because she wouldn't have given it up even if I'd wanted it.

Listen. I have been over what happened next at least forty times. To the police, to my parents. To anyone who cared to hear. But that's nothing compared to the number of times I have rewound and reviewed it in my head. And each time something else came back to me, real or imagined. A glimpse of someone out of the corner of my eye, a snatch of conversation as I passed through the aisles. The supermarket was crowded. There were small children who'd stop right in front of you, oblivious to your presence, so you'd have to swerve around. That definitely happened. There was an Indian woman in brightly coloured clothing who apologised to me when her kid – a little girl with enormous brown eyes and jet black hair that shimmered like silk – skidded to a halt and nearly bailed me up. I smiled at her, but I didn't say anything. The police interviewed the woman, much later, but she couldn't recall anything, not even the apology. I walked to the vegetable section and picked up a pack of pre-sliced mushrooms. There was an assistant – a guy with receding hair, around forty years old – stacking the shelves with broccoli. I remember thinking he was an unlikely employee. And I also remember thinking I was being ageist for thinking it. I guess I believed that when you hit middle age you'd have some kind of career and stacking vegetables wouldn't be part of it. Did he have dreams, when he was at school, of becoming a surveyor or an airline pilot or an inventor or a writer? And what brought him to this point, this balancing of vegetables on steel shelves? I shoved those thoughts away and asked him if they had any fresh dill. They didn't. He told me a delivery was expected tomorrow. He had good teeth and watery blue eyes.

I bought a tube of processed dill – a herb pretending to be toothpaste. It wasn't ideal, but I had to get something. The fruit and veg section was large and full of people. There was a woman scolding her child, who was whimpering about something. She was kind of yelling but pretending not to, as if bawling at a kid was a shameful action in a public place. I guess it is. Her face was doughy and she had a tattoo peeking above her T-shirt at the base of her neck; some kind of Celtic symbol. She grabbed the kid by the arm and gave him a little shake, and then he really started to cry. Her mouth was twisted in annoyance. I remember praying she wouldn't smack her child on the back of the leg. She didn't, but I think it was because she was in a supermarket. There was a guy in a suit on a mobile phone. He kept saying 'Uh huh', 'Yup', 'Uh huh', over and over again while checking out asparagus. They were the only people I remember from that part of the store – the woman with the tattoo, the man in the suit and the broccoli stacker – even though there were probably dozens of shoppers milling about.

I walked past the bread section. Someone's voice came over the loudspeaker asking for all available staff to come to checkout. I remember that because I knew we would probably have to join the end of a long queue, even though we'd only have a few items in our trolley. The confectionery aisle was three-quarters of the way back to the deli and I got there first. I wasn't surprised that I'd made it before Phoebe. There were about five people ahead of her in the queue at the deli and she sometimes gets forgotten about, which is not surprising when the assistants can't see her. It really annoys me when someone who comes after her gets served first, but Phoebe isn't fussed. She can be very patient when it suits her. I have never been very patient.

To while away the time I checked out the specials. Turkish Delight were two for two dollars so I picked up a couple and tried to balance them against the mushrooms and the tube of dill. There weren't many people in the aisle, which was a surprise, given that's where kids normally congregate. I walked down to the end and looked across to the deli, but it was difficult to see. I wandered back. I considered getting Mum a bar of dark chocolate but thought better of it. Where was Phoebe? I walked back down, but this time I went all the way to the deli. After all, Phoebe had nothing else to buy. Where would she go after buying the salmon except to the chocolate aisle?

She wasn't there.

There were only a couple of people waiting to be served at the deli. An assistant was ladling out a tub of potato salad. I walked up to the counter and gazed along the section that housed the frozen food. She wasn't there.

I remember this very clearly. I felt annoyed. It wasn't unusual for Phoebe to take off by herself in a supermarket. There had been a good number of occasions when I'd had to trek most of the way around the store before I found her. In particular, it used to irritate me that I would spy her going along the central aisle and she wouldn't spot me at the top end. I could never bring myself to shout out her name. Not in a supermarket. How dumb is that? So I'd feel like some dickhead in a sad comedy, tailing her across the aisles, trying to get her attention.

Maybe she had gone to the fruit and veg to find me.

She wasn't there.

I walked along the central aisle and glanced up and down each row. Twelve rows, bisected by the central aisle, making twenty-four possible locations to check. Less than a four per cent chance that she'd be in any one at any particular time, given that there are other supermarket areas like the bread and vegetable sections that are not part of an aisle. But the odds would increase exponentially after each Phoebe-less row.

I reached the end. Nothing.

Let me be clear. I was a long way from panicking. This had happened before as well. And the supermarket was busy. It was distinctly possible that I had missed her in the throng. So I retraced my steps. When I got back to the veg area I was feeling...well, this is difficult. I distinctly remember the panic that swamped me, but I can't exactly remember when it kicked in. It wasn't then. I think it came later, maybe when I found the trolley. If I was feeling anything other than that vague sense of irritation, it was probably confusion. How could I have missed her? Phoebe was not the kind of kid who would pull a practical joke. She wouldn't deliberately hide from me. She had to be there somewhere.

How much time had elapsed? The police asked me this later and even now I'm not sure. It could only have been a couple of minutes. I even retraced my steps, afterwards, but that didn't really help. For one thing, I couldn't remember how long I'd spent in the confectionery section. Not long. But *how* long? Two minutes? Five? And how fast was I walking then, when it all happened? From when I left her at the deli to when I really started to feel that hard knot of panic? Between five and ten minutes. That is the best I can do.

This time I was really methodical. I searched each aisle.

I found the trolley in aisle five, right next to the dog food and opposite the toilet paper. There was just one thing in it. A rolled-up package of white, greaseproof paper. I picked it up. The barcode sticker said 'salmon fillets'. Now, as I relive the moment, I realise that wasn't when I panicked. I don't *think* it was. She had to be close. People don't leave their trolley to go exploring the further reaches of the supermarket. They take it with them. This aisle was deserted, apart from a woman who was examining a tin of dog food. She was scrutinising the label as if it contained the key to the secret of the universe.

'Excuse me,' I said. We remain polite, even when the world is in the process of falling apart. She glanced up reluctantly, her face creased in suspicion as if I was about to say something offensive. 'Have you, by any chance, seen a small girl, about eight years old?

School uniform. Blue. She was pushing this trolley.' I indicated it as if that would clear up this confusing situation.

'Sorry, no,' she replied, and went back to her tin.

'Thanks,' I said. 'That's okay.' I have no idea why I said that.

Maybe it was at this point that I became worried. Seriously worried. I didn't want to run. I think I was still keeping hold of a sense of decorum, obeying social convention. What was I going to do when I ran into Phoebe in the next aisle and I'd been screaming her name? Who would be more embarrassed, her or me? This is one of the things that haunted me later. If I had yelled. If I had bellowed at the top of my voice, back there in the confectionery aisle, might she have heard me? Might the person who took her have panicked and run, leaving her behind? Was my determination to stay cool a contributory factor in the tragedy that unfolded? Others have told me this is a foolish line of thinking. I agree. It is monumentally foolish, but that doesn't stop me.

I compromised. I moved briskly down each aisle, increasing pace as I covered the supermarket. Even then, I believed she was going to appear around the next corner. I'd be angry that she had given me the slip. She would raise her eyebrows as if I was a moron and point out that she'd been waiting for me, *exactly* where I'd told her to go. But she wasn't in the confectionery aisle. She wasn't at the deli. I went to the checkouts and she wasn't there either. I went past the checkouts and to the front of the super-market. At some stage I dropped the mushrooms and the dill and the Turkish Delights. The car park was busy; folks loading their groceries into the backs of cars, returning trolleys to the bays. I caught a glimpse of a girl – the back of her head, the briefest hint of a profile – at the far end of the car park. I ran through the ranks of vehicles. Someone swore at me as I nearly collided with a trolley.

It wasn't her. As I got close I knew it wasn't her. She was with a woman, loading groceries, and her shape was all wrong. The school uniform was grey, for Chrissake. I skidded to a halt. A fine rain was starting to fall, though I only noticed because it made it slightly more difficult to see. I needed to think, but there were too many thoughts pushing against each other in my head. I blinked rain from my eyes and approached a couple of people, asked if they'd seen a girl wandering around by herself. I tried to keep my voice level. One woman was solicitous but couldn't help. The others simply shook their heads. I ran back into the supermarket. Think. I needed to think.

If Phoebe had been abducted then any time I spent now was not just wasteful but also damaging. Catastrophic. I thought about that. I did. But the prospect was absurd. Abduction didn't happen to your family. It was something you read about in newspapers. Those things occurred interstate and you saw the photos, read the words and it was all somehow a fiction, like earthquakes in third-world countries or people falling from balconies at inner-city hotels. You knew it was real, but it didn't *feel* real. Words and pictures cushion us from believing in the realm of the emotions, in the gut. I balanced one absurd notion against another. She had gone home. She was annoyed with me for some reason and had left the trolley there (in aisle five, opposite the dog food) to punish me. While I stood in the gathering rain, she was approaching home, her back straight, her lips pursed in annoyance, a secret grievance blooming in her mind. It was dumb, but I was prepared to believe anything that might keep my world intact. Take two improbabilities and select the most palatable.

I ran home. I ran as hard as I could. The rain was heavier now and my shirt stuck to my chest. Once I slipped in a puddle of water and skidded briefly onto one knee. It was much later that I realised I'd torn a hole in my trousers and scraped my leg bloody. Then I simply got back to my feet and kept running, not really aware I had fallen. I must have known, after five minutes, that she couldn't have come this way. I would have caught up with her by then. But I couldn't stop until I was sure. The driveway of our house was deserted and the house itself exuded an air of emptiness. The windows gazed at me and they were blank. I scrabbled in my pockets for keys and found I was shaking so badly that I couldn't get the front door key into the lock. It took three or four attempts and I was muttering *fuck, fuck* and making gouges in the metal. I had to do it two-handed.

'Phoebe!' I yelled when the door finally opened. 'Phoebe!' I let my voice rip then. I was home. I could lose control and no one would judge me. I even checked each room. I looked under her bed. That stupid thought was still with me, that she was punishing me for indeterminate sins, and that I would see her eyes, hard with resentment, staring back at me from the darkness and the dust bunnies. And I would welcome her hatred, accept it and hug her close. Instead, I was running again, back to the supermarket, the front door flapping behind me. I was a stupid fuck. She would be there, in the confectionery aisle, maybe her bottom lip trembling as she wondered where I was, but staying put because that was the kind of girl she was, she was responsible, I told her to go there and that's where she would be and she would be starting to get scared, but she'd trust her brother because he wouldn't let her down, she knew that and she'd yell, 'Where WERE you? I had to go to the toilet and when I got back you weren't here.' The toilet. Of course. Why hadn't I checked that? Because I was a dumb fuck, that's why.

I nursed that small spark of hope through the rain. It warmed me as I ran. It was an explanation and I was in desperate need of one.

I burst into the ladies' toilets because at this stage I didn't care what anyone thought of me. It was deserted. Then I went to the confectionery section. This time a couple of kids were trying to put chocolate bars into their mother's trolley and she kept putting them back on the shelves. The mother took one look at me and gathered her children behind her, moved them down the aisle and away from me. I turned in a circle. I did three-sixties over and over, like a drunk or a deranged dancer.

'Phoebe!' I cried, but I don't think any words came out. It must have been then that I sank to my knees. They told me later that's how they found me.

'PHOEBE!' I screamed.

I think I kept on screaming her name.

# CHAPTER 11

**The manager's office was small, windowless and functional.** I can't remember how I got there. She put a cup of tea and a plate of biscuits in front of me. I don't drink tea. I have never drunk tea. The biscuits were Arnott's and I wondered if she just took a packet off the shelves in situations like this. How did that work? Did she have to fill out a form and what would she put down for reasons? Was there a box to be ticked for 'Missing child'?

Then the manager left. She put a hand on my shoulder and I think I smiled. I might even have said 'Thank you.' Later on, I found out it was Ms Abbott, the woman Summer had so spectacularly insulted on her last day at work. She'd been on leave that day but came in when news filtered through of Phoebe's disappearance. Was it concern, genuine concern, that brought her into work on her day off? Or a sense that potential scandal was best dealt with in person? Forestalling recrimination, protecting her position? I only thought about this stuff later. For now,

I wasn't thinking at all, unless a jumble of images and unrelated ideas counts as thought.

The police officer was female and couldn't have been much older than Summerlee. She asked questions. Name, address, description of Phoebe. I showed her a photograph on my phone. I had taken it about six months before, in our garden at home, and it was a good one. She was blowing enormous soap bubbles from one of those machines you buy in toy shops and I caught her just as a bubble was swelling. It distorted the side of her face, which was one of the reasons I liked it. I wasn't thinking about what would be good from the police's point of view, I just wanted to share the image.

'Pretty girl,' said the police officer.

'Yes,' I said.

Her job was to sit with me. I knew there were other police officers out there somewhere, looking for Phoebe, interviewing people, searching the store one more time. The cup of tea sat on the desk. It was a sickly cream colour and I felt nauseous just looking at it. The plate of biscuits had two flies jostling for position.

'Delaware,' said the police officer. 'That name rings a bell.'

'My sister, Summerlee,' I said. 'She won the lotto.'

'That's it,' she said. 'Summerlee Delaware. Millions, wasn't it? Wow.'

I nodded. The officer smiled and made a note in her notebook. I knew why. At some point – I cannot say when – the possibility had occurred to me. Seven million, five hundred thousand dollars is a sum that attracts attention – and jealousy; how could it not? And here is something very strange. I was aware of hoping – *hoping*, how weird is that? – that someone had taken Phoebe to make money from it. Because, if that was the case, then it would be in their interests to keep her safe. She would become a transaction, and that was better than the alternative that gnawed at me. I couldn't help myself. I saw a man, overweight with thinning hair, combed over to hide a bald spot. Sallow skin and sweaty palms. Dead eyes. He was bundling Phoebe into the back of a van. He'd tell her that if she was a good girl then he would give her chocolate. Maybe a couple of Turkish Delights. But she would have to be a very good girl and do exactly what she was told. And Phoebe would be sobbing and telling him that she didn't want chocolate. She wanted her brother and could the man please, *please* take her back to the supermarket because he would be getting worried about her and she promised not to tell anyone about what was happening if he just let her go…

The pain hit me in the stomach and I bent over and threw up. It flooded the floor and part of the desk. The biscuits were fucked. And then the spasm came again. I retched and retched, even when there was nothing left in my stomach. The police officer had a hand on my back but I kept vomiting. There was a blinding pain behind my eyes and I think I was sobbing.

There is a blank. I can't remember leaving the manager's office but the next thing I'm aware of is sitting on a narrow bed, the kind you get in the sick bay at school. There was a blanket around my shoulders and I was sipping a glass of water. The female police officer had gone. Now there was a man sitting in a chair opposite me. He had a bushy moustache and heavy jowls, and looked like he drank too much. He was asking me questions and his eyes were the kind that bore through you, making you feel that you're almost certainly lying, even when you're telling the truth.

'So the last time you saw her was when she was queuing at the deli?'

'Yes. I told her to meet me in the chocolate aisle when she was done.'

'What time was that?'

I rubbed at my forehead. It was slick with sweat.

'I have no fucking idea,' I said. 'I didn't look at my fucking watch, all right? Why aren't you out there looking for her?'

'Easy, son,' he said. 'I know this is hard, but I need information, all right? And, trust me, we are searching for her as we speak. But I need your help, son. Can you do that for me?'

'I'm sorry,' I said. 'I'll try.'

'Can you estimate how long it was between leaving her at the deli counter and finding the trolley? Just a guess. Five minutes? Ten? Somewhere in between?'

I ran the events over in my mind, tracing my steps and running an imaginary stopwatch.

'What about security cameras?' I asked. It was an explosion in my head. Why hadn't I thought of it before? The place was packed with cameras. Phoebe and I had whiled away many a long wait at the checkout making faces at the cameras and watching the results on the monitors suspended from the ceiling. There was even a camera on the automatic doors, which we used to find disorientating because it always seemed like the image above you was going in the wrong direction. 'They must have caught her leaving. They *must* have.'

'We're going over the recordings now,' said the man. I almost apologised. The police would think of that. I was a prick for thinking they wouldn't. I didn't apologise, though. The guy had given me his name but I'd forgotten it. He looked like he was going to say something else but thought better of it.

'What?' I said.

He screwed up his lips, as if puckering for a kiss. I realised he was sucking his teeth. The moustache writhed like something alive, a salt-and-pepper caterpillar. He blew out his breath and rubbed at the corner of his eye.

'One of the cameras was damaged last night,' he said. 'Someone sprayed it with acid. The one that gave a view of the right-hand side of the car park. A person took a spray bottle, filled it with corrosive and carefully sprayed it through the metal grid protecting the lens. What do you think of that?'

For a moment I thought I was being accused. I felt that familiar sense of panic that comes when your response is certain to be weighed and found wanting. It's not enough to simply tell the truth. Not when you put yourself in the position of the other person who may, for whatever reason, suspect you are lying. Whatever you say can be interpreted as an attempt to hide the truth. Too aggressive, too passive, too defensive, too shifty, too confident. And when you get to thinking about that, you're fucked, because your words, your body language, will inevitably glisten with a guilty sweat.

'Did the camera record who it was?' I said. A thought fluttered. Would he interpret that as me being worried *my* image might have been caught? He tilted his head to one side and sucked his teeth again.

'It was done after midnight, but the car park lights are on twenty-four seven, so the images are fairly clear. Whoever did it brought something to stand on and took great care to avoid the coverage of other cameras. All we get is an image of a hand and then a jet of liquid. After that, nothing.'

'You think this is connected to Phoebe's disappearance?'

'Maybe. Maybe not. It's too early to say.'

'You think she was kidnapped.' I didn't phrase it as a question.

'Too early to say.' He leaned forward on his chair and patted himself on both knees. 'Look, Jamie. There are all sorts of possibilities. Maybe she saw a friend and went off with him or her. Maybe she's playing a joke on you. Nine times out of ten, we find a lost child really quickly and it turns out to be entirely innocent, a communication problem, nothing sinister at all. You know what kids can be like.'

'No, I don't. But I do know my sister. She wouldn't have left the store.'

'So why did you go home to see if she was there?'

'I…I don't know. I wasn't thinking clearly.' The pain in my head was still intense. It felt as if someone was sticking fine needles into my retinas. The cop waved a hand.

'Understandable,' he said. 'Look, let's get back to timing, shall we? We know when you came into the store. All of the interior cameras are working perfectly and you entered at exactly three twenty-two. But that's why I need to know how much time elapsed between entering and finding the abandoned trolley. It will give us specific areas of the recordings to focus on.'

I put my head into my hands and closed my eyes. I reviewed it all once more, the people at the deli, the Indian woman and her child, the broccoli stacker, the woman with the Celtic tattoo. Everything. I answered the questions as best I could, and when he asked the same questions over and over, I thought and deliberated and refined and answered as best I could. I kept my eyes shut to block out the room and focus on nothing but the images as they played out against the darkness of my lids. I knew they would people my nightmares and I knew also that I deserved it. I had lost my sister. She had been my responsibility and I had lost her.

I opened my eyes when something changed in the room. There must have been the sound of a door opening, but that wasn't it. It was something in the atmosphere, a sudden chill that pricked the hairs on my neck. My eyes watered from having been shut so long and it took a moment for them to clear.

Mum stood just inside the door, looking around as if bemused.

She was clutching her purse with both hands, holding it up to her stomach, a flimsy shield to ward off danger. Her mouth was set in a line. I could see the tendons working in her face to keep it fixed. And I knew that any relaxation would crack that foundation, produce a seismic shift and bring her structure down. She was one muscle movement away from destruction.

Mum glanced at the police officer, but I don't think she really saw him. She moved hesitantly towards me and I stood. The next moment she had me in her arms, her head over my left shoulder. She patted my back, slowly, regularly, like she was trying to bring up wind.

'It's okay, Jamie,' she whispered. 'It's okay.'

But we both knew it wasn't. Her voice was cold and the hand on my back felt as inflexible as judgement.

# CHAPTER 12

**It must have been hours later when the police drove us home.** Dad was waiting at the front door. It hadn't even occurred to me he hadn't rocked up at the supermarket. Later, I discovered that the police had discouraged it. They probably had enough to deal with, without the entire Delaware family sobbing intermittently and cluttering up the investigation, but they'd told him to stay at home in case Phoebe showed up there. I have no idea of the agony he must have endured, pinned to the stake of home, helpless and the prey of snarling imagination.

The tooth-sucking cop, whose name was Dixon, had had little to report before we were taken home. The security cameras *had* picked up Phoebe after she'd left the deli but then lost her somewhere before aisle five. So far, no footage had been found of her leaving the premises. Dixon admitted there were blind spots in the surveillance system, particularly at staff entrances and exits through the delivery areas, which struck me as bizarre.

I suspected Dixon felt the same way, though he didn't say anything other than that interviews of staff and customers were still taking place and he was hopeful we'd get news sooner rather than later. He said 'news', not 'good news', and I think Mum noticed. The muscles in her face tightened perceptibly. He asked whether we could find a recent picture of Phoebe and, if so, whether the cop who was driving us home might borrow it. Photographs of Phoebe were not in short supply. Only a month or so earlier, she'd had a school photo done and it was brilliant. She was in part-profile, a Mona Lisa–type smile on her face, and Mum had had it framed.

'Perfect,' said Dixon when we described it. 'She's in school uniform, yeah?' I nodded. 'Ideal,' he added. He escorted us out of the store. I was gratified to notice that police officers were in considerable evidence and that three squad cars were lined up outside the entrance. I was less gratified to notice some of the staff watching us. They whispered to each other and stared at me. *That's the one. That's the kid who lost his little sister. How can you lose your sister in a supermarket? That's just wrong...* I kept my head lowered, like those guys you see on news reports, coming out of court. When that thought struck me, I realised I looked guilty but I didn't care.

Dad hugged Mum when we arrived home and glanced at me over her shoulder. I couldn't read his expression and didn't have the energy to try. When the police officer asked for the photograph, Dad got the picture out of its frame and scanned it into our computer before handing over the print. The officer glanced at the photo.

'She's a lovely girl, Mr Delaware,' he said. 'We'll get this back to you as soon as possible.'

'Just get *her* back,' said Dad. 'Fuck the photograph.'

His words went through me like a jolt of electricity. Dad doesn't swear. I mean *never*. But the officer wasn't aware of this so he simply nodded. He told us we'd be the first to know if there was any news. He shook Dad by the hand, a curiously formal gesture under the circumstances, I thought. And then he left. I suspect he was glad to get out of there, out of the atmosphere of desolation and loss and back to a place where there would be action and colleagues and occasional laughter. Mum paced up and down in the front room, her mobile clenched in her right hand, giving the world a thousand-yard stare. Already the lines around her eyes seemed deeper, more ingrained. Dad waved me into the kitchen.

'Tell me everything,' he said.

I was tired of talking, but I didn't really have a choice. So I went through it all again. It was strange, but the recounting of the story diminished it somehow. Each time I told it, it became more of a fiction, something that belonged in the pages of a novel rather than being a reflection of the real world. Tragedy was transformed into the commonplace through the medium of words. When I'd finished, Dad said nothing, and I didn't know whether to be grateful or resentful. Maybe I wanted acknowledgement that I'd been witness to disaster, that somehow I was therefore more entitled to consideration, to forgiveness. But I also knew that any remark he made would either reveal or hide the true nature of my responsibility. I was already cocooned in guilt. I had no idea if I could take on the burden of any more.

Dad went straight to the computer and opened up Phoebe's photograph. He inserted some text: *Have you seen this girl? Any information, please ring.* Then he put our home number and Mum's mobile at the bottom and printed off dozens of copies. He stood by the printer, drumming his fingers on the machine and avoiding my eyes. The printer ran out of paper and he searched for more, cursing when he couldn't find any on the shelves. I went to my bedroom and brought down a fresh supply, which he took without saying anything. The machine burred once more and he resumed the finger drumming.

Mum came into the kitchen, picked up a sheet and nodded.

'Good idea,' she said. 'Get another twenty done and I'll get these up.'

'What, now?' I said.

She looked at me as if not quite registering my presence. There was another world in her head and she was lost in it.

'Of course, now,' she said finally. 'Is there any point in waiting?'

'Do you want a hand?'

'Stay with your dad,' she replied. 'And try to contact your sister. I've rung her mobile dozens of times and all I get is her message bank. Any news and you ring me first, understood?' I nodded. Mum took the car keys from the pot in the kitchen and gathered up the posters. She glanced over at Dad as if she was about to say something, but then thought better of it. The front door closed and moments later I heard the car start and the crunch of gravel as she reversed out of the driveway.

Dad printed off posters until the ink cartridge ran out, his head bent over the printer. He only spoke once and then it was to himself.

'Computers,' he mumbled. 'My area of expertise.'

I said nothing. I'm not sure a response was expected and it sure as hell wasn't required.

Eventually, silence, like a cat, stretched and curled around the house. I was aware of its claws and knew that at some stage it would use them.

**Dad and I sat for the next two hours locked in our own thoughts.** At one point I considered offering to make us a sandwich but dismissed the idea as soon as it came to mind. I rang Summerlee but had no more luck than Mum. I left three messages. All of them the same. Ring. Now. Urgent. I didn't have Spider's number and couldn't think of a way of finding it.

'Do you want me to go round to Summerlee's house, Dad?' I asked. 'I could get a taxi.'

'Wait till your Mum gets back,' he replied and fell into silence again. I wondered why it was important to wait for Mum. Was he resentful that she had appeared to take complete charge and was spitting the dummy? *I'm not allowed to make decisions so don't ask for one.* Or had he spent enough time alone and couldn't bear the thought of a silent house full of vague, malevolent shadows? Whatever the reason, I was aware we must be sharing mental images. Phoebe, clumping down the stairs after getting ready for bed, that peculiar asymmetric rhythm of bare feet on carpet. Phoebe in the morning, ducking her head as she ate breakfast, trying to get her mouth as close as she could to the bowl of cereal. Phoebe in the evening, bent over her homework, biting her bottom lip and printing her words carefully, methodically. Those were the good images, though they were painful. But others drew me, as they must have drawn Dad. Phoebe in a dark room, scared, her hands tied, the smell of mildew and despair rank in her nostrils. Phoebe in a shallow grave, eyes wide and unseeing...

My phone, when it rang, sent a jolt through both of us. It was as if Dad had been hit with a taser. He snapped upright, eyes filled with something – a cocktail of panic, hope, despair. He must have felt that we were on the brink of an answer he wasn't sure he wanted. And the drop was terrifying. I must have reacted similarly. I slid my thumb over the phone without even checking the caller ID.

'Hello?' I said.

'Yo, Jamie, dude.'

'I can't talk now, Gutless,' I said. 'I will ring you back. Please don't call again.'

'Whadda fuck, man?'

I hung up. Dad had deflated as soon as he heard me say 'Gutless'. Already his eyes were slightly glazed, focused on something within his head, and he appeared to sink into himself.

The sound of the car on the gravel brought us both to our feet. I recognised the engine noise. There were no revolving patterns of light against the wall, something a police cruiser might have generated. The car door slammed just as I opened the front door. Mum looked at me and I shook my head. She brushed past me into the house. Dad had sat down again at the kitchen table and Mum went to one of the cupboards, got a bottle of whisky from the shelf and three highball glasses. She poured an inch or two of whisky into each, put one down in front of Dad, handed me another and raised the last one to her lips, draining half in one swallow. I sipped mine. I'd had whisky before and didn't like it. Now I didn't care what it tasted like.

'You got them up?' I said.

'Yes, all of them. Around the supermarket, in all the adjoining streets. I'll get more up tomorrow.'

'Let's hope it won't be necessary.'

Mum finished the glass. She gulped and twisted her mouth as if the taste was foul. Then she poured herself another.

'And I want you to post as much as you can on social media,' she said. 'Get your friends involved. Spread the word. Facebook, Twitter, whatever.'

I knew this wasn't a good idea, but I didn't know why I knew.

Only later did I think of game theory and the importance of keeping everything close to your chest. At that time, I simply nodded. 'They'll find her,' I said. 'The cops will ring tonight.'

Mum nodded as well, but we were both aware it was an agreement based on nothing but hope.

'I couldn't get Summerlee,' I added. 'Maybe I should go round to her place. I could get a taxi.'

'I'll go,' said Mum. She moved to pick up the car keys again.

'Not after those whiskies,' I said. 'And, anyway, maybe you should stay here with Dad.' They had barely spoken a word to each other and I didn't know why. Maybe there were buried recriminations and their silence concealed an accumulating pressure between them, a dam that could break at any moment. Perhaps it would be good for it to be breached, but I didn't want to be around when it happened. I didn't think I could stand it.

Anyway, the real reason I wanted to go to Summerlee's place was that I could guess what I'd find there. It wasn't something that either of my parents could cope with right now. There would be words. Things would be said that couldn't be unsaid. And, anyway, Mum wasn't the only one who craved the illusion of action.

I rang the taxi company and was told they'd be here in ten minutes. I was vaguely surprised that the transaction was completed in a normal fashion. How could the world go on? How could it not care? I went and told Mum where I was going. She'd sat on the couch in the front room, staring at the blank screen of the television, her mobile still clutched firmly in her hand. She nodded. When I went back to the kitchen, Dad was crying. He was holding another glass of whisky and he was crying. In between curiously soundless sobs, he took another slug. I put a hand on his shoulder and then I went outside to wait for the taxi.

# CHAPTER 13

There were lights on at Summerlee's place. *All* the lights were on at Summerlee's place. Cars ranged along the driveway and halfway down the street. A few motorbikes were dotted among the cars. The noise coming from the house was palpable. The air throbbed.

I walked up the driveway. I heard voices coming from the bushes. A number of the solar lights that bordered the driveway had been kicked over and shards of plastic littered the pavers. The grass was long and turning to seed. Someone was kneeling in the middle of the garden and throwing up. Her body wrenched and buckled but I couldn't hear her puke. The music coming from the open front door drowned out everything else. She had on a dirty white top with spaghetti straps.

Inside the house it was worse. One guy was sprawled just inside the door. He had on leather jeans, a leather jacket and one black glove. His eyes were nearly closed, but I could see a narrow sliver of white beneath his lids. I didn't bother trying to wake him.

The place was trashed. The marble floors were covered in dirt and other things I didn't want to identify. One tile was cracked. How could you crack a marble tile? What force does that require? I poked my head around the living-room door. A few people were dancing, bodies jerking like they'd been connected to the mains electricity. One couple shuffled around a patch of carpet, their heads on each other's shoulder, keeping each other upright. The furniture had been pushed back. A lamp had fallen but no one had bothered to right it and its globe still burned. I followed the sound of voices to the back of the house and into the garden. The pool was full of bodies, most of them naked. I think I spotted a couple screwing on a lounger, but I looked only long enough to make sure one of them wasn't Summerlee. I tried to be similarly efficient with the bodies in the pool. She wasn't there.

I finally found her upstairs in one of the bedrooms. She was sprawled over a bed, her top rucked up exposing a wide expanse of belly and a glimpse of a white, soiled bra. Spider was curled up on the floor next to her. I stepped over him and shook her by the shoulder but she didn't respond.

'Hey, Summer,' I said. 'Come on, wake up.'

She shifted then, but only to turn over on her side. She grunted and I saw a trail of spittle leaking from the side of her mouth. I turned her on to her back. She made a growl of annoyance.

'Summer!' I shouted. I slapped her face, but only gently. The bedroom was like the rest of the house. It was filthy. Things had been dropped on the floor – most of her clothes by the look of it – and left exactly where they fell. The bedside table was littered with junk, an overflowing ashtray, a packet of cigarettes, a lighter, and a plastic bag full of what could only be cannabis. A bong lay next to Spider's outstretched hand. I went into the ensuite and wished I hadn't. There were black things growing on the bathroom walls and the toilet seat hung askew. I emptied a black plastic cup that held a toothbrush, but I would have bet it hadn't been used in weeks. Then I filled the cup with water from the cold tap and carried it back into the bedroom. Summerlee was exactly where I'd left her. She was snoring. I poured the water over her face. That got a reaction. She sat up instantly.

'Fuck off,' she said, but her eyes didn't focus. 'Fuck off, willya?'

'Summer,' I said. 'It's me. Jamie. I need you to wake up.'

She rubbed at her face and screwed up her eyes. Her hands were grimy.

'Jamie? What the fuck you doing here?' She coughed, leaned over and pulled a cigarette from the pack, lit it with the lighter. Then she coughed again.

'You need to come home, Summer. It's an emergency.'

She blew smoke into my face, but I don't think it was deliberate.

'Can't now, Jamie. I'm fucked up. I'm seriously fucked up.'

'Then you'll have to get un-fucked up,' I said. 'It's Phoebe. She's missing.'

It took far too long to get Summerlee to pay proper attention and even longer for her to comprehend what I had said. When she did, her face twisted as if an agonising pain had struck between her eyes. She tried to say something but then staggered into the ensuite. I heard the shower running. I sat on the edge of the bed and looked down at Spider's crumpled body. He didn't look better unconscious than he did normally. He was wearing a red singlet and his right arm was tattooed up to the shoulder and across the side of his neck. There was the normal stuff – dragons and other creatures designed to identify you as someone with a wild personality. But there was also a grinning skull and an impossibly large-breasted girl wearing only a pair of panties. I really wanted to kick the bastard in the nuts but instead I opened the wardrobe and rummaged around for some of Summer's clothes. I came up with a pair of jeans and a plain black top. I cracked open the bathroom door and shoved them inside.

'Two minutes, Summer,' I yelled. There was a muffled reply. At least she was capable of replying. I rang for a taxi. Another ten minutes. I figured I would need that long to get my sister down the stairs and out into the open. When she came out of the bathroom, six minutes later, she was almost normal. Her hair was sodden and she either didn't feel she had the time to dry it or couldn't be bothered. But she was also without make-up for one of the first times in living memory. It transformed her face, made her seem years younger. It almost took my breath away. She seemed innocent, like the girl I remembered, the other girl I'd lost. I could see Phoebe in her eyes.

The party carried on without her. If anyone recognised her as we walked through the hallway to the front door, no one let on.

Most would have been incapable of recognising anyone. The guy with the one glove was exactly where I'd left him.

'Who are these people?' I asked.

'Fuck knows,' said Summer. 'People. Who cares?' She left without looking back. The taxi was waiting for us.

**I had to go through it all again with Summer when we got back to the house.** Now I felt like I was reciting a script that no longer seemed even faintly realistic.

Dad had obviously made further inroads into the whisky bottle. His words were slightly slurred. 'I rang that cop, Dixon,' he said. 'He told me they were following leads, but had nothing to report at this stage. "Following leads"! Sitting around eating doughnuts, more like. At least we got those photographs up. While they were "following leads", your mum and I were actually doing something.'

This wasn't the time to tell Dad that it was not a pissing contest. And he was right. My parents *had* done something. I'd just lost her, and that took no effort at all.

Summerlee said very little, and I didn't know whether that was because there wasn't much to be said or because she was still screwed up by the weed and other shit in her bloodstream. At one point she hugged Mum. She sat next to her on the couch and put an arm around her shoulder, whispered something into her ear. Mum just nodded. I went to sit by them, but Dad took my arm and led me back to the kitchen.

'You think she's been kidnapped?' he said. 'Because I do.'

I shrugged. It wasn't the time to say anything. Dad would have considered the alternatives, just as I had. The whisky was simply a way of diverting that train of thought, maybe trying to derail it. He pointed towards the front room, towards my sister.

'That money is a curse,' he said. 'I thought it before but now I know it. I reckon I'd come to terms with the thought of it killing Summerlee, sooner or later. Sooner would be my guess. But I will not have it kill my other daughter. Why doesn't that phone ring?'

But it didn't. The silence wore us down, made the hours longer. At some point, around two in the morning, I went to the bathroom. I needed to piss and I was feeling nauseous again. Phoebe's bedroom was next to the bathroom, but her door was closed and I was grateful. I looked into the bathroom mirror. What looked back was something old, haunted and defeated.

When my phone rang, I had to scrabble to get it out of my pocket and nearly dropped it. I glanced at the screen. Caller unknown.

'Hello?' I said.

There was a pause. The voice, when it came, was bizarre, robotic. I remember thinking briefly that maybe someone from school was having fun with a synthesiser, testing it out. It reminded me of that Stephen Hawking monotone, each word enunciated clearly yet devoid of emotion. It wasn't even possible to detect a gender.

'I have your sister. Listen carefully to what I'm about to tell you...'

'I can't talk to you right now,' I said. 'I'm busy. Ring me back in an hour.'

I hung up. And then I turned my phone off, just so I couldn't be tempted. Finally, I bent over the toilet bowl and threw up.

# CHAPTER 14

I knelt on the bathroom floor, my hands gripping the side of the toilet bowl. I'd had nothing to eat, so there was nothing to throw up, apart from a few thick strings of mucus. I wiped my mouth with the side of my hand.

What had I done? What was I thinking? I was *busy*? Fuck's sake. I was light-headed and I had to concentrate to stop the toilet bowl from floating to the right of my vision. My thoughts floated as well, drifting, mixing, difficult to separate. Game theory. It was classic game theory. Don't think about what you *must* do, think about what the other person *might* do. Someone who takes a child knows they are in control; they rely upon the balance of power being firmly on their side. How does it go?

*Please don't hurt her.*

*I will do anything you say.*

*Whatever you want, just don't hurt her.*

I was altering the balance of power. I was refusing to acknowledge that this was how the rules worked. There were two players in this game and it's my mind against yours. You think you hold all the cards, but you don't. Stew on that for an hour, fucker.

I knew, of course I knew, that this was a gamble and I was dicing with Phoebe's life.

Actually, I hadn't thought that when I got the call. I had simply reacted, the words spilling from my mouth directly from my unconscious, where I must have been mulling over the situation from a game theory perspective and finding possible strategies. But what if he was so angry he'd hurt Phoebe, just to teach *me* a lesson? Cut off a finger and send it through the post? Want to play games, fucker? Want to fight with both hands tied behind your back? Bring it on.

I clung to the toilet bowl and tried to keep my world from shifting.

I realised I was assuming it was a man. Was that an automatic response because statistics tell us it is men who commit crimes, that less than ten per cent of convicted criminals are women? Was a woman emotionally incapable of kidnapping a little girl? I imagined not, but I didn't know and why would someone change their voice so that it was gender-neutral unless she was female? Then again, maybe a man would want me to be thinking along those lines...

I shook my head and tried to focus. He, she, whoever, might hurt Phoebe, but I didn't think it would happen like that, not then, staring at the blank whiteness of the porcelain. *This guy is organised. He plans. He knows our routines, he took out a security camera, he got Phoebe from a supermarket, past cameras and guards, without anyone seeing. Wouldn't that be easier for a woman? Don't think about that now. Deal with what I know or can reasonably surmise. He is meticulous. He has my mobile number. How did he get that? From Phoebe? Would she give that up willingly? Can't think about that either. This has to be about money and nothing else. Phoebe is an asset to him and there's no point damaging an asset because then the price goes down. He's demonstrated he is intelligent. An intelligent person doesn't give way to anger, because it's not profitable.*

Among all the flotsam swirling in my mind, it was this piece of logic I held onto; without it I would drown.

I glanced at my watch. About five minutes since I'd received the call. Why had I said an hour? Wouldn't fifteen minutes have been enough? No, I decided. It wouldn't. An hour was right. I got to my feet, though I had to steady myself with a hand on the cistern. Whether I was right or wrong, I had to follow this through. But there were people downstairs who deserved the information in my head. I couldn't keep all of this to myself. But even then, I was thinking game theory. They were players but that didn't mean they had to know everything.

The scene in the front room hadn't altered much. Mum still

sat. Summerlee had fallen asleep, or passed out. Dad paced. I disrupted the tableau.

'I just got a call,' I said. 'The person who took Phoebe.'

For a second or two there was a stunned silence. Maybe Summerlee picked up on the sudden charge in the atmosphere because she opened an eye and struggled to straighten herself. Then it was verbal mayhem.

'Is she all right?'

'What did he say?'

'Oh my God.'

'Did you talk to her? Is she okay?'

I held up a hand.

'He…she…didn't say anything. Just that he had Phoebe. He or she's ringing back in fifty minutes.'

'You couldn't tell if it was a man or a woman?' Dad said.

'The voice was disguised. I think he or she must be running it through a computer program. Kind of a vague North American accent, but androgynous. Could be anyone.'

'We should call the police.' This was Mum.

'No police,' I said. 'He said no police. He will only talk to me. No one else listening. He said that he would know if anyone else was listening in.' My mind had suddenly cleared and the lies tripped off my tongue. Would anyone notice the discrepancy between my first statement and the qualifications I was now making? *He only said he had Phoebe. He didn't say anything else.* Apart, it seemed, from plenty. But no one noticed. Mum and Dad were too drunk on hope and Summerlee was probably just too drunk. I held my mobile phone in my hands and trusted no one would notice it was turned off. Mum gave me instructions, as I knew she would. What she really wanted was to be the one doing the talking on the phone, but if that wasn't possible she'd go for the next best thing and jerk my strings, to give herself some semblance of control.

'Insist on talking to Phoebe,' she said. 'Don't even engage with him until you've established she's safe and unharmed. Listen out for background noise. Anything that might give an indication of where he might be. You know, the sound of a train or a plane or something.' It occurred to me that Mum had watched more thrillers than I'd realised, but I didn't say anything. Just nodded. 'When he talks about money, don't try to negotiate. Just agree to his demands whatever they are. There will be ways to trace the money later.' Maybe her head was full of exploding bags of cash that painted red dye onto the perpetrators, or serial numbers that could be traced or GPS devices hidden in the lining of a suitcase. I nodded.

Mum went on in the same vein for twenty minutes. Ideas bubbled from her. Dad tried a couple of times to interrupt, but she ran over his words and didn't even notice she was doing it. Was it possible for me to record the conversation on my mobile phone? Perhaps we could record the entire conversation if I put it on speakerphone? Maybe we should let the police know anyway. Couldn't they track a phone? If I kept the guy talking they'd be able to trace him. SWAT teams going in while he talked to me.

Phoebe being swept up in the manly arms of a good guy while the kidnapper was gunned down as he resisted arrest.

We wallowed in Hollywood horseshit, but then again, even Hollywood horseshit has to be based on *something*, doesn't it? The simple truth was we were all out of our depth.

But Mum's pronouncements made me aware of something buried deep within my character. Those movie scenes. The vigilante doing whatever it took to defeat the bad guy. *You messed with the wrong person, motherfucker*. The realisation surfaced slowly. I could be that vigilante. If it was a man, I could kill him. If it was a woman, I could kill her. Maybe even if it wasn't necessary.

The last fifteen minutes, for me at least, were worse than all the hours that preceded them, possibly because I was the only one who knew my phone was switched off. Dad sat down on the couch and instantly Mum got up and started pacing, as if they were on a roster and had switched duties. I went out to the kitchen and all eyes followed me. I'd thought about fixing myself another drink of whisky, but decided against it. I poured myself a glass of milk instead. It tasted horrible, but I forced it down. If I was going to throw up again, I wanted something in my stomach. Anyway, it was an act that mimicked normality and I needed that. I opened the fridge to return the carton of milk and, using the door as a shield, switched on my phone. Two missed calls. Caller unknown. I closed the fridge and returned to the living room.

Mum screamed when the phone rang, and then stuffed her

hand into her mouth. Five minutes early, but I couldn't do any more. I let it ring twice before touching the answer symbol. Suddenly, the milk wanted to make a reappearance. I swallowed.

'Hello?'

There was a long pause.

'You were *busy*?' That computer voice, leached of feeling. Yet I detected (imagined?) the emphasis on the last word. I tried to focus. I even followed Mum's advice and listened for background noises, but there was nothing. I didn't reply. Let him give information. Dad was waving to try and attract my attention, so I turned my back on him.

'Are the police there?' It didn't even sound like a question. Emotions, intonations, give us cues. We can read them easier than we think. It was disorientating, almost alarming, to listen to a voice and not pick up anything other than basic meaning.

'No,' I said. 'No police.'

'That's probably a mistake, Jamie. I expected you to call the police. It's what I would have done in your situation.' I didn't say anything. But I felt perversely pleased that I hadn't met those expectations. 'Or maybe you're lying to me and the police are there. It makes no difference one way or the other. You should know that.'

'What do you want?'

'It's very simple. I will return Phoebe unharmed as soon as I receive two million dollars in cash.'

'I want to talk to Phoebe,' I said.

'Sorry. That's not happening.'

'How do I know you've got her?'

'Ask me a question only she would know the answer to. I'll ask her and relay it back to you.'

'That's complicated. Why can't I just talk to her?'

'Because I say so. Now, do you want to ask that question, or not?'

I thought, but my mind was blank. How dumb was that? When it came down to it I couldn't think of one thing that only Phoebe and I would know. It seemed emblematic of my betrayal of her, but I couldn't afford to dwell on guilt. I racked my brain.

'Ask her what the suitors want when they have their ninja rats at the ready.'

There was silence for a beat or two. 'You are serious?'

'Ask her.'

There was no change down the line, but I knew he no longer had the phone to his ear. I focused intently but could detect no variation in the quality of the silence. Then the voice came back.

'Princess Phoebe's hand and her other bits.'

I bit so hard on my bottom lip that I tasted blood. 'Okay,' I said. 'How do we do this?'

'I'll call you at midday tomorrow. Try not to be busy. Oh, and Jamie. I would seriously think about involving the police, if I was you. Ring them now, get it set up so they'll be ready when I call you. This really isn't something you can handle by yourself.'

*He knows game theory*, I thought. *He knows game theory.*

'Tell Phoebe I love her,' I said. 'Tell her we all love her and we will get her back safe.'

There was that blank silence again.

'I will, Jamie. I'll tell her. But it's up to you to make that last bit come true. I mean, you didn't do a good job of looking after her today, did you? This is your chance at redemption. Don't fail.'

He hung up. I stared at the phone, put it in my pocket. And then I answered my family's questions. There were many and they came quickly.

# CHAPTER 15

**We were all at the cop shop by ten in the morning.** A car came to pick us up – me, Mum, Dad and Summerlee. It was driven by the guy who'd taken Phoebe's photograph. He didn't say much during the drive. Neither did we.

Mum had rung Dixon the previous night, as soon as I'd told everyone about the call. He'd listened, asked a couple of questions and then made arrangements for the morning. He suggested we all try to get some sleep. Summer took his advice but only because I don't think she had much choice. At some stage during the night – around five, I'd guess – I tried to ring the guy back by accessing the last call on my phone's menu. Yet another robotic voice told me I could not be connected. At least this one was recognisably female. Dad watched as I tried. When I shook my head he took the bottle of whisky and poured what was left down the sink. Then he resumed his pacing. The night crept into day.

The police station was disturbingly normal. A couple of

people were sitting in chairs and a guy in uniform was behind a counter, listening to a woman reporting a crime. From the brief snippet of conversation I overheard I think it was something to do with a stolen purse. It crossed my mind to tell her that she was belittling herself by being there. She'd lost her purse? The sun was shining, people were laughing and joking, the day was going on, just like any other day. A purse. I'd lost a sister. She should go through those doors, raise her face to the sky and thank whatever god would listen. I'd lost all tolerance for the trivial and wondered if I'd ever find it again.

We were taken through a locked door and down a corridor to an interview room. I was expecting to see Dixon, but he wasn't there. A guy in a sharp suit sat behind a desk. He was probably in his late thirties. A woman, slightly older, stood at his side. She was dressed in a business suit that looked expensive. I noticed she had a thin dusting of moustache on her top lip. It seemed at odds with her general appearance which could have passed for that of a company executive. They smiled as we entered. Not a full smile. Not the kind of smile that said, *we are having a great day. Isn't this fun?* More a smile that conveyed the deadly seriousness of our collective business while retaining the human touch. Did they get training in that? Practise it in front of the mirror each morning? I was tired. I was close to shutting down. My brain was making wild, bordering on chaotic, connections. Everything was absurd.

They introduced themselves. Detective Inspector Gardner

and Detective Moss. Mum leaped straight in and asked about progress. Detective Moss briefly left the room to find us a couple more chairs while her colleague answered. He did his best to give the impression of considerable and ongoing industry and I'm sure that was true. Many people had been interviewed: all of the supermarket staff on duty and a fair number of customers. Police were working to track down other people who were in the store at the time in question. They had been planning an appeal for information on local radio and a special broadcast on television had been arranged, complete with the photograph of Phoebe. Now, with the news that the kidnapper had made contact, they were rethinking. Maybe it was a good idea to keep the media out of it for the moment, until more information was forthcoming. They didn't want to add another factor into an already volatile situation. Nonetheless, the police had already gathered considerable intelligence – he really used that word – and were confident of gaining more as the investigation proceeded.

He talked a lot, the Detective Inspector, but it all boiled down to fuck all. No one had seen anything. It wasn't surprising when I thought about it later. The man in his suit talking on his phone. The woman with the Celtic tattoo and the troublesome kid. All those people going about their daily lives, orbiting their own individual suns. What to make for dinner. How to sort out that problem at work. Is that lump on my breast cancerous? It's what I'd done. I'd been absorbed in dill, mushrooms, Turkish Delight and maths homework. Why would I pay particular attention to worlds that brushed my own but never made proper contact?

Mum asked questions as if by doing so, she could force meaningful answers.

Detective Moss made me go through the conversation I'd had with the kidnapper the previous night. She was gentle but persistent. Mum kept trying to put in her version, but Moss steered the conversation away in a diplomatic fashion. I kept to my fiction that the first call had been simply a statement that he/she would ring back in an hour. I couldn't tell the truth because no one would understand. I tried to convince myself the lie wouldn't matter or wasn't important. Detective Moss led me through the second conversation time and again. She seemed particularly interested in the remark that I had been poor at looking after Phoebe at the supermarket and that this was my chance at redemption. I noticed she doubly underlined something in the notes she was taking and put an exclamation mark in the margin.

'Where's Dixon?' I asked after I'd been through the same version for the fourth time.

'He's not on this case,' said Gardner. 'Not now it's no longer a missing person but a suspected kidnapping.'

'Why?' I asked. 'I liked him.' It was strange. Until I said that I had no idea it was true.

'Not his area of expertise,' said Gardner.

'I want him involved,' I said.

Gardner pursed his lips and glanced at his colleague. 'Sorry,' he said. 'Not possible. But I'll tell him what you said, if you like.'

That was the first time I understood we were no longer in charge; though, come to think of it, we had never really been in charge from the start. Protocols existed. My sister was not my area of expertise. These strangers, who didn't know her, had abducted her also.

My phone was hooked up to a computer, presumably with recording software, so we could all listen through the speakers. We were offered tea or coffee. I accepted the coffee on the grounds that caffeine might just keep me going a bit longer. Mum and Dad didn't have anything. The strain was showing. Dad seemed to be withdrawing into himself and his skin was shrivelling in response. Mum, perhaps to compensate, was becoming bigger, her voice louder and more strident. She asked about tracking conversations, establishing locations via GPS. Gardner was respectful but his answers didn't give much away. Eleven-thirty arrived. Hours later it became eleven forty-five. Gardner told us how the situation was going to be handled.

'I want you to let me deal with this wherever possible, Jamie,' he said. 'It's impossible to predict how this might pan out, so we can't lay down any hard and fast rules. You were told to contact us, so it's reasonable to assume the perpetrator wants us to handle the negotiations.' I couldn't believe he'd used the word 'perpetrator'. He continued. 'He or she wants to talk to us directly. Are you sure you couldn't tell the gender from the phone conversation?'

I nodded.

'Okay. We'll call the perp "he". It'll save time.'

I nodded again.

'Then again,' said Gardner, 'he may want to deal with you and let us listen in, for reasons of his own. I guess what I'm saying is that we should play this by ear. What I do insist on, however, is that no one says anything at all unless specifically asked to.' He looked long and meaningfully at Mum as he said this. 'No off-the-cuff comments. Keep quiet. If you can't, then you'll have to leave the room. Is that understood?' We all nodded. Gardner turned to Summerlee. 'It's possible he will want to talk to you, given you're the one who can afford the ransom money. If he asks, just say that Detective Gardner will handle all negotiations on your behalf. Okay?'

Summer bit her lip and nodded. She'd tidied herself up at some stage during the night, even put on a little bit of make-up. I noticed that the skin around her eyebrow piercing was red and raw. It looked painful. We settled into our chairs as best we could and watched the clock on the wall as its hands crept in glacial fashion towards noon.

I suspect we all held our breath as the minute hand clicked onto twelve. Two hands merged into one but the phone didn't ring. It wasn't until five past that the call came in. I was embarrassed by my ring tone. Its cheeriness was an affront. Why hadn't I changed it to something more appropriate? Because I had other things on my mind. Gardner gestured to me to answer it. My finger trembled as I swiped the pulsing icon.

'Hello?' I was appalled by the poverty of the opening. There was that silence again. I was starting to understand that there are different textures to silence. This was not the absence of noise. It was something more solid, weighty. The absence of noise wrapped in something thick and buried underground.

'Not busy, I hope?' said the mechanical voice.

'No.'

'That's good, Jamie. Now. Tell me where you are and who's with you.'

I glanced at Gardner who nodded.

'I am at the police station, in an interview room. With me are my Mum and Dad, my sister Summerlee and Detective Inspector Gardner and Detective Moss.'

'Good. You are on speakerphone or Bluetooth, I can tell. Good afternoon, Detective Gardner.'

'Good afternoon.'

'You are the officer in charge?'

'Correct.'

'Excellent. I want you to listen carefully. All of you. First things first. Phoebe is fine. Obviously she is scared and misses her family. But I am looking after all her needs. She has eaten, though not much I must admit. She is hydrated. She got some sleep last night. Physically, she is in good shape. I have not harmed her and I will not harm her, provided you do what is necessary. Is that understood?'

'Perfectly,' said Gardner. 'Is it possible to speak to her so that she can confirm what you've told us?'

'Not now. Possibly later. In the meantime you will have to take my word.'

'That's not fair on her family,' said Gardner. 'As you know, they are distraught with worry. This would be a small gesture of good faith on your behalf.'

'Possibly later.'

Mum made as if she was about to say something, but Moss placed a hand lightly on her shoulder and she shrank back into her chair. I could tell something was building inside and the pressure was becoming unbearable.

The voice continued.

'Here is one piece of information I am prepared to give you about me. I once worked briefly for a mobile phone provider. I was exceptionally good at my job. In fact, I am confident there are very few people in Australia who know more about the technology of communications than I do. If you have any notions of tracking me through these conversations, then I advise you to forget them right now. It will not happen. No GPS. No triangulation of signals or any of that nonsense. You will be searching for Phoebe and, of course, me. I understand and respect that. But you will not find me through phone conversations. I'm trying to save you time. I'm being cooperative in the hope you will reciprocate.'

He paused again.

'Summerlee Delaware won seven million, five hundred thousand dollars recently on Ozlotto. My price for returning Phoebe Delaware is two million dollars in cash. Once I receive that I will release her unharmed. I will not ask for more money. Two million is sufficient for my needs and I am professional. I think it would be better for all concerned if we considered this a straightforward business arrangement. Are we clear so far?'

'Yes,' said Gardner.

'Okay. Here is the last point. I will no longer talk to anyone except Jamie Delaware. This is not open for negotiation and I will hang up if anyone else attempts to talk to me. This includes, in fact it especially applies to, the police. Obviously I cannot control what is happening at your end of the phone and I imagine Jamie will want to have the advice and support of experts whilst I am talking to him. This is fine by me. But no one else is to talk. If I even hear another voice in the background I will hang up and the release of Phoebe will be, at best, delayed. Understood?'

'Yes,' said Gardner, and the line went dead. 'Shit,' he muttered and rubbed his brow. He looked up at us sheepishly and for a moment I thought he was going to try to explain. *I didn't realise he meant starting now.* The room was quiet.

Mum started crying. It was a stifled sob at first but then it got messy and loud. She hunched over in her chair and really let rip. Her pain, I realised, had been an avalanche waiting to happen. The drift of one snowflake would set it into unstoppable motion.

A snowflake had drifted in that mechanical voice.

It was difficult to believe a body so small could contain such anguish, and I wondered if it would physically tear her apart. Dad tried to help. He really tried. But the only strategy he had at his disposal was an arm around her shoulders, and it didn't work. He looked at Summerlee and his face was filled with helplessness. I was learning much about my family. Mum's explosive energy, her determination to act, was a thin veneer, a film protecting a deep, possibly bottomless, pit of fear. Dad was simply out of his depth. Summerlee had chosen her path and every step took her further and further away from the family. Phoebe had always been the best of us. But Phoebe wasn't here.

Detective Moss took over.

'I know this is hard,' she said, 'but I would like a favour from all of you. Can you all, independently, write a list of anyone – and I mean *anyone* – who could conceivably wish you harm?'

Mum jumped in and her voice, though shaky, was strong enough. Barely.

'But this is just about money, isn't it?' she said. 'I mean, that's what the voice said. Two million dollars. Not about doing us harm. Not about harming my baby...' Her voice broke once more.

'I'm sure it is,' said Moss. She put her hands flat on the table as if somehow that was reassuring. 'But we have to explore all possibilities, Ms Delaware. It won't do any harm and might, conceivably, give us another lead to work on. Can you do that for us? Please?'

'Of course,' said Dad.

'Thank you,' said Moss.

The meeting finished soon after that. Gardner practically ejected Mum and Dad through the police station's main door and

Summer and I followed. But before we left, Gardner took me by the arm and pulled me to one side.

'When he rings again, I want you to contact me immediately. Understand?'

'Of course,' I said.

'Day or night. Any time, okay?'

'Sure.'

He nodded, but kept his eyes on mine for longer than strictly necessary as if, for indeterminate reasons, I might be lying. He gave me a card with his mobile number on it.

'Get some sleep,' he said, not unkindly. 'You look like shit.' Even that wasn't unkind. And I felt certain it was true because I absolutely *felt* like shit.

It was only when we were in the car park that we realised no one had arranged a lift home for us. Dad took the opportunity to rail against the inefficiencies and lack of consideration of the police and used his mobile to call a taxi. He stormed into the road, his back to us, and rang while glancing up and down the main street. I might have pointed out that the detectives were hopefully busy doing their jobs and that we were still capable of finding our own way home, but I kept quiet. I knew enough to know Dad needed indignation right then. It was performing a similar function to the whisky. Mum had calmed down a little and Summer was hugging her close. When she broke off, I tapped Summer on the arm and she moved with me a couple of metres away.

'I'm going for a walk,' I said. 'I'll be home later. Tell Mum.'

'You can't just leave us, Jamie,' she replied. 'What if he rings again?'

'Then I'll ring you guys immediately.'

She looked as if she might argue, but then she shrugged. Even under these circumstances she couldn't bring herself to consider me as anything other than an irrelevance. I stepped into the road and turned left. Dad was talking on his phone and raising a hand towards a taxi that was quite obviously already occupied. He didn't see me and I was grateful.

# CHAPTER 16

**I had no idea I was going to school until I got there.** And I didn't know I was tracking Gutless down until I went to Mr Monkhouse's classroom to find him.

I knocked on the door and waited. Mr Monkhouse could get grumpy if someone just burst into his classroom. It interrupted his flow, he said, and he liked flow. I did too. When Mr M was chasing after a mathematical idea it was kinda beautiful, even if very few of his students were able to follow the mental path he was beating. He didn't mind that. In the end he often taught to an audience of one – himself – and if others were able to join in, that was fine. It just wasn't obligatory.

The door opened and a different teacher stood there. He was short, bald, and sported a salt-and-pepper beard, trimmed close. My mouth opened and closed again. Mr Monkhouse was *always* in class. Some students reckoned he slept there.

'Can I help you?' said the man.

'I was looking for Mr Monkhouse,' I said.

'He's off sick. I'm the relief teacher.' He went to close the door so I put the flat of my hand against it. The teacher regarded me for a moment and any trace of friendliness evaporated. There wasn't much to start with.

'I need to see Gutless Geraghty,' I said. 'It's an emergency.'

'Who?'

'Sean. Sean Geraghty. He's a student in this class.'

'And do you have a note from reception?'

'No. It's just that...'

'Then I suggest *you* get to class, young man. The students here are working.' This time, the door closed with unmistakable finality.

I went out into the pale and sickly sunshine and sat down on the grass bank overlooking the basketball court. The entire school was deserted.

Sick. Mr Monkhouse was sick. I remembered a time when Mr M broke his arm and didn't miss a day. He had one of the students write on the board for him. I pulled my phone from my pocket and found his number in contacts. He'd given it to me a year back, when it became clear I was his best student. Hell, I'd even been round to his house for personal tuition a couple of times. I rang and didn't feel the slightest bit guilty. He might be ill, but there was a thought rattling around at the back of my head and I wanted to talk to him. The phone rang and rang, and just when I was sure it was going to voicemail, he answered.

'Hello?' It's only one word, I know, but he didn't sound sick.

'Mr Monkhouse. It's me, Jamie Delaware.'

There was a pause, like he was trying to place me. 'Jamie,' he said. 'Look, I'm sorry, but I'm not in school at the moment. I'm not well.'

'What's the problem, Mr Monkhouse?'

Another pause.

'That's none of your damn business, Jamie. Don't ring me again.' The line went dead.

I put the phone away and got to my feet. Something strange was going on.

Mr Monkhouse was nearly always patient. I had seen him explaining something to a student, carefully and meticulously, though he must have wanted to scream at the lack of understanding, the apparent inability to grasp the obvious. Mr Monkhouse was the gentlest man I had ever known.

Our conversation had *not* been gentle. He had been brusque, insensitive, and he sounded stressed out rather than sick. True, there was no reason he would know about Phoebe. There'd been nothing on the news, so I shouldn't have been expecting sympathy or any consideration for my feelings. But, still ... he liked me, or I always thought he did, and I was ringing to check on his wellbeing. Why would he be so rude?

His house was a five-minute walk from the school. Maybe he'd bought it to cut down on the time spent away from the classroom. Who knows, who cares? I got to his place in three minutes and sat on a wall opposite his front door in the shade of a large tree.

Every curtain in his house was drawn closed. I spent half an hour watching and a curtain didn't so much as twitch. I could have knocked on his door – why should I worry about other people's sensibilities when they didn't worry about mine? But I didn't. I sat and thought. Detective Moss had given me much to think about.

My phone buzzed. Text message. I didn't know whether to be relieved or disappointed that it was from Gutless.

Dude. u wantd 2 see me. dooshbag relf teacher. fuck him. meet greesyspoon in 20. Da Horse.

I texted back. *Make it 45*. At some stage I would have to have another word with Gutless about his text messages. Who wrote shit like that? He signed off as The Horse because someone had once pointed out his initials were gee-gee, a tacker's name for a horse. Gutless is undoubtedly pitiful and I probably won't be able to change him. Maybe that's okay.

Just as I was about to leave, Mr Monkhouse's front door opened and the man himself stepped into the yard. I shrank back against the bole of the tree, though there was little chance of being spotted anyway.

Mr M took a cigarette from a pack and lit up. He doesn't smoke. I've never seen him smoke, which I know doesn't mean a great deal. What you do in your own house is your own business. But I would have smelled it on him, even if he was a light smoker.

He smoked it down to a stub, then tossed the butt into the

garden and went back inside. I watched him for between five and ten minutes. He didn't seem sick, he seemed agitated. Why would he be agitated?

**Ten minutes later I was outside the supermarket where Phoebe had been taken.**

I didn't want to go there. In fact, when I arrived, I had to stand for a few minutes and fight against something heavy and churning in my chest. I took long, regular breaths because I knew I was on the verge of hyperventilating. Even when I'd regained control, it was still a massive effort to go through the automatic doors and approach the customer service desk. The air inside was heavy with loss and I felt like throwing up again. I put both hands on the counter and swallowed hard.

Eventually, a young girl with bad skin and a mouthful of chewing gum approached me. I wondered if she was Summerlee's replacement. Her eyes were a touch glassy, but maybe that came with working in a supermarket. Summer's eyes were normally glassy, but that was probably due to what she smoked.

'Can I help you?'

'I wondered if it was possible to have a word with the store manager, Ms Abbott,' I said. My voice sounded relatively normal, but my heart was pounding. I needed to get out of there.

'Are you a rep?' She didn't stop the gum chewing.

'Sorry?'

'A rep. Are you selling something?'

'Oh, no. It's personal.'

She picked up a phone, tapped a number, mumbled something and then put the phone down. 'Ms Abbott will be with you shortly,' she said. I smiled but she didn't smile back, just watched me, her mouth working continuously. Fortunately, I didn't have to endure the uninterested spotlight of her glare for long because Ms Abbott rocked up in less than a minute. She took one look at me and recognition swam into her eyes.

'You're the brother of that little girl,' she said.

'Phoebe,' I said. 'Her name's Phoebe. And I'm Jamie.'

She put a hand flat against her chest. 'Is there any news?'

I tilted my head towards the gum-chewing employee.

'Any chance of a word in private?' I said.

'Of course. Please follow me.'

It was strange walking through the supermarket aisles, and a wave of nausea hit me as we went past the deli counter. It was even stranger being back in that office. I remembered the plate of biscuits and the pale tea and the female police officer. But it was as if all that had happened in some other era to some other person. My stomach clenched.

'Is there any news?' repeated Ms Abbott, sitting behind her desk.

'Nothing so far.'

'I'm so sorry. If there's anything I can do . . .'

'Well, actually there is.' I hadn't sat down. Maybe I'd entertained some stupid idea of exerting dominance by towering above her, but suddenly I wanted to sit. I wasn't sure my legs would support me for much longer. 'Could you explain how Phoebe left this store without any of the security cameras picking her up?'

Ms Abbott frowned. 'I really have no idea. I told the police that as far as I know . . .'

'But you *must* know which parts of this supermarket are blind spots for the cameras,' I said. I tried to smile but I think it came out wrong. 'The police told me there were plenty, so I'd really appreciate it if you walked me through the place. You know, so I can better understand.'

Ms Abbott's frown deepened and she placed both hands flat on the desk.

'I don't want to be unhelpful,' she said, in a tone of voice that indicated she was about to be just that, 'but I think the police have all the relevant information. Perhaps you should talk to them.'

'But I did talk to them. I just told you. Now I'm talking to you.'

Ms Abbott brushed imaginary specks of dust from the surface of the desk. 'I'm sorry,' she said, 'but I can't simply show people – even you – potential security breaches at work. I really am sorry, James, but you should talk to the police.'

'It's Jamie.'

'Pardon me?'

'My name. Jamie. Brother of Phoebe and also Summerlee Delaware. You probably remember Summerlee.'

That got a reaction, though she tried to hide it. For a fleeting moment her face filled with loathing.

'Of course I remember Summerlee. How is she?'

I ignored her. 'Perhaps you could let me know if there are any staff members who might have a grudge against my sister?' I said. I tried that smile again. 'She rubs some people up the wrong way, as you probably recall.'

This time Ms Abbott got to her feet.

'I'm sorry,' she said, 'but you know I cannot answer a question like that unless it's to the police. I'd really like to help, Jamie, but unless there's something else I think it might be better if you left.'

'I appreciate your help and concern,' I said but if she spotted the sarcasm she gave no indication.

Ms Abbott personally escorted me to the front of the store as if she couldn't relax until I was gone. She watched me all the way out through the sliding doors. I could tell from the itch beneath my shoulder blades.

I could only breathe properly when I'd turned a corner and the supermarket was out of sight.

I met up with Gutless at the small cafe we'd occasionally visit after school. It's a really bad cafe, the sort of place where choosing from the menu feels like a game of Russian roulette with food poisoning. Anyway, that's one of the reasons we like it so much – it's not often that eating becomes a high-risk activity. Gutless was already there and had ordered a couple of plates of chips and gravy. He was most of the way through his. I sat opposite and pushed my plate towards him.

'That fuckin' relief teacher, man,' said Gutless. 'What a wanker. Some kid near the door told me it was you outside, that you wanted to see me and I'm like, why didn't you let me know – to the relief teacher – and he's like get on with your work and I'm like, fuck this shit, I'm outta here, so I go and he's like, I'm reporting this and I'm like...'

'Gutless,' I said. 'I need to talk to you. I don't need *you* to talk. Just listen, okay?'

He put a chip into his mouth and shrugged.

I told him about Phoebe. Some people, I realised, must have known already. Word from supermarket staff would have got around, and there were those posters that Mum had put up, though maybe the lack of news might have led some to believe she'd been found, that the drama had been resolved. Or maybe people just forget. Isn't that what I always did? If it wasn't in the news, then it floated away into oblivion. We all have busy lives. Other people's problems simply dissolve into the relentless flow of time.

Gutless listened, his mouth open, one half-chewed chip resting on a back tooth, and it was obvious from his reaction that he hadn't had a clue. Video games, let's be honest, rarely allow the real world to penetrate.

'Fuck, man,' he said when I'd brought him totally up to date.

'Couldn't have put it better myself, Gutless,' I said. 'Anyway, I've got a few ideas I want to run by you. Detective Moss – one of the cops I was telling you about – asked my family to draw up a list of people who might be behind this. You know, people with a possible grudge.'

Gutless nodded and closed his mouth. I was pleased. That chip was getting on my nerves.

'I want to apply game theory to the problem,' I continued. 'But game theory works much better when you have some idea of the other players in the game. You know, their personalities and how that might affect their decision-making.' Gutless nodded again. 'Okay,' I continued. 'I'm gonna throw out a few thoughts. Just listen, all right, and tell me if anything I say sounds right or wrong or just plain weird or stupid.'

Gutless started on my plate of chips.

'It's important to know whether the kidnapper is working alone or if he or she has an accomplice,' I said. Gutless opened his mouth, but I beat him to it. 'Because if he is working alone, then I can rule out the people with me when he made a call.'

'Like?'

'Like Mum and Dad, Summerlee and a few of the cops.'

'Whoa, man.' Gutless dropped a chip back onto the plate. 'You serious? Your Mum and Dad? Summerlee, for fuck's sake? You think she's extorting cash from herself? That's fucked-up thinking, man. True.'

'Just because it's unlikely, doesn't mean I should rule it out,' I replied.

'But your Mum and Dad?'

'Both have motive. They've spent eighteen years bringing up

Summer and she doesn't give them a cent from her winnings. Can you imagine the resentment? And who better to kidnap Phoebe? She'd be looked after, loved. And she'd have gone with either of them from that supermarket without thinking twice. '

'You're fucked up, man.'

I took a chip from the plate. It was cold and greasy.

'I know, Gutless. Trust me, I know.' I had to swallow hard to get the chip down. 'But I've ruled them out. And Summer. Partly because I think the kidnapper *is* acting alone – two million dollars is shitloads, but if you start splitting it, it might not be worth the risk.'

'Still a million each if there's two of them.'

'In which case, they would've asked for four. No, I think it's just one person. Plus, Mum and Dad are not great actors. There's all sorts of shit going down at home and they can't hide their feelings. Mum thinks Dad is useless and Dad kinda agrees, but resents Mum for making it plain. No. They couldn't hide this. And you're right about Summer. It's not like she has any kind of motive.'

Gutless was looking at me as if I'd lost my senses. I tried to ignore him and continue my train of thought. 'So, if it's one person acting alone, that would also rule out Gardner and Moss, because they listened in to a phone call. But it doesn't necessarily rule out *every* cop, like Dixon, the one who first interviewed me. Or the female officer who stayed with me in the supermarket. In fact, she brought up Summer's win on the lotto.'

'You think the cops could be involved?' Gutless clearly felt I was moving further and further from reality, which is ironic for someone who spends his entire life in computer games.

'The police crave money, like everyone else.'

'Yeah, but…'

'Then there's Spider,' I said. 'True, he's with Summer and she bought him a car, but that doesn't mean he's got access to all of her cash. Maybe he wants to start his own drug cartel, needs a little seed money.'

'You hate Spider, man. You could be biased.'

'That's for sure. And anyway, I don't think he has the brains for this. Most of the time, he's stoned out of his head. Unless that's just an act…'

Gutless shook his head and took another handful of chips.

'I'm thinking Mr Monkhouse could also be a suspect,' I said. Gutless choked and spluttered a mouthful of half-chewed chips across the table. When he'd recovered, I told him about Monkhouse's 'sickness', our phone conversation and what I'd witnessed at his house.

'Yeah, but that don't mean shit. I mean, c'mon, man. You can't be serious…'

'He has the brains, all right,' I continued. 'He's the smartest person I've ever known. And everyone knows teachers get paid peanuts. In fact, he mentioned that himself when he asked about Summerlee. Said it would take a teacher a hundred years to earn that kind of cash. Said it just before Phoebe was taken.'

'Yeah, but he wouldn't've if he'd been planning to do it, man. Come on. He's smart. Your words.'

'Maybe that's exactly what a smart person would say. Throw off suspicion because no one would expect a guilty person to say that.'

Gutless took a swig of Coke, wiped his mouth with the back of his hand and muttered something. I think it was, 'Fuck's sake.'

'And then there's Ms Abbott,' I said.

This time, Gutless nearly lost it.

'Who da FUCK is Ms Abbott?'

The cafe went silent. Actually, I think the cafe had always been silent because only one other table was occupied. Nonetheless, we had the full attention of a guy with a grizzled beard and a bacon sandwich. The owner of the cafe moved towards us, a dirty tea towel slung over his left shoulder.

'You watch your language, you kids,' he growled, 'or you will leave. I won't put up with that kind of talk in my restaurant.'

Gutless raised both hands in the air. 'Sorry, dude,' he said. 'Won't happen again. We love your *restaurant*.' He winked at me.

The owner regarded us for a moment and then moved back to his counter. 'Fucking kids,' he muttered at the guy with the bacon sandwich, who nodded and took another bite. It was the closest I'd come to laughing since Phoebe had disappeared. I leaned towards Gutless.

'The manager of the supermarket,' I whispered. 'The one Summer gave such a hard time to. Think about it, Gutless. That woman was humiliated in front of everyone. Wouldn't you want payback? And it's more likely Phoebe would leave with a woman – a woman who knows the back entrances and how to avoid surveillance cameras. I went to see her and asked for information. She was tighter than a duck's arsehole and it was obvious she hadn't forgiven Summer for what happened.'

'How about it's someone you *don't* know?' said Gutless. 'You think of that? Your sister's lotto win was plastered all over the news. Hell, man. It could be anyone, probably a complete stranger.'

'Yeah,' I said. 'In which case all of this is a waste of time. But that is something I have no control over. If it *is* someone who knows me, then it'd be criminal not to at least think through the possibilities.'

The proverbial light bulb appeared over Gutless's head. It was disarming in a way. His eyes widened and his jaw dropped. He was never very good at hiding what he was thinking.

'That means you thought *I* could've done it,' he whispered. 'Shit, Jamie. You had me down as a suspect as well?'

I smiled. Inwardly, at least. Yeah, I'd thought about Gutless. Of course I had. But unless he had spent the last five years carefully building up a persona to fool the world on the off-chance someone who knew him would win the lotto, then I could discount him. Where would he keep Phoebe? In his bedroom? She'd sneak out while he was blowing someone's head off on his computer and probably wouldn't notice she'd gone for a couple of hours. Anyway, I knew Gutless. There wasn't a bad bone in his body. Or that many brains in his head. I opened my mouth to tell him just that – minus the brain part – but I didn't get the chance.

My phone rang. Caller unknown.

# CHAPTER 17

**I scrambled from my seat, knocking it over in the process, and bolted out the door.** I heard the cafe owner's voice raised in anger behind me. I thumbed the screen.

'Yes?'

The heavy, portentous silence. And then the computer-generated voice.

'Are you alone, Jamie?'

'Yes. No. I mean, someone will probably be joining me in a minute or two. But I am now. Alone, I mean. And I'll tell him to go away, okay?

The velvet silence.

'Calm down, Jamie. That's fine. I won't hang up. Is it Gutless?'

'Yes.' I stopped. My brain was not at its sharpest. It took a few seconds for me to process even basic things. I thought of Monkhouse. 'How do you know about Gutless?'

'You'd be surprised what I know, Jamie. Think. Elementary

research. Would I take your sister without careful research and planning?'

It was disorientating, the posing of a question without the accompanying inflection. I tried to get past the monotone delivery to find some trace of personality. Something I might recognise.

'I am a professional. Never forget that.'

The door to the cafe opened and Gutless emerged, blinking, into the sunshine. I held up one hand in the stop position and kept the phone raised, but away from my mouth.

'Gutless,' I shouted. 'This is an important call. Wait for me here, okay? I'll come back for you.'

Gutless was mouthing something at me. I think it was *Is that him?* But I was already walking down the road. After thirty metres I put the phone back to my ear.

'Okay,' I said. 'I'm back.'

'Did you ever wonder why I am dealing with you and not your sister, Jamie? After all, she's the one with the obese bank account. Did that thought cross your mind?'

'Yes,' I said. 'You think I am smarter than her and that appeals to you. You think this is a game and you want a worthy opponent. You know me. Personally. We've talked in the past.' Game theory might be more difficult when dealing with an unknown opponent, but that doesn't mean you can't try to disorientate and confuse with unexpected information. If I'd hit on the truth, would it elicit some response? The problem was identifying whether I'd hit a nerve when the words coming back were so robotic.

'Are you into mathematics?' I added.

A pause.

'Mathematics? No. I am not like you or Mr Monkhouse. However, I can count up to two million and that's all that matters.'

'You're lying.'

'Always a possibility.' Silence. 'How about some homespun philosophy, Jamie? Life is unfair. Your sister won an enormous amount of money. Not earned. Won. And yet, at the risk of offending your sensibilities, she is nothing more than a slut.' *Process this, Jamie*, I thought. *He is intelligent. He likes the juxtaposition of articulate vocabulary like 'sensibilities' with slang like 'slut'. Does it help? Look for a fissure in his personality and maybe you can insert a knife blade and prise it open, reveal his identity. Concentrate. His words are your only resource.*

'No comment,' I said.

'She is someone who will not willingly part with her winnings, so you might have to do some persuading, Jamie.' Another small clue. He might know a lot about my family, but he didn't know everything. Whatever else Summerlee was, she loved Phoebe with every fibre of her being. She'd pay and count it a bargain.

The voice continued. 'Tell her she should look at it like another person came up with her numbers and it's simply another form of sharing. Who knows, Jamie? Removing two million from the equation might mean she won't kill herself quite as fast.'

Was the word 'equation' a taunt?

'Let me speak to Phoebe,' I said.

'No. Perhaps tomorrow.'

'How long does this have to go on? Let's finish our business. I get Phoebe back, you get your money. Why wait?'

The curtain of silence was drawn once more.

'There's no point rushing.' The words were carefully enunciated. 'We must be careful that we both come out winners. I know it's hard, but Phoebe is well looked after. Trust me on this, if only because you don't have a choice.'

'At least can we talk about *when* you want the money? That needs organisation. You can't simply walk into a bank and draw out two million dollars in cash. It'll take time.'

'Actually, you can just draw out two million. It's a bank. It's your money. But yes, it might take some time. Get onto that straight away. The police might be useful in that regard. They'll be able to pull strings, exert pressure. Tell them when you ring after we've hung up.'

He was fond of throwing in the occasional remark designed to make me think he knew my every move. Was that arrogance, or a tactic designed to unsettle? Arrogance is often a weakness. Something else to file away.

'Okay,' I said.

'I'll call you soon. Maybe you'll get the chance to talk to Phoebe, though I am not promising anything.'

'Can I ask you something?'

A slight pause.

'Make it quick.'

'How did you get Phoebe to leave that supermarket with you?'
The question had been bubbling ever since her disappearance.
My sister wasn't dumb – she was a *long* way from dumb – and she
would never leave with a total stranger. She'd had the stranger-
danger sermon at home and at school on countless occasions. It
was the main reason why I felt he *wasn't* a stranger. But even then,
she wouldn't go without telling me. It wasn't in her nature. Yet
the two of them must have left, avoiding security cameras, and
got into a car. And no one had raised an eyebrow because it must
have appeared entirely normal. He couldn't have been holding
a weapon, because there were too many people about. And that
meant, until she was in the car, there were plenty of opportunities
to raise the alarm or show distress or simply run screaming. But
Phoebe must have gone without fuss. In some way she must have
been complicit in her own abduction.

'Do you have any theories?' Again, the question that didn't
sound like a question.

'She's met you before.'

'Still harping on that, Jamie? No. She had never seen me before.
The truth is, everyone has their weakness. We are all capable of
doing things that seem entirely out of character if that weakness
can be found and exploited. That's all I did. I used Phoebe's weakness.'

I kept quiet. He wanted me to ask but I knew he'd tell me
anyway. He wouldn't be able to resist.

'Phoebe's weakness is you, Jamie. That is both wonderful and tragic. I approached her in one of the aisles, the aisle where the trolley was found. I told her that her name was Phoebe Delaware and that her brother Jamie was in the supermarket. I also told her – no, I *promised* her – that unless she did exactly what she was told, her brother would die. She looked me straight in the eyes and she believed me, Jamie.'

It was a lie. I knew it was a lie. Or maybe I wanted to believe that. Either way, I found it difficult to breathe. There was a hard constriction in my throat, blocking off air. Later I found my right hand was curled so hard that my fingernails had left crescent-shaped gouges in my palm. Suddenly, I needed to sit down. The voice continued, unemotional and relentless.

'She is remarkable. She walked out of that place, at my side, and didn't give one indication that there was anything out of the ordinary. Nobody would have been able to tell I wasn't her mother or her sister.'

Another lie. A deliberate attempt to confuse. He wouldn't make a mistake like that, not after going to all the trouble to make sure his voice couldn't be identified, even to gender. It seemed more likely to me that a man would be so devious and arrogant at the same time. Or was I deceiving myself? In the end, it probably didn't matter.

Regardless of whether he was male or female, I could kill this person. That was a cold certainty in my gut.

The phone went dead.

# CHAPTER 18

**Gutless bombarded me with questions, but I didn't answer.**

Instead, I took my phone out again and rang Mum. She was pissed off I'd disappeared but the annoyance was tempered by the urge to know what the kidnapper had said. She made me go over it twice, even though, when everything was said and done, there was not much in the way of new information. The only thing she could hold onto was the bit about money. I knew that she would be getting something organised as soon as we hung up. Action. Just keep moving. I promised I would be home soon and got off the phone by expressing the simple truth that I had to ring Gardner and fill him in. I did that as well. Gardner made me go over it another three times and said he and Detective Moss would be around to the house later to get a formal statement. I had the impression he really wanted to pick me up and take me to the station right there and then, but I made it clear that there was nothing new to add to what I'd told him. 'He's playing a game,' I said. 'This call was just to string me along, keep me focused.' I wasn't sure Gardner agreed with my analysis, but he didn't push it.

Gutless walked me to my front door. He offered to stay, but I told him I was fucked and had to get some sleep.

'Ring me, dude,' he said. 'I won't ring you. I imagine you shit yourself when your fucking phone goes off. But day or night, man. I'm here for you. True.'

'Thanks, Gutless,' I said. He's no wordsmith, but he meant it and I was grateful. 'There is one thing you can do for me, though.'

'Anything, man.'

'Keep an eye on Mr Monkhouse for me. Check what he's doing, try to find out whether he's really sick or not.'

'Whoa.' Gutless grinned. 'I can do that,' he said. 'Gutless Geraghty, P.I.'

He was so pleased with himself that he was heading off without Monkhouse's address. I called him back and gave it to him. At least it might keep him away from video games for a while, and anyway, it was easy to underestimate Gutless. I knew he'd do his best to help out.

I opened my front door, dreading what lay beyond it. Not just the pain and the fear and the stultifying sense of helplessness, though they were bad enough. What I really dreaded was more words. Words that go round and round and round and never get anywhere. I wanted sleep. No. That's wrong. I *needed* sleep. But as soon as I walked into our front room I knew I wouldn't get it.

**Dixon was hunched into Dad's chair.** He looked like some kind of down-at-heel Buddha, a broad band of gut bulging against his shirt, straining the lower buttons to the extent that I could see patches of hairy skin peeping like strange eyes. The belt of his trousers was lost beneath the swell. He stroked his moth-eaten salt-and-pepper moustache and his eyes flitted around the room. Maybe he was looking for a drink. He certainly appeared in need of one. Summerlee and Spider sat on the sofa across from him. Spider was still wearing that singlet from the night before. It was nearly as red as his eyes.

Dixon lumbered to his feet as I came in, hoisted the waist band of his pants up a notch.

'Your mum said it would be okay for me to wait for you here,' he said, like I was on the point of questioning the legitimacy of his presence. I shrugged. 'Your parents are not here,' he added. 'They went to the hospital.' He raised a hand to ward off an anticipated question. 'It's okay. But your dad...well, he was complaining of chest pains, you know, and your mum thought... better safe than sorry.'

Summerlee chipped in.

'She rang ten minutes ago,' she said. 'All good. They gave him shitloads of tests but they came out clear. They'll be home soon.'

'Okay,' I said. Maybe we were all becoming strung out and overly suspicious of everything, but I wondered if Dad's chest pains were psychosomatic, an unconscious attempt to evoke sympathy. I imagined the same idea had crossed Mum's mind. It was uncharitable and, anyway, it didn't really make any difference.

I glanced at Spider. He half-waved his hand and then nodded at me. Two guys bonding. What a shit. Dixon hoisted his pants again. Fat guys have two choices with pants. I'd noticed this with Gutless. They either go for the band above the waistline where the stomach's diameter keeps everything in place, or the waistband beneath the overhang, in which case the belt keeps slipping. The first option offers security for your stomach but makes you look like a dick. Dixon had obviously decided not to look like a dick, and hoisting pants at regular intervals was the price he was prepared to pay.

The longer I went without sleep, the more bizarre were my thought patterns.

'How can I help you...er, Inspector Dixon, is it?'

'Just Dixon will do.' He sat back down again. I was pleased. I was becoming obsessed with the movements of his pants. 'I believe you wanted to pass on a message to me.'

'Why aren't you on the case?'

He shrugged. 'Not my area. That's okay, son. Detective Inspector Gardner is an expert at this stuff. He has degrees. He's been on courses.' Tired though I was, I could pick up on subtext. The new educated cop, fast-tracked to promotion, versus the old guard who'd been round the blocks more time than you could count, earning their expertise through erosion of shoe leather. This was the fabric of television drama and I wasn't interested. Well. I *was*, in a way, but exhaustion was diluting my attention.

'So why are you here?'

He stroked the moustache again.

'I'm off duty. Thought I'd pop round. I might not have a degree, but I know a bit about how the world operates. It crossed my mind you might like to chat.'

*I want to sleep*, I thought. But he was on my mental list of possible suspects and this was a good opportunity to do a little digging.

'I would,' I said. 'I appreciate it.'

Dixon gave an almost imperceptible glance towards Spider and Summerlee.

'How about we go for a walk?' he said. He got to his feet and adjusted his pants one more time. An image of a nail gun crossed my mind but I pushed it to one side.

'Sure,' I said.

We walked around the block. It was hometime at the local primary school and kids bustled everywhere. Mum and Dad hadn't sent Phoebe to the local school. They'd done their research and chosen one in the next suburb that got better NAPLAN scores. I'd never been convinced those kinds of things mattered, but I wasn't allowed a vote. Small tackers on skateboards weaved around us and parents ushered children into cars. Off to homework and playtime with the dog and dinner and all the unappreciated, disregarded normality of family life. I swore I would never take that for granted again, but it was too late for that. So I walked, kept my eyes to the ground, a sense of injustice surging like a tide. How dare these people behave normally? What gave them the right?

'You reckon the kidnapper knows you?' said Dixon.

The question startled me. I'd said as much to the guy on the phone not half an hour earlier. Why would Dixon say that? If he was the person behind the voice, then why would he bring it up now? And wouldn't something that coincidental indicate his innocence? I was so tired. My thoughts wouldn't assume any shape.

'Maybe,' I replied. 'He knows a lot about us, that's for sure. My mobile number, for one thing.'

Dixon waved a hand and then ran it across his brow. It wasn't particularly hot, but he was sweating anyway.

'Easily found,' he said. 'Phoebe might have given it to him. More interesting is that he wants to talk to you and not your sister.'

'He said she's stupid and a slut,' I replied.

'You believe that?'

'That she's stupid and a slut? No comment.' I watched Dixon's face but it was impassive.

'No, do you believe that's the reason he wants to deal with you.'

I gave that some thought. We walked for probably two or three minutes in silence and Dixon didn't try to make conversation. He let me process his question. Out of the corner of my eye I saw him hitch his trousers a couple more times. I went through the possibilities. I had been with Phoebe in that supermarket, so maybe the kidnapper was tapping into my sense of guilt. I was the one who had lost her, therefore I was the one most emotionally qualified to move heaven and earth to get her back. The redemption motive. Plus, Summerlee was nothing more than a bank account to him. Did it really matter if he talked to her directly or used me as a go-between? Perhaps all of this was simple common sense. Maybe, logically, I was the ideal candidate for negotiation. Dad couldn't cope, Mum was wired, Summer was fucked up on drugs and alcohol most of the time. I was the mathematician. I was more likely to respond in a controlled and rational fashion. But something in my gut rebelled against the argument. It was all that, but it was something more.

'I think he wants to play games,' I said. Still no decipherable reaction, though he took out a handkerchief and mopped his brow. It really *wasn't* that hot.

'Meaning?' he said.

I held up my hands. What did I mean? What evidence could I put forward in support of that assertion? Was I elevating myself to a position of importance that couldn't be justified? *I'm at the centre here. It's all about* me. But the feeling persisted. What I had said on the phone was true. I felt sure this was a game and the kidnapper knew it, was in some way relying on it.

'I get the impression,' I said, 'that he wants me to understand that he knows my thoughts, my feelings, my motivations, and that he is one step ahead of me all the way. Almost like he wants us to be friends, for fuck's sake.' I stopped on the pavement and Dixon turned towards me. 'No. Not friends. He wants me to *admire* him. You know, two minds in battle, two chess players moving towards an endgame and he is the one with the skill to see it through. He wants my applause.'

Dixon stroked his moustache and examined his shoes, which were old, scuffed and dull. A small strip of the sole was coming loose and one lace had broken at some stage and he'd had to shorten it to make it fit. He sucked at his teeth.

'You think I'm full of shit,' I said. 'Over-complicating.'

He looked up at me then and seemed genuinely surprised.

'No. Not at all,' he replied. 'Seriously.' He kicked at one shoe with the other. No wonder they looked like crap. 'You're the one he's been talking to, Jamie. You're the one qualified to make judgements based on your conversations. Certainly not me. If that's what your instincts tell you, then that's good enough for me. The real point, though, is does it help? Assuming you're right.'

I shrugged. Dixon hoisted his pants and moved on. I think he needed shade.

'What about you, Jamie?' he said a moment later. 'Are you a game player?'

'Not when it comes to Phoebe's life,' I replied. Then I thought again. What about that first phone call when I told the kidnapper I was busy? What was that about if it wasn't game playing? And did it really matter if that was an instinctive reaction? Christ, how much did I have in common with this guy?

I was so tired. My suspicions of Monkhouse and Abbott, and Dixon himself, were starting to appear absurd. Why not anyone who had ever known me, passed a casual word in the street? Fuck, I might as well work on the telephone directory as a list of potential suspects. Mum and Dad? Christ, what was I thinking? Suddenly I felt the urge to just answer honestly, without worrying about what was going on in the head of the person I was talking to. I was tired of games, especially my own.

'Game theory,' I said.

'Game theory?'

I gave Dixon the potted version, the establishment of game theory as a respected branch of mathematics and economics. 'Essentially, it's the analysis of decisions made between at least two independent and rational players and how outcomes are influenced by those decisions.' Dixon scratched his head and sucked his teeth. He gave me a shucks-I'm-just-a-humble-cop smile.

'I'll give you an example,' I said. 'One that should appeal to you as a police officer. Answer this: is it true to say that if we all became better people, the world would be a better place?'

Dixon looked at me as if I was a bit simple.

'Sounds to me,' he said, 'like that goes without saying. I suppose you're going to tell me it's not true.'

'You're right. It isn't true. It's absolutely false and I could prove it to you with mathematics.'

Dixon held up a hand.

'Spare me,' he said. 'I always sucked at maths.'

'The fallacy of composition,' I continued. 'What applies to an individual doesn't necessarily apply to the group.' I looked at Dixon's face and decided to press on quickly. 'Let's say that one definition of being 'better' is that we think more about other people's feelings and do things specifically to make them feel good. Yes?'

Dixon nodded.

'Okay,' I continued. 'So criminals behave better, but we also behave better in response to criminals. Punishment is less harsh, which means that there's a greater incentive for criminals to behave badly. That would make the world a worse place, wouldn't it?'

Dixon screwed up his eyes and sucked his teeth. He opened his mouth and closed it again.

'Whatever,' he said finally. 'You think this game theory is useful as far as the kidnapping goes?'

'Possibly,' I replied. 'It has applications in most areas where there are winners and losers.'

He chewed on that for a while. We had circled the block and he shambled over to his car, an old Ford that looked as battered as his shoes. I thought he might be overdoing the down-at-heel persona, the gritty cop with no formal education but high on street-smarts. Did it work to lull suspects into a false sense of security? Did Dixon, in his own way, employ game theory to maximise his chances of success in the game of good versus evil? He motioned me to the passenger seat and then turned on the engine, which coughed for a moment before catching. Almost immediately a blast of cold air poured from the vents. He might not spend money on the car's bodywork, but he hadn't stinted on the air conditioning. Dixon mopped his face with his handkerchief and lay back in the seat.

'So,' he said. 'Two possibilities. One, your interest in this game theory is clouding your judgement of the crim's motivations. In other words, you're finding an interest in game-playing because that's what *you're* interested in.' He took a pack of cigarettes from his jacket pocket, tapped one loose and put it into his mouth. He glanced over at me. 'You mind?' he asked.

'It's your car and your lungs,' I said.

'Well, your lungs as well, in this instance.'

'Go ahead,' I said. He lit up and gave a sigh of satisfaction. 'You were saying?' I added.

'Two, the kidnapper knows about your interest in game-playing. He has, you say, considerable information about your family. It might be reasonable to assume he also knows about your personal interests.'

'And how does that help?'

'It makes it more likely you know the kidnapper. Phoebe left the supermarket with him, after all, which suggests it was some-one she might have reason to trust.'

'He explained that.'

Dixon took a long drag and flicked ash out of his window.

'Yeah,' he said. 'But that doesn't mean we have to believe him, does it? Pulled your strings, I reckon. Worked on your guilt. Maybe he was making a calculated move to get just that reaction. To gain an advantage in the battle between the two of you. Am I getting the hang of this game theory of yours?'

I thought it over. Bad shoes, poor diet, as witnessed by the waistline and the fast-food wrappers in the car's footwell, but an intellect that was sharp and well-maintained. Yes. Dixon might well be spot on.

'Not just getting the hang,' I replied. 'I think you might be an expert player but aren't aware of it. You've been using game theory all your professional life but just didn't know the term.'

'I called it police work,' said Dixon. 'But then I'm just a dumb cop.'

'Oh, please,' I said. 'Don't play *me*.' He smiled at that and I tried to smile back but it turned into a yawn. 'I've got to get some sleep,' I said. 'I'm on the point of dropping.'

'Sure,' said Dixon. ' He flicked the butt of his cigarette out onto the road, then reached into his pocket and took out a business card. 'I have no jurisdiction in this, you understand. But if you want to talk – if anything else occurs to you and you'd like to bounce it off someone, then call. I like to think I still have my uses sometimes.'

I took it. 'Day or night?' I asked.

'Hell, no. I need my sleep. But up to ten in the evening is good and I'm generally out of bed by five in the morning. One of the lifestyle changes that comes with age.'

I opened the car door.

'One other thing,' said Dixon. 'This business about disguising his voice, so you can't tell if it's a man or a woman. You think he'd bother doing that if he was a stranger to you?'

I put the card into the top pocket of my shirt.

'Yes. If the cops might recognise his voice,' I said.

'True,' said Dixon. 'Worth thinking about, though.'

I got out and closed the door. His car took off trailing a plume of smoke from its exhaust. I watched until it disappeared around the bend at the end of our street, then I went back inside the house. Summer was where I had left her, though she'd slumped over the side of the couch and was snoring gently. Spider was leaning forward and rolling a joint on the coffee table.

'If you're smoking that, you can go into the backyard,' I said.

'Sure, man,' said Spider. 'No worries.' He stuck the end of the roach into his mouth, twirled it round to wet it, then put it behind his ear.

I went into my bedroom and fell onto the bed. I wasn't sure if I would manage to sleep, and anyway, I was too tired to undress. Adrenaline was surging, as it had for the last twenty-four hours. It was as if every corpuscle of blood, every firing neuron, was jumping in its own electrical dance. But I had barely closed my eyes before I fell asleep.

**I dreamed.** I was in the supermarket, carrying a basket, and putting carrots into it, one by one. The woman with the tattoo was there, as was the guy on the mobile phone. This time, though, he wasn't saying, 'Sure, yeah, sure'. He was saying, 'He's here with me. In the veg section. The coast is clear.' I met his eyes and they had no whites to them, just black holes containing the dim reflections of the fluorescent lights. I glanced from side to side. Where was Phoebe? She'd been here a moment ago.

I spotted her: a glimpse of the back of her head as she disappeared round a display of baked beans. Her dark hair swayed and was gone. I saw the red denim material of one of her sneakers, its heel tilted. 'Hey, Phoebe!' I called, but she didn't come back. I went to the aisle and looked along it. Phoebe was turning right at the end. This time I thought there was a man with her. The flap of trousers, a flash of a dark shoe. I ran to the end, looked left and right. Nothing. I went to the next aisle. She was at the far end, turning left. I ran. There was no way Phoebe could outrun me. I was only two metres behind her. At the end I looked right and left. Nothing. Then I saw the back of her head, the tilt of red denim sneaker, as she turned the corner. Was she holding someone's hand? 'PHOEBE!' I yelled. 'YOU CAN'T RUN THAT FAST.' She didn't come back.

I moved as if in a maze. Now the supermarket was deserted, except for Phoebe and me and the faintest hint of another presence. Someone, something dark. The aisles stretched and twisted and went on forever. I ran headlong through each one, and each time caught a glimpse of hair, the tilt of a sneaker. I never got closer.

And then a sound. I stopped halfway down one aisle. Baked beans were on all of the shelves. Thousands, millions of cans, stretching to infinity. The sound coalesced. A hum. It made my heart leap in my chest.

I jolted upright in bed. My phone was buzzing. Not a call. A text message notification. I fumbled with the screen. Unknown caller. I pressed to bring up the message, but there was no message as such to bring up.

I had received a video.

# CHAPTER 19

**Phoebe sat in front of a completely blank wall.** It was obviously brick-work – I could see the classical outline of staggered individual bricks – but it had been painted an off-white. She wasn't wearing her school uniform, but something I'd never seen before. A kind of green smock with a bright bow at the neckline. Definitely not something she would have chosen to wear. It was too girly for her taste. Clearly, the person who'd taken her had picked this. It was exactly the kind of dress that someone who didn't know kids would have chosen. It spoke of conventional fashion, a sense of what little girls *should* look like. Questions rose like bile in my throat. Had she been forced to change into this from her school uniform? Most importantly, had she been given privacy while she struggled into this monstrosity? I wanted to shut my eyes to keep the appalling alternative at bay.

Phoebe was cross-legged on a plain concrete floor. She wasn't wearing socks or shoes. In her lap she held a newspaper. It was local and it was today's. She held it up to the camera and it was as if she was embarrassed doing it. Then she folded it neatly – of course she did – and placed it at her side. The image swam and rippled but I didn't have the time or inclination to wipe my eyes. She smiled at me – a strange, lopsided smile – and a sob stuck in my throat. Then she spoke.

'Hi, Jamie. I'm fine and not hurt in any way, so please don't worry. Say hi to Mum and Dad and Summer. Tell them I miss them and I love them and I can't wait to get back home.' Her eyes shifted briefly to a point just off centre of the lens. She nodded. 'See you soon, Jamie. Love you. Bye.' And then she froze, the image went a pale shade of grey and the 'play' icon appeared over her face.

I stumbled down the stairs, the phone in my hand. The day had been crazy. It was about to get crazier.

**Summer had gone off somewhere with Spider but Mum and Dad were home.** Dad sat on the sofa and wore the befuddled expression that was becoming his habitual mask. Mum paced behind him. It was difficult to resist the urge to put both hands on her shoulders and force her to stand still for a moment. I thought if I did, she might crumple, as if someone had pulled her plug. Maybe she needed that.

I took Mum into the kitchen and showed her the video. She watched it twice and glanced towards the shelf where the whisky used to be kept. Then we took my phone in to Dad. He gazed at the screen in silence. His eyes filled with tears and he reached out at the end and touched the frozen image of his daughter. It was unbearable. I was overflowing. I had no resources to stem the flood and wouldn't have used them anyway. In the end, I simply put my hand on his shoulder. He didn't react, didn't say anything, just kept his finger on Phoebe's face. I left him with the phone.

Mum called Gardner and he and Detective Moss turned up within half an hour. They watched the video – it took some time to get the phone from Dad's grasp – and downloaded it onto a laptop. Then Moss took a detailed statement from me about my conversation with the kidnapper earlier that day. I sat at the kitchen table and combed my memory. Then I re-combed it. Mum and Gardner, off to one side, talked. Just occasionally, I caught a flash of emotion, of frustration, all of it coming from Mum. But, like Dad, I was removed, locked in my own world of recollection. I was grateful for the act of memory, recalling what had been said, pinning down snatches of words. It meant I didn't have to think. Maybe Dad was right. Maybe he was in a good place where the outside world couldn't reach him. Or maybe he was in a nightmare from which there was no escape. And no one he could turn to for help. From time to time he pressed a hand against his chest as if to stem a pain, or stop something escaping.

'We have a number of leads,' said Moss, 'and this video has definitely given us more to work on.'

Mum stopped talking. The silence was palpable. There are words that have more power than others, I realised. 'Leads' was one. It parted a curtain of despair through which we glimpsed a landscape called hope.

'Yes?' said Mum.

'We have a team of tech guys, specialists, trying to trace the phone calls and also working on the recordings of the kidnapper's voice.'

'And?'

Gardner pulled at the knot of his tie as if it was constricting his breathing.

'The voice is obviously being disguised by some kind of program or app, but the problem is there are so many of those available that it's not really a productive line of enquiry.'

'He said he used to work for a phone company,' Mum said. 'Have you followed up on that?'

'Yes. But there are many providers and we don't know when, or where in the country, he might have been employed. Of course, he could simply be lying, giving us false leads to tie up our time. But we're working on it.' He paused, undid the top button of his shirt, and pulled his tie down a few centimetres. 'Our guys have come to a tentative conclusion about his gender, though, based on an analysis of speech patterns and vocabulary. The probability is the kidnapper is male, and educated, possibly to degree level.'

'Probability?' I said.

Gardner sighed. 'This isn't an exact science, Jamie,' he said. 'No guarantees, but that's what they're thinking.'

'So,' said Mum. 'The *probability* is he's male and he *might* have a degree. That's great.' She wasn't even trying to hide the bitterness in her voice. 'What does that leave? A hundred thousand suspects. Is that the *probability*?'

Moss interrupted.

'That's not all we're working on, Ms Delaware,' she said. 'We've conducted many face-to-face interviews and we're chasing down new leads. For example, three people in the supermarket car park remember a girl matching the description of Phoebe getting into a car with a middle-aged person.'

Mum tried to interrupt, but Gardner raised a hand.

'You have to understand,' he said, 'witnesses are always unreliable. There's nothing strange about a young girl getting into a vehicle in a supermarket car park. So they may not have identified your daughter at all. Nonetheless, it's vital we chase this up.'

'Did they get a car rego?' asked Mum.

'Not even close,' said Gardner. 'Remember. These are people putting shopping into their cars. Who notices vehicle regos in that situation?'

Mum went to interrupt again, but Gardner raised a finger this time.

'However, two people remember the make of car and the colour. A green Commodore. Their descriptions generally agree. That means we can attempt to narrow down the year, which means we can make investigations regarding possible owners.'

'What about the third witness?' I asked.

'Didn't see the car,' replied Gardner. 'Just saw – thinks he *might* have seen – your sister in the company of a woman.'

'A woman?' said Mum. She ran a hand across her eyes and sighed. 'Description?'

Gardner shook his head. 'Middle-aged, possibly younger. Of average height or maybe above average height. Dark hair, or it could have been grey, long or it might have been shoulder length. Please understand, Ms Delaware. You catch a glimpse of someone in a supermarket car park. How reliable would your description be? If you knew it was going to be important you'd pay more attention. But you didn't know. You're putting shopping into the boot of your car. A day later you probably can't remember what your own shopping looked like, let alone someone passing by.'

Mum mulled things over. She looked like she wanted to challenge the irresponsibility of someone not picking up crucial information, but couldn't think of a counter to Gardner's point.

'How about hypnosis?' she asked.

Gardner blinked and sagged a little. It occurred to me he probably hadn't had much sleep either. At least, I *hoped* he hadn't slept. He was clearly searching for a diplomatic response. Equally clearly, he was having difficulty finding it. In the end, Moss came to his rescue.

'Hypnosis, despite what you might see on the television, is rarely successful, Ms Delaware. In fact, it often brings up things that never actually happened – trace memories from the un-conscious, stray bits of imagination. Obviously, that confuses the investigation. Not to mention that any evidence gathered from hypnosis is not admissible in court because of its unreliability.'

Mum wanted to argue the toss. I could see it in the set of her mouth and the way her shoulders straightened. I thought it best to head this off.

'So how do we trace the car?' I said.

The look Gardner gave me was tinged with gratitude. 'Legwork, Jamie,' he replied. 'Old-fashioned legwork. We go through the vehicle registration records and draw up a list of cars in the immediate area that fit the description. Then we send out officers to interview the owners, find out where they were at the time Phoebe went missing...'

'What's to stop them lying?' I said.

'Nothing,' said Gardner. 'And obviously the kidnapper, should we interview him, would do just that. But we have considerable experience in dealing with suspects and witnesses. Believe me, none of us will rest until we find your sister.'

Moss took over.

'And this video is another lead, possibly a number of leads. The dress that Phoebe's wearing, for example. The suspect clearly bought it and it's certainly distinctive. We'll find out who manufactures those dresses and get a list of retailers who stock them, locally and nationally. Then, as Detective Inspector Gardner mentioned, it's a matter of legwork, checking invoices at retailers, interviewing shop owners. The same goes for the newspaper – some retailers print their names on the papers and we'll have an expert examine the video to see if we can see it. It's even possible that we might be able to find out the camera or, more likely, the phone that took the footage. That gives us another line of enquiry.'

Gardner stood.

'It's my experience,' he said, 'that most breaks in these situations come from leads like the ones we're pursuing. It's not glamorous, but that's not important, is it?' He glanced at his watch. 'And if you'll excuse us, we'd better get back to the station. The sooner we get this video analysed, the better.'

I took them to the front door. Moss stopped just outside and turned back to face me.

'By the way,' she said. 'Tell your parents and your sister that we've been in touch with Summerlee's bank and that getting the cash won't be a problem. They'll require as much notice as possible but can get it in a few hours if necessary. That's not information you should pass on to the kidnapper, obviously.' I nodded. 'If he rings to discuss the transfer of the ransom,' she continued, 'ask him to call back in a few hours, while you find out when the money's available. Then call us straight away, obviously.'

'Of course,' I said. She turned to go. 'Oh, by the way,' I added. 'Here's the list of people I think might have a motive to do this.' I'd written down just two names in the end – Mr Monkhouse and Ms Abbott. I didn't think it was politic to put down 'and every police officer involved in this case.' She put the slip of paper into her pocket without looking at it.

'Thanks,' she said. 'Your mum rang in her list.' Moss smiled. 'Summerlee told me it would be easier to make a list of people who *didn't* wish her harm. In the end, hers came to five pages.'

I wondered if my name was on it or if I was the only one who was so fucked in the head they'd seriously considered other family members. I nodded.

'How's it going in there, Jamie?' She inclined her head towards the house.

I shrugged. 'We're enduring,' I replied. 'I'm not sure if I'll know the extent of the damage until this is all over. But, for the time being, we're functioning. Nothing more.'

She shook my hand. Her grip was firm. Then she joined Gardner, who had already started their car. I watched as they drove off. The sound of tyres on gravel faded and the world was quiet. Night had drawn in. How long had I slept? I glanced at my watch. Eight-thirty. I stood on the doorstep for ten minutes, listening to the silence and taking deep breaths, like I was trying to purge some kind of infection. It wasn't so much that the night was clear and fresh and a good place to be, though it was. I was avoiding the world behind our closed door.

That was muddied, stale and a bad place to be.

**Mum drove to the fish and chip shop at nine o'clock.** No one felt like eating, but it gave her something to do. She put the greaseproof paper parcel on the kitchen table so we could help ourselves. I tried a piece of fish; it was oily and the batter was stodgy, but I forced it down. Mum and Dad didn't touch anything. We didn't speak.

No one acknowledged it, but we were all waiting for the silence to be broken by the trill of an incoming call. I kept the phone balanced in my palm. Delicately, like it was dangerous and could explode at any moment. I suppose that wasn't far from the truth.

Minutes crawled by and turned into hours. I found myself thinking about Summerlee. Where was she, and what was she doing? I didn't ask Mum, because silence had become so ingrained that it was almost impossible to disturb it. I wanted to talk to my older sister. I was tired of us all living in our own heads, separated by pain rather than united by it. And I knew that Summer, for all her obvious faults, her little cruelties and self-absorption, loved Phoebe and would be in her own private hell. My family. Islands of suffering and not a bridge in sight. Maybe all families are like that.

It was gone eleven when the walls in the front room became washed in waves of light. I blinked and for a moment couldn't understand their source. Then I heard the sounds of car engines, the slamming of doors, the murmur of voices. Mum moved to the curtains and peered through a gap. One side of her face lit up, the other plunged into shadow. Dad had stood and he glanced at me. I shrugged. Then there was the sound of footsteps on gravel, followed immediately by a hammering on the front door.

At almost the same moment, every phone in our house rang. I looked down at mine, still resting on my palm, and for a moment or two, didn't understand what it was.

# CHAPTER 20

**Mum was raising her mobile to her ear, Dad was moving towards the landline.** I went into the kitchen. Caller unknown.

'Hello?'

'Is this Jamie Delaware?' A woman's voice. It threw me.

'Yes.'

'This is Yvonne Murrell from *The Clarion*. I wonder if it would be possible to talk to you about your sister's disappearance…'

I hung up. The hammering on the front door intensified. My phone started ringing again. I saw Mum finish her call with a jab to the screen that threatened to crack the glass. Dad was placing the landline back into its cradle, but it rang again immediately. I went back to the kitchen and swiped the icon on my phone.

'Jamie, I just need a statement from you…'

'Don't call this number again,' I said. 'Please.' I hung up, but almost immediately it rang once more. I moved a few paces closer to out-and-out terror. How could I not answer my phone? Even if there was only a one per cent chance it was the call we were waiting for? I put it into my pocket but its vibration against my leg was indistinguishable from agony.

Then I heard voices from the front room. Mum had flung open the door and admitted a blaze of light. I caught sight of a group of people but they were silhouettes against a backdrop of car headlights. A dozen voices were speaking at once. I went to join her.

'Mrs Delaware. I'm sorry to disturb you but…'

'Do you have a statement to make, Mrs Delaware…?'

'Jamie, is there any news of your sister…?'

'Ms Delaware, have you heard from the kidnapper yet…?'

Mum and I stood shoulder to shoulder, too stunned to say anything, washed in light and a babble of words. My phone continued to ring. Finally, Mum raised her arms and the voices immediately stopped. I caught a glimpse of microphones being thrust forward. A few flashes popped and Mum flinched as if wounded.

'I have nothing to say,' said Mum. 'There is no news. But I would ask you to give us privacy. As you can imagine, this is a difficult time.' I was staggered by her understatement and also impressed at her self-control. I'd expected her to explode like one of those flashes. 'In particular,' she continued, 'I would ask you please, do not ring our phone numbers. When we're ready to make a statement then we will do so through the police. Thank you.'

She made to close the door, but the questions redoubled in volume.

'So are you saying there's been no contact with the kidnapper yet, Mrs Delaware...?'

'Jamie, Jamie...you were there when she was taken. Can you...?'

Dad pushed his way past us. Even out of the corner of my eye I could see his face was flushed an angry dark. It occurred to me that his chest pains could be a symptom of something really wrong – that there might be a bomb inside his chest that was ticking. Then again, the whole family was surrounded by ticking bombs.

'Have you people no shame?' he yelled. 'What part of "we have nothing to say" don't you understand? Now piss off, the lot of you. You are trespassing and I'm calling the police.'

He slammed the door so hard the glass in one of the panels cracked. A young reporter at the front nearly got her fingers trapped between the door and the frame and I was almost disappointed she didn't. Judging by his expression, Dad felt the same. But it worked. There was a murmur of conversation and then the sound of people retreating down the path. I moved to the curtains and peered through. Some of the reporters got into cars and drove off. Others milled around on the street, just outside the boundaries of our property. Someone handed round cardboard cups of coffee. A young woman started preparing for a television report. A colleague set up a floodlight and someone else unloaded a camera from the rear of a van. I let the curtains fall.

'They could be here for the long term,' I said.

At least my phone was silent.

**Mum rang Gardner, and he assured us we wouldn't receive any more calls from the press.** Not on my mobile, at least. He was sorry the news had leaked, but he told Mum that it had only been a matter of time, anyway. This wasn't the kind of thing you could keep quiet for long. And maybe it wasn't such a bad development. News coverage was an effective way to gather information from the public. More people would come forward.

Gardner sent a policeman round to guard our door and we returned to what had become our normal state of affairs, sitting or pacing in the front room, the television silent. One part of me wanted to check out the news, but I didn't think any of us could bear it. Now that it was doubtless on television, I guessed it would be sensible to use social media – at least we might have some control over that – but I couldn't bring myself to do it. The thought of Phoebe's face shared on strangers' Facebook pages, mingling with inspirational quotations and videos of cute cats made me feel sick.

It was close to two in the morning when the three of us started to talk. Mum had finally stopped pacing and sat next to Dad on the couch. He hadn't said anything since his outburst to the reporters, but his face had regained a colour bordering on normal, and his breathing was regular. I sat on the rug in front of the blank TV screen, facing them.

'Do you remember when she was born, Jamie?' said Mum.

I thought. To be honest, most of it was lost now. I had been nine years old and I could recall the sense of excitement, but few of the details. Going into the hospital and seeing Phoebe for the first time. I remembered that. She was so tiny, with this faint covering of hair, like the fuzz on a peach. I remembered putting my little finger into her hand and feeling her clasp down on it. That was special. Some of the early stuff, too, when she was a baby. Most of it seemed to involve her crying at all hours of the day and night. Poo figured prominently, as well. I guess I only paid attention when she became a human being, when I could recognise the dawning of her personality. When she became…Phoebe. When I became something more to her than a shadowy presence and she started to love me. All of those sensations, feelings and memories came back and I had to clamp my jaws together not to cry out.

Mum's question, it turned out, was rhetorical. She started talking. The little details that I'd never learned or paid attention to. The influenza when she was three. The time she had turned blue and had to be rushed to the hospital. No one knew what had caused that, but it made Mum and Dad paranoid. Dad smiled when she said that.

'You didn't sleep for months,' he said to Mum.

'Neither did you,' she replied. 'Not really. We took it in turns, Jamie. I'd grab a nap when I could and your dad would do the same. We felt that if we took our eyes off her she'd stop breathing.'

'Remember her first day at school, hon?' said Dad. 'I couldn't bear it. She was so tiny and it was like we were giving her up, putting her into the system, you know? A system that would swallow her and we'd never get her back. Not the same child, anyway.'

'I came home and sobbed for three straight hours.' Mum slipped her hand into Dad's. 'You cried for four, I seem to remember.'

I smiled as they shared their memories. They became lost in the moments, living them again. The fear and the joy. Mum and Dad talked for twenty minutes, holding each other's hand. There had been no time to consider this, but I suddenly knew their marriage was in danger, that in enduring this they had been split apart, each of them locked into their own individual pain. Now, sharing the past, they were happy and together, but I knew the present was lying in wait, and suffering was only one word away. The word was 'Jamie'. I had lost my sister. I was responsible for all this.

'Do you think he will kill her, Jamie?' Dad said.

I glanced at Mum. She didn't avoid my eyes. The expression of a thought we all harboured wasn't terrible, she seemed to be saying; in some ways, it was a relief. My brain instinctively phrased a lie, but I stopped myself in time. Mum and Dad deserved better than a trite reply. It wouldn't have fooled them anyway.

'I don't know,' I said.

They both nodded as if my comment was an echo of their own thoughts.

'If he does,' Mum said after a moment, 'I will find him and I will kill him. I will tear his heart out with my bare hands. That is a promise.' I knew she would. The truth was embedded in her tone. Quiet, almost matter-of-fact. Under other circumstances I would have found it chilling. Dad smiled after she said it.

'You'd both have to get behind me in the queue,' I said.

Mum nodded. A few minutes later their hands had slipped apart and they stared past me at the wall, each retreated into a private space where I couldn't follow.

No one said anything else.

**At three in the morning I shimmied down the drainpipe outside my bedroom window.** Dad had gone to bed just after two, but it was unlikely he was going to find sleep. I think he wanted a physical space to match his mental space. A place where he could explore Phoebe's life without distractions.

I understood. Our house seemed steeped in desolation. The silence was filled with an unbearable longing, but there were also echoes of other emotions if you listened closely: fear, obviously; anger, without doubt. And there, far in the background, that faint tinnitus of recrimination. I wasn't sure who created it. Maybe it was only me, but I didn't think so.

The night was cool and clear. Trees stood out in silhouette

against a milky sky. I edged my way around the side of the house and looked towards the street. Most of the reporters had gone home but there were still a few cars parked outside, and I could see the shadows of people in them. Through the passenger window of one I caught the glow of a cigarette butt. A wisp of smoke coiled from the partially opened window. I found it difficult to understand. Did they really expect something to happen at three in the morning? Even if it did, was it *that* important to be the first to hear or see it? Everyone, it seemed, wanted a piece of Phoebe now. She had become important. The difference between them and us was that she had always been important in our family. For them, when this was all over, she would dissolve into insignificance. They would move on to the next fleeting moment of drama. Chasing smoke.

I went into the back garden and hopped over the fence into the neighbour's property. Then I went into the next. I would have gone into the third but the fence was too high, and I couldn't remember whether or not they had a dog. If the reporters were looking anywhere it was at our property, so I slipped past the far side of the house and into the street. There were trees on the nature strip and they provided some cover. Even so, I didn't relax until I'd turned the corner of our road. I pulled out my phone and called a taxi. They had no problems picking up a lone male from the street at three in the morning. It seemed dangerous to me, but maybe I was just looking at the world differently now.

Everywhere and everyone was coloured with potential tragedy, but I guess it hadn't always seemed that way.

**Summerlee's house was in darkness.** Party time was over. I rang her and she picked up on the second ring. Within two minutes I was sitting at her kitchen table, twirling the neck of a beer bottle between my finger and thumb. I didn't want a beer, but I needed something to fiddle with. Summer sat opposite, smoking with an air of desperation. She sucked the smoke into her lungs as if afraid a single tendril might escape. When she finished one cigarette, she lit another from the end and crushed the old one into an overflowing ashtray. Every movement was charged with violence and helplessness.

'No news?' she asked. I shook my head.

'Not from the kidnapper. But the media are onto it big time. They're camped outside our place. I guess it won't be long till they track you down here.'

'Fuck 'em. They'll get nothing from me.'

'How are you doing?' I asked. She tapped her cigarette hard against the side of the ashtray. There was no ash to get rid of, but she did it three times anyway.

'I'm not stoned,' she replied. 'And I'm not drunk.'

'Makes a change,' I said, but I grinned slightly to show I wasn't being nasty. She didn't pay attention anyway. All of her attention was focused on the cigarette and getting rid of non-existent ash.

'I thought being out of my head would help. You know? Deaden things. But it didn't. It just gave everything an…edge. I hated it. So I got straight.'

'You feel better?'

She glanced up at me. 'Nothing can make me feel better. Except getting Mouse back.' She welled up then, brushed impatiently at her face and lowered her eyes.

'Summer, I…'

'Do you want to hear something weird, Jamie?' She looked up again. Held my eyes, continued without waiting for a response. 'I was thinking about old Mrs Morris, today. Remember her? That crabby old bat of an English teacher. I had her in Year Nine, I think. You had her as well.'

'Yeah,' I said. 'She could strip paint at ten metres with one glance.'

'What a bitch,' said Summer. 'I hated her. Then again, she hated me. Couldn't blame her, though. I was *so* rude to her. Even by my standards, I was really rude.'

I didn't say anything. Wherever Summer was going with this, I knew it was important to give her time. She lit another cigarette and coughed.

'And I remembered something from one of our lessons. A poem. Fuck knows what it was. As you know, I never paid much attention. Especially to poetry, which seemed like the biggest waste of time in a continual waste of time. Something stuck, though.' She gave a thin smile and examined the glowing end of her cigarette. 'No matter how hard you try to let it all wash, some things stick. Education, huh? They screw you one way or another. Anyway, this poem. The only thing I remember was a line. Maybe it's two lines. And it goes something like, "We need to be kind to each other, while there's time". She looked up at me and it was almost like she was pleading for something. 'What do you think?'

'Doesn't ring a bell,' I said.

'"We need to be kind to each other, while there's time." It's been going round and round in my head all day. Like a song lyric, you know? A lyric you hate, but it just keeps looping in your ears, buzzing away like an annoying insect.'

I smiled.

'Hey,' she continued. 'I know what you're thinking. I think it too. I'm a walking fucking cliché. Not appreciating anything until it's gone. But, I dunno, Jamie.' She ran a hand through her hair. I could see her widow's peak and it was dark where it was growing out. The old Summer was still there, but it had been bleached away. Maybe in time she could grow back.

'The thing is, it's so true,' she continued, urgency in her voice. 'I mean, it's true. Even with old Mrs Morris. The last thing I said to her – hell, I can't remember the exact words, but they were full of hate. And she died. You know that? She had a heart attack the following year and that was it. And the last thing she heard from me was hate.'

'She probably didn't think about it, Summer,' I said. 'Lots of kids were horrible to her.'

'That's not the point,' said Summer. She was really intense, as if this was something I *had* to understand. She took another deep drag on her cigarette. 'I had a choice and hatred was what I chose. Now there's no time to take it back.'

'You were never hateful to Phoebe,' I said. 'You love her.'

'They were your numbers, Jamie,' said Summer. 'You know it. I know it. They were *your* numbers.'

'It's not important. None of that's important.'

'Yeah, it is.' Summer looked down at the kitchen table, brushed ash onto the floor. 'And I'm sorry. While there's still time, I wanted to say I'm sorry.'

I reached over and put my hand on hers, but she pulled away as if scalded. I took a drink from the beer. The house was silent, apart from a gentle thrum of rain on the roof.

'I need a favour from you, Summer,' I said finally. 'Well, from you and Spider.'

'Name it.'

So I did. Summer listened. I thought she'd laugh at my plan, but she didn't, and when I was done, she stubbed out her cigarette.

'I hate to be the one to break it to ya, Jamie,' she said, 'but you're not James Bond, little brother, you're a fuckin' nerd.'

'I know, Summer,' I replied. 'Trust me, I know. But that's the whole point. The kidnapper, he thinks he knows me, he's done his research and he has me classified as a nerd as well. Someone who can think but can't take physical action. So I need to make decisions he won't have anticipated. It's basic game theory.

Do whatever the other player isn't expecting. And he won't expect this.'

'Because it's fucking dumb.'

I didn't say anything. I wasn't going to convince Summer with words, but I knew she liked my idea, despite her objections. Sometimes a fantasy is extremely attractive, and I just needed to let it work its magic. She took another cigarette from the pack, but then slid it back and stood.

'Okay,' she said. 'But if this puts Mouse in greater danger, I'll hold you responsible, Jamie. And then *you'd* better watch your back. Do you follow?'

I nodded.

Summer turned towards the door. 'I'll wake Spider up now.'

'Hey,' I said. 'That's not necessary. If he can help me it can't be until later.'

'I'll get him up anyway,' said Summer. She had one hand on the door handle when she turned back to me. 'Spider. He's a dick, Jamie. I know he's a dick and I know you guys can't stand him.'

I shrugged.

'But he's been kind to me, you know? Spider's been kind to me, even before the money. That's gotta count for something.' She left, and all I could hear was the whisper of the rain.

# CHAPTER 21

**Spider said he would pick me up later, about eleven.** I told him I would come round to their place, assuming the media wasn't lying in ambush. One thing I could guarantee – it would be a total disaster if anyone followed me and Spider.

Summer offered to let me sleep at her place, even though it was six in the morning. She could probably read in my face and the way I moved that I hadn't slept for…God knows how long. But I turned her down. I'd only been there a few hours but already the fabric of the building seemed to be contracting. No matter where I was, claustrophobia stalked me. So I walked. The rain had stopped, though I really didn't care about that. Dawn was bleeding over the horizon and birds sang. Summer, not surprisingly, lived in the best suburb. Huge houses with imposing facades and beautifully kept lawns. I wondered what the neighbours thought about having Summer and Spider move in, thereby reducing property prices at a stroke. Then again, each house was so insular, so tucked up in its own exclusive world, that maybe they didn't notice.

I passed a woman walking two Dalmatians and she nodded at me as our paths crossed. I said good morning. The dogs were entirely in keeping with the neighbourhood, classy and elegant. I was far from classy and nowhere near elegant. I couldn't remember the last time I'd showered or changed my clothes. I also couldn't find it in myself to care. The dogs didn't seem to notice. They walked past, heads high, assured of their superiority.

I walked through a section of the city that was coming to life. People were out and moving, performing their early morning rituals and full of purpose. I had none myself, but I walked briskly, giving the illusion of it. My phone was tucked into my top pocket. It was like carrying around a cancer. I was obsessed with its presence, even when it gave no signs of activity. *Especially* then. I bought myself a takeaway coffee from a place that catered for business types coming to work early. It was scalding hot and bitter, but I felt slightly better with it inside me. I also stopped for thirty minutes in a park and watched joggers passing. Most had music plugged into their ears and shirts damp with sweat. No one paid me any attention.

I hadn't been aware of heading there, but I found myself on the boundaries of my school just as the students were arriving for the first lesson of the day. I stood and watched. Kids played basketball on the courts. Some performed tricky manoeuvres on skateboards. Most just stood around in groups, chatting.

I felt curiously detached from it all. It was a familiar world, but irrelevant now.

Gutless was dropped off by his mum. I recognised her car as it turned into the gates and I certainly recognised his bulk as he eased out of the passenger seat. He had a backpack slung over one shoulder and was wearing his baseball cap, the peak turned to the back. I'd told him about that before, that the peak at the back made him look like a wannabe dick, but he hadn't listened. *You wouldn't understand, man*, he'd said. *It's called style*. I picked my way around the knots of kids and headed towards him. I think some of the students called out to me, but I didn't respond. Many fell silent as I passed. The news must have been full of Phoebe this morning. Gutless himself didn't see me until I tapped him on the shoulder. He had his back to me. His baseball cap had some logo I didn't recognise. Almost certainly something to do with a computer game. It swung away from me as Gutless turned.

'Hey, Jamie, man,' he said. 'How are you, dude?'

I tried to say something. I opened my mouth, but there weren't any words there, so I closed it again. He put a hand on my shoulder.

'Jesus, man. You look like shit,' he said. 'Any news?'

I might have shaken my head. I'm not sure. Suddenly, I was spent. Whatever energy store I was functioning on had suddenly run dry. My left leg started to tremble and I felt the world move away from me.

'Say something, man,' said Gutless. 'You're starting to freak me out.'

I tried again, but my mouth wasn't obeying instructions. It twisted and the muscles in my face twitched and jumped. My skin was slick, with sweat or tears or both. There was a thudding in my ears.

'I'm scared, Gutless,' I whispered. 'I'm so scared.'

And he hugged me. He put his arms around me and drew me into his chest. I imagine we were the focus of everyone's stares, but I was beyond caring. I sobbed and it all came out, the hurt, the fear, the guilt. It washed through me and Gutless hugged me, there in the schoolyard. He hugged me.

## The call came half an hour later.

Gutless had wanted me to come into the school, maybe see the nurse or, at the very least, get someone to take me home, but I couldn't bear it. So I'd gone to Phoebe's school. The kids were in class by then, so I had the yard to myself. I sat on the low-slung swing and didn't care if I looked like a paedophile. The grounds had been recently mown and the air smelled of freshness and innocence. My ringtone dispelled all of that.

'Listen carefully, Jamie,' said the voice. 'In twenty-four hours you will have Phoebe back. I want you to arrange for the money to be delivered to your home today. Two million dollars in cash, in one-hundred-dollar bills. I also want you to buy a backpack large enough and strong enough to carry the money, which will weigh in excess of twenty kilos. Keep the money in the backpack at all times and wait for my call arranging the drop-off, the exchange.

I will ring again at six o'clock. I strongly suggest you do not let the police listen to our conversation then, since what I have to say is for your ears only. Tell me you understand.'

'I understand.'

The phone went dead.

Here is something remarkable, something powerful. All of my tension, my tiredness and my fear drifted away on the grass-scented breeze. Maybe living in a kind of suspended animation had leached my spirit, dissolved my spine, but I had things to do now. I rang Gardner and told him the call had come. He wanted to talk but I hung up. Then I rang Mum and gave her the same information. She wanted to know when I would be home, but I couldn't tell her. *Later*, was all I said before cutting her off, too.

I pushed up from the swing and my legs were solid. I walked back to the city and found a camping store. I went for a top-of-the-range backpack. The assistant assured me it could easily cope with a weight in excess of twenty kilos.

'This is a serious piece of equipment,' he said. 'Check the stitching and the zips. Built for a lifetime of heavy use. The light-weight frame is designed to spread the weight and…'

'I'll take two,' I said. 'As long as they're identical.'

They cost a fortune and I worried for a moment that there wouldn't be enough in my account, and I'd have to call Summer-lee. But the eftpos machine gave a large green tick. Then I went to a cafe and bought myself the special breakfast with my last twenty-dollar note. Sausages, bacon, hash browns and two fried eggs with doorstop slices of toast. I finished all of it. I looked at my watch. Ten-thirty. Time to get to Summer's place.

Gardner rang me a couple of times on the way, but I didn't pick up. I'd decided that the only use he could be to me now was to arrange for the money delivery, and he didn't need to talk to me to do that. But I did ring Summer. She told me a number of things. First, there was no sign of the media; second, Gardner was coming round immediately to take her to the bank, and she wouldn't be there when I arrived. Finally, she said that Spider had made some phone calls and was ready to go. I asked her not to mention this call to Gardner and she agreed without asking why.

I picked up my pace. It was a beautiful day and I almost felt good.

# CHAPTER 22

**Spider took me to see his Spider.**

To be strictly accurate, his Ferrari Testarossa Spider. It was a monument to rampant consumerism – low-slung, all streamlined contours and bright red. An engorged penis on wheels. I tried to look impressed, but I'm not sure I succeeded.

'Wow. Cool wheels,' I said, but only because I couldn't think of anything else to say. A few alternatives sprang to mind. *Awesome*, was one. *What are you, some kind of dick?* was another, but I needed this favour, so I kept quiet. Of one thing I was sure, however. It was a cast-iron certainty he was about to tell me how much it cost.

'Any idea how much this baby cost?' he said.

'A lot?' I hazarded.

He told me. I whistled.

'I was thinking of just getting a Ferrari, you know? But then I saw this Spider and I thought, hey, that's my name. It was kinda fate, man, you know what I'm saying? Calling to me. Like it literally had my name on it. Cool, huh?'

'Absolutely,' I lied.

'Some bastard pissed in it,' he informed me, mournfully. I adopted an expression of horror. 'Yeah,' he continued. 'Me and Summer parked up at the local mall and when we come back, the seats are wringing wet. The stench was fuckin' disgusting, man. Can you believe that? It's just jealousy. I know that. But to stand there, in a car park and whip out your trouser snake to piss in someone's Ferrari Testarossa Spider. I mean, what's the world coming to?'

'It's the downfall of western civilisation,' I replied.

'Too right. Cost me four thousand bucks to get it cleaned and detailed.'

'Well, you can afford it,' I said. 'Or should I say, Summer can afford it.'

Spider shook his head, lost in despair at the evil in the world. I felt cheated. If I'd known they were going to park up at the local mall, I would have pissed in it first. Well, probably not, but the concept was really appealing.

'Did they put that huge scrape along the side at the same time?' I asked.

'Nah,' said Spider. 'I did that. Took a bend too fast. I was doin' about a hundred and eighty and it slid a tad. Hit these fuckin' barriers. Tellya, man. You should've seen the sparks.'

I thought that if I had hit barriers at a hundred and eighty

I would have pissed in the car with no help from jealous passers-by at local shopping malls. Time was moving on, however, so I opened the door and slid into the passenger seat. The man himself strolled around and vaulted into the driver's side, one hand on the windscreen, the other on the plush leather headrest.

I hate Spider. Despite Summer's heartfelt testimonial, I can't express how much I hate Spider.

He turned the ignition key and the car growled into life. Whatever the engine was – I couldn't say, I'm not into cars – it exuded an air of being unhappy in a state of rest. The whole car shook with pent-up energy, a validation of Newton's laws of physics. Potential momentum demanded conversion into actual momentum. Spider slipped the car into first and took off with a wail of wheels and the smell of burning rubber. My back pressed into the seat.

'You might want to slow down, Spider,' I suggested.

'This car doesn't do slow, man,' he yelled against the wind. He was probably right. It didn't matter, anyway. We couldn't hear each other even when we shouted. I didn't relax until we left the city, which took about half an hour. Under other circumstances, I might have appreciated the looks of admiration we received driving along the highway, but I had too much on my mind. Particularly since I was concentrating on keeping the car away from any crash barriers by sheer force of will. Only when the traffic eased slightly did I force my fingers to relax and stop digging gouges into my palms. I took the opportunity to breathe as well.

Spider reached down into the glove compartment, pulled out a joint and lit it. Even with the wind rushing around our ears, the smell was pervasive, cloying and instantly recognisable.

'Spider,' I said. 'You think it's a good idea to be smoking pot while driving a car like this well above the speed limit?' I might have gone on to mention that he was a barely post-adolescent bogan and, therefore, a prime target for the police even if he was driving a Corolla, but I'm not sure he would have taken the point.

'WHAT?' he yelled.

I repeated the question with a higher decibel count.

'No worries, man,' he replied. 'I don't have a baggie in the car, just some pre-rolled joints. The cops pull me over, I ditch the smokes into the slipstream.'

I shook my head. It wasn't the police I was worried about, really. In fact, I probably would have welcomed the sound of pursuing sirens, if only to minimise the chances of some stoned dickhead driving me into a wall at one hundred and fifty kilometres an hour. I reminded myself why I was here in the first place.

'You're sure this guy can get me a gun?' I screamed, then regretted it. It wasn't a question that should be yelled.

Spider inhaled deeply. He even did the pinched cheeks bit and held the roach between the middle finger and the thumb, glowing end against his palm. I couldn't bear to watch.

'No problem, man,' he replied. 'There is nothing this guy cannot get. But it'll cost.'

'I know that, Spider. I'm taking it you brought along enough cash.'

'Well, yeah, but you need to pay me back, man.'

I pinched the bridge of my nose with a couple of fingers. Summer was worth an obscene amount of money. Spider, by association, was scarcely hard up. The car was a subtle clue.

'Are you serious, Spider?' I asked. 'You've got seven million big ones in the bank.'

'Down to four and a half now, what with the house and the car.'

'Still sounds more than enough to me.'

'Yeah, but it's the principle, man.' He glanced over at me, tossed the roach out of the car. 'Everyone should pay their debts.'

'Summer won that money,' I said. 'Have you paid her back for the car yet? And half the house?'

'Hey,' he said. 'We do things together, me and Summer. She bought the tickets but I paid half. So half the winnings are mine. That's the law, dude.'

'You paid her…what, six bucks? When?'

'Soon as I heard we'd won.'

'Okay,' I said. There seemed little point in pursuing this. 'I'll pay you back out of my pocket money. How does two dollars a week sound?'

He shrugged and reached down for another spliff.

'Look. When we get there, let me do the talking, man. This dude…he's kinda…well, unpredictable, if you catch my drift.'

'How unpredictable?'

'Like, may gut you with a boning knife if you look at him the wrong way kind of unpredictable.'

'Jesus, Spider,' I said. 'Who is this guy?'

Spider took both hands off the wheel to light his joint. We were only doing a hundred and forty now. Maybe I wouldn't have to worry about a maniac gutting me with a boning knife.

'You're buying an illegal gun,' Spider pointed out. 'What were you expectin', Jamie, a freakin' nun? Nah, man. He's a big cheese in a local bikie gang. But he's all right. Generally.'

'Oh, fuck, Spider,' I said. I didn't feel like talking anymore.

I spent most of the journey going through my plans, such as they were. Did it really make sense to buy a gun? There were so many things that could go wrong. I could blow my own head off for one thing. Or I could hurt Phoebe, which didn't bear thinking about. Summer had made this point; it had shaken me then and it shook me now. And there was no sense in buying a gun if I wasn't prepared to use it, which presented further problems. I had never fired anything in my life and I probably couldn't hit a barn door at five paces. Was it physically possible for me to level a firearm at another person and then pull the trigger? Even if it was, if I could stop shaking long enough, was it psychologically possible? I wasn't sure. I didn't want to find out.

Ultimately I had to face the real reason I was on this journey with Spider. Oh, I could fool myself by saying it was a move consistent with game theory, the argument I'd used with Summer. The kidnapper had researched me, he appeared to know my physical movements and my personality. If that was true, then he would also know that it was exceptionally unlikely I would come armed to any meeting. I was middle-class, I was a mathematician. People like me did not carry guns. People like me wouldn't have a clue how to get a gun in the first place. So I needed an advantage, an edge in this game. That was the theory and it sounded fine. It was logical.

But, fundamentally, there was another, much darker, reason.

Phoebe had seen this man's face. She would be able to identify him. Maybe if she'd been snatched on the street, bundled into a car and whisked away before anyone could witness anything, it might be different. He could have hidden his face, or put something over her head. But she knew who he was. You can't walk up to someone in a supermarket wearing a stocking or a latex mask. So was it reasonable to expect him to let her go when he'd got the money? Wouldn't it be more logical, safer for him, to kill her so she could never testify? It was this underlying suspicion that gnawed at me. I couldn't afford to adopt a position based on wishful thinking. I had to look at it from his viewpoint. And his viewpoint led to only one conclusion.

I knew the odds were against Phoebe coming out of this alive. And *that* was the reason I wanted the gun, because if she died, then he would too. Under those circumstances, there would be no psychological problems about pointing a gun at another human being. I would level a gun at this man's face, look him in the eyes and pull the trigger. I wouldn't hesitate and I wouldn't care. I'd even reload and do it all again.

Maybe keep one bullet for myself.

**The countryside became drab and featureless.** We had left the main road many kilometres behind. Farmers' fields flanked us, but if they were growing anything it was difficult to tell. Most seemed given over to grass and they didn't even house any livestock. An occasional barn appeared on the horizon and once or twice I caught sight of distant farm buildings, but other than that, we were far removed from civilisation. Spider appeared to know where he was going, however, which raised another question. Why would Spider be in contact with a bikie gang? The guy was a hopeless stoner and an even more hopeless bass player. I thought I knew the answer. What does a hopeless stoner do when he comes into money? He imagines himself a businessman with an empire to build. And his specialist commodity, his area of expertise? Drugs. Who runs drugs? Bikie gangs.

The way I figured it, Spider would be dead within a year. He'd either choke on his own vomit, have one too many brushes with crash barriers or find himself on the wrong side of a boning knife. I wasn't convinced the world would be a poorer place.

Spider turned off the road onto a dirt track. There were no signs that I could see. At least he was forced to slow down to about sixty. Even then, I could hear the car's undercarriage scraping the ground when we went over ruts, which was nearly all the time. A Ferrari Testarossa Spider with a resale value plummeting by the second. I checked out the countryside, but only because there was nothing else to do. The land was still dry and featureless, the odd scrawny gumtree providing the only relief from terminal monotony. It was difficult to believe anyone would want to live out here. Apart from a member of a bikie gang, I guessed, who was not necessarily keen on being close to good restaurants and nationally recognised operatic performance centres.

Ten minutes later, we passed through a ramshackle gate that clearly marked the entrance to a property. There was a sign next to it, but it was impossible to read because it was completely pock-marked with dents. Someone had been discharging a shotgun, repeatedly. Despite the purpose of my mission, I did not find this encouraging. Nonetheless, we drove on for another two minutes, before rounding a bend and stopping. We stopped because we couldn't go any further. A small, low-set shack sat in our way. Its roof was completely oxidised, window frames rotted. Two things adorned the small, weed-riddled yard fronting the property. One was a large motorcycle. The other was a large dog.

I didn't like the look of either.

**At least the motorcycle wasn't snarling.**

The dog was something like a German Shepherd or a Rott-weiler. I'm not great at recognising breeds. But I knew enough to realise this wasn't a canine bred to curl up at your feet, fetch tennis balls or beg to have its belly rubbed. This dog had only one thing on its mind: death. As I got out of Spider's car, it eyed me with interest, as if I had suddenly been promoted to number one on its desirability list. Black lips curled, revealing large yellow incisors. A froth of drool gathered at one side of its mouth. A low growl built and then erupted into a frenzy of barking. It lunged towards me and came up short, only because of the chain that kept it tethered to a post. The chain snapped violently, but held. I eyed the post. It seemed secure enough, but this beast was all muscle, and it appeared... motivated. I backed against the car. Pity it was a convertible.

'It's all right, man,' said Spider. 'He won't bother you.'

'He *is* bothering me, Spider,' I muttered.

The door to the shack opened and a man appeared on the verandah. He growled at the dog, which instantly dropped to its belly and rolled over. I felt like doing the same. This guy was every bit the bikie gang leader stereotype. A massive belly swelled against an inadequate singlet. And it wasn't a belly that spoke of too many fast food meals and an overindulgence in full strength beer. It was all muscle. He had a lot in common with his dog, including large yellow incisors. Where he differed was in the ink that covered every centimetre of exposed flesh. Most of the tattoos appeared to be of women in various stages of undress, though a few featured snarling jaws and dripping blood, or racist insignias. His head was shaved but, to compensate, his beard was luxuriant enough to curtain his chest. One long and vivid scar ran from his left ear towards his mouth. My mouth felt dry and I swallowed.

'Spider,' he said, and nodded towards my driver. Spider nodded back.

'Hello,' I said. I took a couple of paces forward and extended my hand. The dog growled, but subsided at one glance from its owner. The man looked at my hand and ignored it. 'This the guy?' he asked Spider.

'Yeah,' said Spider. 'The brother of my chick, man.'

*My chick*? Had I gone back in time a few decades? I let my hand hang for a few moments, then dropped it.

'You'd better come in,' said the guy. He turned and went back up the front steps. I could hear the floorboards of the verandah complaining. He disappeared through the front door and Spider followed. I followed Spider. I didn't really have much choice, and anyway, I had come this far. I was determined to see this through, even if I died in the attempt. The odds appeared pretty good in that respect.

The inside of the shack was consistent with its exterior. It spoke of neglect. A plain wooden table sat in the centre of what passed for the kitchen. The sink was full of dirty dishes and there was a vague smell of decomposition in the air. This might have been the result of an old woman who sat at the far end of the table. She had an excessively wrinkled face and her skin had that sheen you associate with leather left in the sun for too long. When we came into the room she got to her feet, displaying a surprising sprightliness. Liquid brown eyes glittered.

'We have guests, Darcy,' she said. 'How lovely.'

*Darcy?*

'Yeah, Ma,' said the man. 'Just a couple of business associates.'

I extended my hand a second time. The old woman took it and her grip was surprisingly strong.

'My name's Jamie,' I said. 'It's delightful to meet you.'

'Jamie,' she said. She cocked her head to one side and regarded me as if I was a long-lost, favourite grandchild. 'Charmed. Please sit. Would you like a cup of tea?'

'That would be lovely,' I said. I didn't drink tea. I never drank tea, but I guessed it wouldn't be a great idea to spurn hospitality. Darcy didn't give the impression he would take rejection well. I sat at the table and the old woman started to struggle towards the bench.

'Take a load off, Ma,' said the biker. 'I'll put the kettle on.'

'You're a good boy, Darcy,' said Ma, settling back down. As he passed she reached up and pinched his cheek. 'Remember to warm the pot.' She smiled at me. 'Sometimes he forgets to warm the pot and that doesn't make for a good cuppa, does it?'

'Certainly not,' I said. Darcy shot me a glance as if suspecting I had been dissing his tea-making prowess. I wanted to point out that contradicting his mother might not have been wise under the circumstances. Basically I was screwed whatever I said.

While Darcy busied himself with tea-making, his mother tilted her head to one side and regarded me benignly.

'So what are you, then?' she asked. 'A criminal or a policeman?'

'I beg your pardon?'

'Anyone who comes to see my Darcy is either a criminal or a policeman. Isn't that right, Darcy?'

'Sure is, Ma.'

I considered my answer.

'Well, actually, Mrs...'

'Call me Ma. Everyone does.'

'Well, actually, Ma, I'm neither. I'm a high school student.'

There was a sharp intake of breath. Out of the corner of my eye I saw Spider shaking his head. Darcy dropped a teaspoon into the sink and turned to face me. The temperature of the room suddenly plummeted and the atmosphere darkened. I was the centre of attention and it wasn't pleasant. I wondered where the boning knife was kept.

'I'm a mathematician,' I added, as if that would make everything okay.

'I think you'll find I'm right, aren't I, Darcy?' said Ma. She still smiled but her eyes had lost their sparkle. 'We get policemen and we get criminals. We don't get mathematicians. I can't remember a mathematician ever visiting.'

Darcy strolled over to the table and put a hand on his mother's shoulder. He didn't take his eyes off me.

'No, Ma. No mathematicians. Criminals or cops. That's it. You're absolutely right.'

I spread my hands to the sides and grinned, though it didn't come out right. I could feel my facial muscles twitching. Suddenly I needed to visit the toilet.

'What I *should* have said,' I spluttered, 'was that I am a criminal mathematician. I do study maths, but I'm a criminal first and foremost. That's my main job. The maths is nothing more than a sideline really.' I tried to stop, but it was difficult.

Ma softened, but her son didn't. I couldn't make up my mind who was the more dangerous. I also couldn't understand how I had found my way into this room, in the presence of a brain-dead stoner, a deranged biker and a geriatric psychopath. For once, game theory offered no useful strategies.

'Oh,' said Ma. 'What type of criminal are you, Jamie?'

'I'm a murderer,' I said. In for a penny, in for a pound.

'That's nice,' said Ma. 'We normally get drug dealers. That's our standard visitor, isn't it, Darcy? We don't often get murderers.'

'Only now and then,' agreed Darcy. He wandered back to the kettle, which had boiled. I was grateful when his attention turned to the teapot. I noticed he warmed the pot carefully.

'So, you're buying a gun, then?' asked Ma.

'Yes, please,' I said. *Please?*

'We've got plenty of guns,' said Ma cheerfully. 'I'm sure you'll find one to suit you. Is there anything in particular you're after?'

'I'm prepared to take advice,' I replied.

'But you're the murderer,' Ma pointed out. 'You must know what type of gun you want.'

'I'm a beginner, really,' I said. 'Still learning.'

She regarded me for a long moment and then nodded.

'Well, you *are* very young,' she said. 'So. Is this to be a close or long-range kill?'

'Errr...close, I think.'

'Sawn-off shotgun would be best. We have a good range. Unless you need to have the weapon concealed.'

'I think that would be best. Perhaps small enough to fit in a pocket.'

'Ah, pity. The shotgun doesn't require much in the way of expertise. Basically, you point it in the general direction and pull the trigger. Boom!' She smiled, revealing a set of intensely white and intensely artificial teeth. 'Then it's just a matter of scraping the guts off the walls. But if it's a concealed weapon you need, then a handgun is the obvious choice... Ah, thank you, Darcy.'

Her son had placed a bone china cup and saucer in front of his mother. In the other hand he held a chipped mug, which he thumped down on my side of the table. The tea splashed out of the mug and burnt my hand. I suppressed an 'ouch', which probably wasn't the response you'd expect from a murderer, albeit a young one.

'Thank you,' I said. Darcy scowled.

'A few biscuits would be nice,' said Ma. Darcy smiled and pulled down a tin from a shelf, opened it and placed an assortment of biscuits onto a plate. He put the plate next to his mother's cup.

'You're so sweet to me, Darcy,' she said. 'Now, be a good boy and get the selection of handguns from the bedroom, would you?'

'Of course, Ma.' And off he trotted. Ma took a biscuit and dunked it into her cup. I sipped from my mug. The tea was disgusting, but I was determined to swallow every drop. What I really wanted was to put distance between myself and this shack. A considerable distance. Buy the damn gun and get the hell out of there. But it appeared that, even for gun dealers, there were protocols to be followed. So we sat in uncompanionable silence, drinking our tea and nibbling at a selection of Arnott's. Spider stayed up against the wall, smoking yet another joint, not saying a word. Maybe he had more sense than I gave him credit for.

Darcy lumbered back into the room, carrying a large tool bag. He placed it carefully on the table and started unpacking the contents. Handguns of various sizes and colours. He lined them up close to his mother, butts facing towards her. He unpacked eight in total. She looked at me. I looked at the guns. I raised an eyebrow as if engaged in expert appraisal. I resisted the urge to simply grab the closest and finish the deal.

'What would you recommend?' I asked.

'This is a nice gun,' said Ma, picking up the third one along the line. It had a polished handle and looked murderous. Then again, they all looked murderous. I guess that was the point. 'It's reliable,' she added. 'Rarely jams. You don't want a gun that's liable to jam at the crucial moment.'

'Absolutely not,' I said. She offered the weapon to me, butt first. I took it. It was heavier than it appeared but I managed not to clunk it onto the table, possibly discharging it and taking out Ma.

I couldn't imagine that would endear me to her son. He wouldn't be offering me any Iced VoVos under those circumstances. I hefted the weapon in my hand and nodded sagely. It was the equivalent of kicking the tyres in a second-hand car dealership.

'Feels good,' I said. 'I'll take it.'

'Don't you want to try it out?' asked Darcy.

'Nah, I'll be right.'

'You should try it out,' said Darcy. He fixed me with that gaze again.

'Yes,' said Ma. 'Darcy is quite right. Never buy a gun you haven't tried. I mean, it's not like Target here. You can't bring it back for an exchange or your money back. We don't work like that, do we, Darcy?'

'No, Ma. We don't.' The silence gathered.

'I promise you I won't be returning it,' I offered.

No one said anything.

'Maybe I'll try it out,' I said.

'Good idea,' said Ma.

Darcy rummaged around in the tool bag and brought out a box of bullets. He took the gun from me and slapped it open – I'd seen that kind a million times in movies; it had a revolving chamber with six tidy holes to accommodate the bullets. It made me feel more comfortable that I had some notion of how it worked. Darcy inserted the bullets and then slotted the chamber back. It engaged with a satisfying clunk. He offered the butt to me and I took it.

'Let's step outside,' he suggested. I wasn't in a position to argue. We all trooped out onto the verandah, me first, flanked by Darcy, with Spider behind and, finally, Ma. She plopped herself down on a rickety old rocker and folded her hands into her lap. The dog got to its feet and growled at me. Then it glanced at Darcy and put its ears back.

'What do you want me to fire at?' I asked. I wasn't looking forward to this. Whatever the target, I was sure to miss, but that wasn't what bothered me. It was the thought of the recoil and the loud noise. I could envisage myself screaming and dropping the gun onto the ground as if it was red hot. Not that I minded making myself look like a dick in front of these people. But Darcy might take offence. I was coming to the conclusion that he was a guy who would take offence at almost anything.

'The dog,' said Darcy.

'What?'

'The dog, man. Shoot the dog.'

I looked from one to the other. Darcy's eyes bored into me, Spider shrugged and Ma grinned in a manner that reminded me of Norman Bates in that old movie, *Psycho*.

I laughed, but I was the only one.

'I can't shoot your dog,' I stammered.

'Why not?'

'It's your dog.'

'But I'm giving you permission,' said Darcy. 'I mean, yeah, if you'd just rocked up and shot my dog I would've been pissed off…'

'Watch your language, Darcy,' said Ma.

'Sorry, Ma,' said Darcy. 'I mean I would have been ticked off if that had happened. But this is different. I *want* you to shoot my dog.'

'But...'

'I've never liked that dog,' Ma chipped in. 'It makes too much noise. And, anyway, I want a Labradoodle. Labradoodles are cute. So you see, Jamie, it would be killing two birds with one stone... Oh, dear, I've made a joke.'

Darcy laughed. It was good to know he was capable of laughter. Not *very* good, though. 'Nice one, Ma,' he said.

'This way,' the crazy old bat continued, 'you save Darcy having to shoot him *and* you get to see if the gun is what you want. So, please. Go ahead.'

My mouth had gone completely dry. I looked at the dog. He had stopped growling now and I could see something I hadn't noticed before. His tongue lolled from the side of his mouth and it appeared as if he was grinning. I knew he wasn't, but it seemed that way. This was a pet, even if he hadn't been trained to do anything but be aggressive. He didn't deserve to die. Even if he did, I couldn't be the one to put him down. I let the barrel of the gun droop towards the floor of the verandah.

'How about I shoot at something else?' I suggested. 'Maybe that post over there.' I wasn't even sure I could shoot a post that hadn't done me any harm.

'How about you shoot the dog?' Darcy responded.

Nobody said anything. I shifted from one foot to the other. I could run for it, but even though I'd done some athletics in school, I thought it unlikely I'd be able to outrun a Harley Davidson motorcycle.

'Tellya what,' Darcy continued. His tone was reasonable. 'If you don't shoot the dog, I'll let him off the chain. He doesn't take to strangers, does he, Ma? And you and Spider are strangers. So that's your choice. Shoot the dog or take your chances.'

Ma chuckled. 'No, you're quite right, Darcy. He really doesn't like strangers at *all*.'

I glanced at Spider. He rolled his eyes wildly towards the hound. It was easy to read him. *Shoot the dog, man. Shoot the fuckin' dog.* It was a sign of desperation, anyway, looking to Spider for support.

I stepped down from the verandah, my legs shaking violently. I really did need the toilet now, but guessed a request would not go down well. I took a few paces towards the chained animal. It didn't snarl this time. It didn't hurl itself towards the end of the chain. It just lay there and gazed up at me with huge brown eyes. I lifted the gun. Partly because it was so heavy, but mainly because my hands were fluttering, the barrel roamed a shaky diameter of four or five metres. I had no chance of hitting the poor thing, even at a distance of two metres. But I also suspected that if I was to miss I would have to do it again. Darcy seemed that kind of guy. So maybe it was better to do it right first time round. I couldn't bear to think of the dog suffering. So I took another pace forward.

If it decided to attack, there was no way I could escape. I almost hoped it would. A badly bitten leg might get me off the hook. But it just lay there, its eyes on my face. I think it was beginning to like me. We were forming a bond.

I closed my eyes and forced myself to exert pressure on the trigger. It was stiff and I knew that the more I pressed, the greater the arc described by the barrel. Maybe I'd shoot my own foot off. *Don't think, Jamie. Just do it.* I pressed harder, my teeth grinding together. Nothing happened. Just how much pressure did you have to exert to get this damn thing to fire? My fingers were cramping.

'You've got the safety off, have you?' asked Darcy. He stepped over, took the gun from me and glanced at it. 'Nah. Here you go.' He flicked a switch and gave the gun back. 'Surprising how many people forget the safety.'

'You're not a very convincing murderer, are you Jamie?' said Ma. She appeared enormously cheerful. 'Please hurry. It's nearly time for my afternoon nap.'

This time I grabbed the gun, pointed, closed my eyes and jammed down on the trigger. I couldn't bear it. There was a very loud explosion and the gun jumped violently in my hand. A smell of burning assaulted my nostrils and my ears rang. I waited for a few moments before opening my eyes. I didn't want to. I didn't want to open them until I was home. Maybe not even then.

The dog hadn't budged. It continued to stare up at me with those soulful eyes. I scanned it for blood but there was nothing.

Then I heard the laughter. Darcy was wiping tears from his eyes and Ma was rocking back and forth in merriment. I gazed at them.

'I'm so sorry, Jamie,' said Ma after a minute. It took her that long to recover from her chuckling fit. 'But you should have seen the look on your face. It was priceless.'

I tried another unsuccessful grin.

'Blanks, mate,' said Darcy. 'I put blanks in the gun. You didn't really think I wanted you to kill my dog, did you?' He chuckled. Ma chuckled. Spider joined in. Even the dog panted as if laughing. What an honour to be in the presence of people with such highly developed senses of humour. Darcy suddenly stopped laughing.

'Right,' he said. 'Two thousand dollars for the gun. Here is a box of proper bullets. Now pay me and get off my land. Ma needs her afternoon nap.'

'Two thousand?' said Spider. 'But you said...'

'I think you'll find I said two grand,' replied Darcy. 'You have a problem with the price?'

'No,' said Spider. He took out his wallet and grasped a bundle of green notes. 'Two thousand,' he said. 'It's been great doing business with you.'

Darcy took the cash, counted it and tucked the wad into his jeans pocket. Then he turned and went back into the house. The door closed behind him. Ma continued to rock.

'Bye boys,' she said.

'Goodbye, Ma,' I said. 'It was nice meeting you.' *And even nicer to get as far away as I possibly can. Maybe a couple of states distant.*

Spider and I hurried to the car and hopped in. I didn't bother opening the door this time. The engine roared and Spider backed up, did a three-point turn and burned off down the track, the undercarriage scraping wildly. I noticed his hands on the wheel were shaking.

'Maybe you can drive quicker, Spider?' I said.

'No worries,' he said, and floored it.

It was only when we were on a proper road and I hadn't heard the sound of a pursuing Harley that I relaxed. And I use the word 'relaxed' in its loosest sense. The only thing really relaxed and loose about me was my bowels. I put the gun down into the footwell very gingerly and then rubbed at my eyes.

'By the way, Spider,' I said. 'I really appreciate how you did all the talking back there. Made it so much easier.' I think he had uttered a dozen words in total.

'WHAT?' yelled Spider.

'Never mind,' I said. I could do without the noise anyway. I wasn't listening for a Harley anymore. I was keeping my ears peeled for the sound of police sirens.

There was a gun sitting in the footwell and I couldn't think of any convincing explanations for its presence.

# CHAPTER 23

It was three o'clock when Spider dropped me off at home. Gardner and Moss were there and so was Summer. Mum was pacing back and forth in the front room. I was pleased to notice that only one strange car was parked outside. Maybe Gardner had put some pressure on the media.

Everyone wanted to talk to me but I excused myself on the grounds that I needed to visit the bathroom. In fact, I had an illegal handgun tucked into my butt crack and it didn't seem like a good idea to let Gardner notice the bulge. I went into my bedroom and put the gun under my pillow. Funnily enough, I didn't feel tough. I felt silly. Then I unzipped the newly purchased backpack, removed its twin from inside and put it under my bed. I kept the other in my hand.

When I went downstairs, there was a meeting convened in the kitchen. I was made to go over the phone conversation with the kidnapper while Moss took notes in a small notepad. I told them everything except the time when he said he would ring again. I also didn't mention his advice to keep the police out of the next call.

'It was a short conversation,' I said. 'Just get the money, put it into a backpack and wait for another call. He said that wouldn't be before seven, to give us enough time to get the money.' I put the backpack onto the table. 'I bought a pack this morning. He was pretty specific about the kind he wanted,' I lied.

Gardner picked it up and examined the zips and the seams.

'Big enough and strong enough,' he conceded. 'Good. Listen, everyone. Summerlee and I went to her bank and the money was delivered to her home by a security firm. Two million dollars in one hundred dollar bills.' He pointed to a couple of sacks in the corner of the kitchen. 'The money is there and soon I'll transfer it to this backpack. Then it's simply a question of waiting for the next call and finding out the location of the drop. Now, Jamie. You said he said that Phoebe would be returned in the next twenty-four hours. You're sure about that?'

'That's what he said.'

'That at least gives us a time frame,' said Gardner. 'He will ring, therefore, some time between seven this evening and ten in the morning. I suspect it will be this evening. He may want the cover of darkness. Either way, I will not leave your house from now on. I'll be joined by another police officer and we will spend the night, if necessary, in your front room. If that's okay with you, Mr and Ms Delaware?'

'Of course,' said Mum.

'Obviously we want to protect your money, but we also want to ensure that we are in place when the call comes through. To that end, Jamie, I need you to stay here as well. I take it that's not a problem.'

I looked at my watch. It was a quarter past three.

'I have to go out soon for an hour but I'll be back by five at the latest.'

Gardner screwed up his face.

'Is it important?' he said. 'He may ring earlier and I don't want you to take the call while you are by yourself. I want it on speakerphone.' He held up a hand. 'I know what he said about no one else speaking and that's fine. No one else will. But I need to hear exactly what he wants and when he wants it, so that we can put plans into effect.'

'What plans?' asked Mum.

Gardner frowned and glanced at Moss. He was weighing things up.

'Look, Ms Delaware. I understand your priorities. You just want Phoebe back unharmed and it might *seem* to you that the best way to achieve that is simply to do everything this person wants, without question.'

'Yes,' said Dad. 'That's *exactly* how it seems to us.'

'We see things differently. It's our experience that if we get the chance to apprehend this person we need to take it immediately. I hate to say this to you, but it's best to be brutally honest. Most kidnappers are greedy. They say they just want a one-off payment, but when that goes through without a hitch, they think, *Hey, that was easy. Why not go for some more?* And that only prolongs the agony and increases the danger for your daughter.'

'And you think he might harm Phoebe anyway?' Mum asked.

At least it was out there. Gardner paused and then nodded. 'I can't lie to you, Ms Delaware. That is a possibility. Phoebe can presumably identify this man and...' He shrugged, left the rest unsaid. 'So it's even more important that you let us handle this in our own way. We will call on specialist people. They are *very* good at what they do. Professionals. Once we know where the money is to be delivered, they'll move into place. No one will know they're there. And when they move in, it's all over in seconds. Trust me, it's far and away the safest way to get your daughter back unharmed.'

There was silence. I could imagine what was running through everyone's heads. We'd all seen the movies. The guys with acronyms on their backs and steel in their spines. High technology, shadowy figures, overwhelming force applied in a few explosive seconds. Game over. The child returned to the family embrace. Good guys win. Maybe Gardner wanted those images in our heads. He certainly wanted us to bend to his will. Another practitioner of game theory.

'What if he's already harmed her?' asked Summerlee. 'Before the money gets there?'

Gardner shrugged. 'All the more reason to bring him down, I would have thought.'

There was another silence while we absorbed this.

'You're the professionals,' said Mum, finally. 'Of course we will follow your advice.'

'Good,' said Gardner. 'Now, if you'll excuse me, I have a number of calls to make. Detective Moss is also following up the leads from the video and from the eye witness reports. We are making good progress in some of those areas.'

Moss took over.

'We have a number of leads on the green Commodore. Same with the clothing that Phoebe was wearing in that video. There are officers pursuing those leads as we speak…'

I zoned out. One of the few advantages of watching television drama was that I recognised when busywork was masquerading as constructive work. Within twenty-four hours the game would be over, one way or another. Green Commodores appeared, to me at least, supremely irrelevant. I excused myself and slipped out of the house. I was grateful Gardner hadn't pushed his plea that I stay put – I think the flood of questions had distracted him. When I left, he was transferring piles of money from the canvas bags into the backpack, his mobile phone pressed up against his ear. Under other circumstances I would have been fascinated at the sight of so much cash. Now, the fat wads of notes seemed as irrelevant as Commodores.

Once I was out of the house, a reporter opened a car door and approached me, but I held up a hand and, to my surprise, he let me walk away. It might have had something to do with the policeman outside our front door who took a few steps towards him. I crossed the road and headed to the local park. Only when I was out of sight did I take my phone out and ring.

'Dixon.' He clearly didn't waste energy on unnecessary greetings.

'It's me, Jamie. Jamie Delaware.'

There was a pause.

'How you doing, son? Any news?'

'I'd like to take you up on your offer to talk, if that's okay.'

'When?'

'Now.'

I could hear him sucking his teeth. It was a vaguely sinister hiss down the line.

'Tell me where you are and I'll meet you.'

I gave him directions and he said he would be there in half an hour. I sat on a bench and waited. There was a small lake at the centre of the park and a few ducks wandered around my feet, hoping for bread. I wished I'd brought some. The sky was flawless. It was a beautiful day.

Dixon shambled along a footpath and raised a hand when he saw me. He was wearing a greatcoat and it looked like he hadn't shaved in a week. If this was an image he was cultivating, I wondered what that said about the man.

He plopped himself down next to me with a sigh, as if the act of sitting was wearisome. He took a pack of cigarettes from the side pocket of his coat and lit one.

'What's the development?' he asked.

I told him. Again, I left out the part about the kidnapper's next call and the advice not to let the police listen in. Naturally, I also said nothing about what lay concealed under my bedroom pillow. Dixon leaned forward in his seat as I spoke, his forearms resting on his thighs, examining the state of his shoes. He didn't say anything until I'd finished.

'Sounds like it's all coming to a head,' he said.

'Yes. One way or another, this should be over soon,' I replied.

'So what do you want my advice on?'

'Inspector Gardner was really convincing about setting a trap for the kidnapper.'

'And you're not convinced. You think it might be an idea to go it alone.'

I supposed I shouldn't have been surprised. Dixon was sharp. I guess you couldn't be a cop for so long and not develop an instinct about what's going through someone's head.

'I'd have to be dumb to think that, wouldn't I?' I said. 'I mean, you guys are the professionals.'

Dixon dropped his cigarette end between his feet and carefully ground it beneath a heel. He sucked his teeth for a while, but remained silent. I did the same.

'This is not a call I can make, Jamie,' he said eventually. 'You have to understand that. My advice must always be to follow police advice. But bear with me for a second, while I go through what I *believe* are your thought processes.' He lit another cigarette. 'You think the idea of a police trap is very seductive. Getting your sister back and bringing the bad guy to justice. That's a vision you find…attractive. But there are other images as well. What if it all goes wrong? What if the trap itself brings harm on your sister? Under those circumstances, maybe it would be better to hand over the money and let the bad guy get away. It's only money, right? Whereas your sister is precious. Am I wide of the mark so far?'

I shrugged. 'Go on.'

'But what eats away at you is the thought that either course of action could result in disaster, and then you have nowhere to hide. If the police operation goes wrong and your sister is harmed, then obviously you made the wrong choice. Then again, if you hand over the cash and *that* goes wrong, then obviously you should have let the professionals deal with it. It's a classic lose–lose situation and you will never forgive yourself.'

He stopped for a moment as a jogger went by.

'I understand and I sympathise, Jamie,' he continued. 'I really do. But that very dilemma is also *my* dilemma. I can't give you advice because I couldn't live with myself if it was wrong. And no one can know how this thing will pan out. So, I repeat. Stick with police procedures.'

He didn't finish the thought, but he didn't have to. *If Phoebe*

*dies, at least you will be able to share the guilt. Go it alone and it's*
*all on your shoulders.*

'What would you do in my situation?' I asked.

He stood and put a hand on my shoulder.

'I'm not in your situation, son. And if there *is* a good lord,
I thank him for that...'

My phone rang. I glanced at the screen. Caller unknown.
I took a step away from Dixon and slid my thumb across the icon.

'Surprise, Jamie.' The mechanical voice. Instantly, my heart
rate accelerated and a film of sweat broke out on my forehead.
'I said I would ring at six, but sometimes it's good to disappoint
expectations. Are you alone, Jamie?'

Dixon must have known who was on the line by the expression
on my face. He was mouthing *Is that him?* at me and pressing an
imaginary button, presumably a plea to put the conversation on
speakerphone. I turned my back.

'Yes,' I said.

A long pause.

'Do not use speakerphone, Jamie. Trust me, I will be able to
tell. Now, I will talk and you will listen with no interruptions.
Firstly, let me disillusion you about a few things brought up in the
media. The police will not track me through green Commodores
or children's clothing. I have never owned a Commodore, green
or otherwise. The clothes for Phoebe were purchased at a charity
shop a number of months ago. They cannot be traced. Secondly,
you will have received advice from Inspector Gardner, a good

man but one who cannot conceive of doing anything that's not straight from the manual. He will want to take charge of the exchange. He wants officers staking out the rendezvous point, ready to take me down. I imagine he has been very persuasive on this point. But think about this, Jamie. I will know if you have company. And if that's the case, you will not see your sister again.'

I sat down on the bench before my legs gave out, bent my head. Dixon's cigarette butt was in my direct line of sight and I focused on it. The voice continued.

'But here's the positive. You worry I will harm Phoebe regardless of what happens. That I would...eliminate incriminating evidence. Believe me. Once I receive the cash, Phoebe will be released. I will not ask for more money. I do not need it. And as for your sister identifying me in court, I will be out of the country within an hour of receiving the money. I will not return to Australia and it would not be in my interests to provoke an international murder manhunt.'

I stood and walked to the edge of the lake. My legs were numb and my feet tingled with pins and needles. I was dimly aware of Dixon in my peripheral vision. He had stopped gesticulating.

'We are approaching the endgame, Jamie,' the voice continued, 'and we can both come out winners. It all depends on the choices you make. Now, listen carefully and do not write anything down. Here is what I want you to do with the money...'

I listened carefully and I didn't write anything down. The phone went dead. I stood for a few moments, watching the ducks as they sailed peacefully over the lake. I guess I must have appeared like them – at peace on the surface, but underneath it was all churning movement.

Dixon appeared at my side. He'd lit another cigarette. For a moment we watched the ducks together, thin trails of smoke drifting across my vision.

'Anything you want to tell me, son?' he asked finally.

I shook my head and put the phone back into my pocket.

'Sorry,' I said. 'But I think I need to talk to Gardner.' I put out my hand and Dixon regarded it for a moment, his moustache writhing as he sucked at his teeth. Then he gripped it and we shook.

'Thanks,' I said. 'You've been a great help and I appreciate it.'

He held onto my hand for a few more seconds. 'Police procedure, Jamie,' he said. 'Remember that.'

I nodded, turned and headed towards home.

The endgame was approaching and I had to make my move.

# CHAPTER 24

The adrenaline that had kicked in at Phoebe's school had returned, and in some curious way I was relieved. The kidnapper was always one step ahead. And that made my decision easier. I even found myself believing him when he said he had no interest in harming Phoebe. There was something authoritative, not in his tone, because there wasn't one, but in the logic of his words.

I knew what I had to do.

Gardner was not pleased at my prolonged absence. Neither was Mum. Luckily for me, both were heavily engaged in planning. Well, Gardner was, and Mum was following one side of the conversation as he spoke to people on his phone. Another cop had turned up. He was a huge guy, obviously chosen for his bulk rather than his conversational skills, since he didn't say a word. He just nodded at me when I came in. Gardner covered the mouthpiece of his phone and glanced over.

'Has the call come through?' he asked. I could tell he really wanted to say, *where the hell have you been?*

I shook my head and he returned to his phone conversation. I went into the kitchen. Summerlee sat at the table, looking like hell. Even so, without makeup she still managed to look years younger. She raised her head at my entrance.

'I need your help, Summer,' I said.

'What?'

'In fifteen minutes I want you to get those cops, and Mum and Dad, into the kitchen and keep them here for five minutes, tops. That's it. Close the door when they're in.'

'Dad's having a lie down.'

'Where?'

'In their bedroom, I guess.'

I nodded. 'Okay. Just whoever's down here, then.'

'And how am I going to get them into the kitchen?'

'I dunno. Make them a sandwich or something.'

She raised an eyebrow.

'C'mon, Summer. Throw a screaming fit. Use your imagination.'

She looked at her watch. 'Fifteen minutes?' I nodded again.

'Okay,' she said.

I went straight to my bedroom and got the remaining backpack from under the bed. I stuffed it with what was left of my printer paper, but I only had a ream of that. So I added maths text books. Fortunately I had plenty of those, and they were heavy as hell. The shapes were all wrong, but I was banking on no one examining it too carefully. All I needed was around twenty kilos in weight. I picked up the backpack. It felt heavy enough, like a suitcase being checked in on holiday. It would have to do.

I opened my bedroom door carefully, keeping the bag concealed. Just as well, because the door to Mum and Dad's bedroom opened and Dad stood there, gazing at me, his eyes blank and distant.

'Jamie.'

'Hi, Dad.'

'What's going on?' He ran a hand through his hair.

'Nothing. No news. Go back to bed.'

He continued to stare as if not comprehending my suggestion. Maybe he didn't. I was almost tempted to take him by the arm and lead him back, but he was so wired I couldn't guarantee he wouldn't scream. It was a stand-off. His hands twisted against each other, like he was washing them.

'I can't sleep,' he said eventually. 'Whatever I do I can't sleep. Need the bathroom.'

I nodded and waited. He continued to stand, but then seemed to remember why he was there and shambled off down the corridor. I waited until I heard the door close and then I lugged the pack down the stairs. I propped it up outside the front room and listened at the door. Gardner was still speaking on the phone. I glanced at my watch and prayed no one would think to open the door to the hallway. What was keeping Summer?

Then I heard her scream.

There were sounds of scrambling feet from the front room. I waited about twenty seconds and opened the door. The room was deserted but the kitchen door was slightly ajar. I could see a slice of Gardner's suit. Summer's voice was loud and panicky.

'I saw someone through the kitchen window,' she said. 'A man. He was there a moment ago.'

The slice of suit moved. I rushed over to the pack in the corner and exchanged it for the one full of textbooks. Mine sagged in a way the other didn't, but there was no time to do anything about it. I took the money and went back out into the hallway. Dad was coming down the stairs, his previous lethargy gone, face filled with terror. I dumped the bag against the stairwell and stood in front of it.

'What is it, Jamie?' he said. 'I heard screaming.'

'In the kitchen,' I said. 'Summer thought she saw someone in the garden.'

Dad brushed past me and I took the pack and hefted it up the stairs. It was damn heavy and I was relieved when I finally had it stowed under my bed. Then I went down and joined the others.

The big guy had gone into the garden, presumably in pursuit of Summer's imaginary intruder. Gardner was on the phone again. Dad had his arm around Mum, whose fist was pressed halfway into her mouth. Summer gave me a questioning look and I nodded.

'I might have imagined it,' she said. 'My nerves have been playing up recently.'

There was considerable bustle, but it all calmed down after fifteen minutes. The big guy came back in and shrugged. Eventually we all went back into the front room and settled down to wait for a call I knew wasn't coming.

I got a text message, though. At nine-thirty my phone buzzed and everyone reacted like they'd been tasered. I held up a hand. 'It's just Gutless,' I said. I opened up the message.

steakout at monkhouse place. dude hasnt bin in school 2day but shitloads gossip. maybe wife or mhouse bin shagging sumone els. sumone moving out. seen car loaded up with own eyes. fuckin worldwar going on in his house. Da Horse.

I deleted the message and while I was at it, went to settings and deleted the record of the last incoming call.

At midnight I excused myself and went to bed, promising I would come down if my phone rang. Gardner vetoed the idea. He insisted that if I wanted to go to bed I would have to leave my phone with him.

'Trust me,' he said. 'When it rings, I will be in your bedroom in five seconds.'

I thought about it. I didn't think I would have further use for the phone, especially as I had already received directions. In some ways, it was to my advantage. Gardner's attention would be focused entirely upon my phone, which meant he wouldn't be checking up on me during the night. Or, even worse, posting the big guy outside my bedroom door. But I worried a little anyway.

What if the kidnapper changed the instructions and tried to tell me at six in the morning? Gardner would come rushing to my room and find it deserted. The shit would hit the fan in a very big way. In the end, I decided I would have to take my chances. The phone would ring out or Gardner would be forced to answer it. Either way, the kidnapper would understand I wasn't in a position to take further instructions.

So I handed over the phone and went to my room. I had no idea what the morning would bring, but I thought it wise to get what rest I could, even though I knew I couldn't sleep. More than anything else, however, I needed space and time to think.

Time to prepare.

# PART THREE

# CHAPTER 25

**I keep to the track of broken lines in the middle of the street.** Everywhere is dark. Everywhere is quiet, except for the soft kiss of rubber soles on tarmac.

I'm conscious of the weight of two million dollars on my back, but the backpack takes that weight and distributes it, just as the man in the shop said it would. After half a kilometre, I almost forget it's there. I keep my head down, focusing only on the lines. At the back of my mind is the possibility that someone might step out in front of me. Perhaps an addict. Maybe just an ordinary thief, looking for a few bucks in a wallet, a backpack to sell. I imagine his face when he opens up his prize and finds two million dollars in neatly packed bundles, rather than dirty socks, T-shirts and torn jeans. I know it's unlikely. I also know I have a gun tucked into my waistband. For the moment at least, I'm glad it's there.

Time passes and, as it does, loses meaning. It is one step in front of another. Another broken line and then another. I think of Phoebe's face. For some reason, I think of her expression when she is mad. At me. Or the world at large. The way her mouth sets in that determined, thin line, her little brow scrunching. Putting her hand on her hip, turning a foot. The classic body language of annoyance. And then I think of how quickly that changes. When I tickle her or make her smile by saying something silly. Her irritation dissolves. Solid and immutable one instant, insubstantial the next, gone entirely a moment later. How life floods into her eyes and her lips part, revealing small teeth with that tiny gap between the front two.

I feed on those images and the belief that every step takes me closer to her.

The meeting point is an hour's walk away. I know the general area. It is run down, a suburb that used to be home to an industrial complex before a new development on the far side of the city brought about its death. Now it's a landscape of desolation, empty buildings, vast car parks where the tarmac is cracked and weeds invade, chain-link fences full of gaping holes. It's a year since I passed by it, on a trip with Dad to a destination that escapes my memory. I suspect chaos will have made further inroads. It's a good choice, at least from the point of view of the owner of the mechanical voice. It is far from residential property, yet the roads that once serviced it are still there. Any movement in the complex would be easy to pick up, for someone observing. A difficult place to infiltrate without being seen. Yet also ideal for escape, the roads branching off in every direction, so that, within fifteen minutes, a car would be lost among a multitude of possible highways.

I will be early for my appointment, but I understand that I will almost certainly not be early enough. He will be there already. Possibly, he was always there. I see him in my mind's eye, on top of a building, perhaps, scanning the landscape through night-vision binoculars, waiting for the signs of those grey-suited figures with guns slung over their shoulders, threading their way across fields, through fences, swarming into buildings and finding holes in which to hide. He is listening for the drone of a helicopter. Yes, he will already be there. Prepared to follow through on his threat at the first sign of scurrying movement. Is Phoebe at his side, shivering in the chill night air, her hands tied in front of her? Does she, too, watch, wait and suspect her world is on the cusp of ending? What thoughts will go through her head? Is she aware that I am coming for her? Does that help keep her darkness at bay? The questions are insistent but I try to push them away, and focus only on the road markings and my feet as they move in and out of vision.

I have no plan and that is curiously liberating. Game theory has fucked me, filled my head full of stratagems and suspects, the illusion of being in control. What did Summerlee say about me? Something about my overwhelming fucking sense of superiority. She is right. I look back on all my pathetic game-playing, the logical processing of potential suspects, all of it underpinned by the feeling, the certainty, that no one could outsmart me. Not me, Jamie Delaware, game-theorist and complete idiot. And where did it all lead? I still have no idea who is behind this. Probably a complete stranger or someone I don't know who Summer pissed off, just because she's Summer and that's what she does. But I couldn't accept that because it didn't involve *me*. I couldn't bear to be a bit player, a medium to take messages, a packhorse to deliver the money. I have to be centre stage.

So it has come to this. A decision based not on game theory, but on the logic of the gut. Leave it to the police or trust my instinct? Dixon had expressed it well. I was torn between two courses of action and no matter what I did I couldn't see what the future held. I have a gun. Yeah, big deal. And that turns me into Bruce Willis? I am sixteen years old, a high school student who excels at maths. Until this week, the height of my daring was planning to go to university in Sydney to study applied mathematics. I'm a kid, not a superhero. What did the careers counsellor say at school? *Always consider your skill sets.* Well, this is not my skill set. But I believed the kidnapper when he said if the police came, I wouldn't see Phoebe again. I *feel* that truth. So, in the end, I have to acknowledge a number of things. He *is* in control. This is the way he wants it to play out, so this is the most likely course of action to get my sister home safe. These are his rules, and game theory was never going to help.

But the gun is in the waistband of my jeans and I *will* use it. If necessary.

Dawn is gathering force. I glance at my watch. It's five-thirty; I have been walking for forty-five minutes. I have not passed another soul, though a few cars thread through the streets and force me to walk on the footpath. People starting their days. Just another day, another routine. Get to work, do the job, go home to wives, husbands, children. When I glance up, I see the sky lightening almost with every passing step. A few birds sing. One car passes with its window down, and a blast of song from the sound system washes over me. I notice the Doppler effect as it turns the corner and vanishes from my world. I take one step, then another.

I am not calm. I feel disengaged from everything around me, but also disengaged from myself. I'm defined by nothing but the taking of steps, one after another. This might be an advantage, this disassociation. But maybe it won't be. I retreat further into myself. I cannot feel the weight of money on my shoulders. I cannot feel the pressure of the gun against my back.

And then I see the site ahead of me. It's dark and full of shadows, despite the weak sun struggling over the horizon.

# CHAPTER 26

**The instructions were clear.**

*Approach the site from the south. There is a large perimeter fence about two metres high with barbed wire along the top. There is a pair of metal double gates and a faded notice that reads KEEP OUT about halfway along the fence. Go through the gates, which are not secured. Directly facing you are two buildings. The one on the right has a partly collapsed roof. Walk between the two buildings and into a clearing on the far side. To your right, about a hundred metres in the distance is something that looks like a water tower. It has no windows. Go into this tower. The door seems locked, but it isn't, though you might need to use force to open it since the frame is warped. Climb the stairs, which are directly opposite you. When you can go no further, you will find yourself in a large circular room with no fittings. I will meet you there. Even though there are no windows, part of the ceiling has fallen in and this will provide sufficient light to help you see. Be in that room, with the money, at eight a.m. Come alone.*

I have not come directly from the south, so I walk around the perimeter fence for about a kilometre until I recognise the double gates in the distance. It's almost like a film set, a post-apocalyptic landscape where the remainders of humanity light small fires against the chill of a nuclear winter. Parts of the fence sag outwards, a series of distended bellies. The ground is uniformly concrete, though tufts of grass have found purchase in cracks and potholes. In places the concrete has been pushed up by things growing below. It's easy to imagine how, in years to come, green will re-establish itself as structures decay. In time it will all disappear. In time it will all be green.

I walk away from the fence, fifty metres or so from the boundary but approaching a position directly opposite the central gates. The sign is there, but it has faded from what must have been bright red to a washed-out pink. The P in KEEP OUT has almost disappeared and the sign hangs at an angle. One gate is ajar about forty-five degrees, turned inwards. I can see the two buildings clearly, a couple of hundred metres past the fence and beyond another large expanse of cracked concrete. The structures have rows of metal window frames, three storeys high. Only a handful of the windows have glass as far as I can see, and each of those is broken. A factory of some kind. A place where people spent hour after hour operating machinery, churning out some product, before returning to their real worlds. Exchanging time – entire lives, perhaps – for far less money than I am carrying on my back. Now all that labour has vanished and the skeletons of the buildings are reminders of futility.

I squat down on my haunches and watch the site. I am under an old tree and I don't think anyone watching from those buildings would be able to see me easily. But of course I can't be sure.

The sun is still very low in the sky, and patches of shadows shift across the buildings' facades, giving the illusion of movement. A bright flash to my left makes me turn my head. I see nothing. Maybe it was a ray of sunlight brushing a fragment of broken glass. Another movement, to my right this time. But it's only a pigeon scrabbling for something on the ground. I see no signs of human life. But wherever I look, movement occurs in my peripheral vision. It's unnerving.

I close my eyes and try to order my thoughts. I have no idea what I should do next. I am two hours early for the appointment but that affords no advantage as far as I can tell. It had been my only choice, since I was anxious to get out of the house before my disappearance was noted. Now I go through possible scenarios, but none are valid. I will meet him in that water tower, I will hand over the money and hope he keeps his word. And if he doesn't, then I have the gun. The last resort. I pray it doesn't get to that.

At seven-thirty I get to my feet and walk towards the gate. I am feeling light-headed and the sun hurts my eyes. I pass the faded sign and stop just beyond the gate. The huge expanse of concrete must have been a car park at one time. The bays are marked out in faded yellow lines. I walk. The windows in the buildings before me seem to track my every step. The movements in my peripheral vision become more marked, but I try to ignore them and focus on the gap between the structures, a void draped in deep shadow. As I go further into the deserted site, the silence seems to gain substance and my calf muscles begin to cramp.

Between the buildings, it is cold and dark. There are no windows on the side of either building and the alleyway is rank with weeds and the smell of dog shit. I feel goosebumps on my arms. The feeling of being watched has increased and I can't tell whether it's that or the chill in the air that's making me shiver. I have this strong impression that someone will step out in front of me, at the end of the alley, and block my path. He will be large and dark – a silhouette against the backdrop of day – and all my fantasies involving guns and confrontations will dissolve in terror. But it doesn't happen. I step out into the pale sunshine and I am grateful. I glance behind me. There is no one there either. I shift the pack further up onto my back and take a couple of steps forward.

It's impossible to miss the tower. It's not a water tower – at least I don't think so. It's a bleak monolith, almost completely featureless, and made of brick. A central column stretches towards the sky and at the top, blossoms into a circular structure. It's like an attenuated mushroom. From its left-hand side a narrow metal walkway stretches across to a similar structure, though this one has no cap at its summit. Despite what the kidnapper told me, there are slits along the sides of both towers, almost like arrow notches in medieval castles.

I wonder why he chose this location for the meeting. If I had brought police then he could have been easily trapped up there. It might be possible to get across the walkway, but that leads simply to another tower, with no escape. In fact, the more I look, the more the walkway seems derelict. In a few places a rusted metal bar hangs, dangling into space. If he is in that tower, he is trapped. But instructing me to go to the tower doesn't mean *he* is there. Logic tells me he is somewhere else entirely, watching from some vantage point, ensuring I am alone, that I have fulfilled my part of the bargain. No. Neither the kidnapper nor Phoebe are there. But I am not in control. I have no option except to follow the directions and see where they lead.

So I walk towards the tower, conscious now of the hard pressure of the gun against the small of my back. I wonder if that is something noticeable through a pair of binoculars. Everywhere is quiet. Even the few birds have stopped singing. The door to the tower is made of solid wood, though years of exposure have buckled and stained it. I put a hand against its surface and push but nothing happens. I try my shoulder next and it gives slightly. I can't help thinking that this door has not been opened in some considerable time.

It takes three good shoulder charges before the door finally gives way. When it does, a hinge breaks and the door tilts drunkenly.

I step inside. The air has a stale taste with an underlying tinge of rot, as if something has died in here a long time ago and been reduced to bones and a faint aura of corruption. It is very dark, and the doorway admits little light. I stand for a moment or two to let my eyes adjust. Within a minute I can see well enough to determine that there is nothing within, except a spiral metal staircase on the far side of the circular room. Somewhere, something clanks and I freeze. The noise is not repeated, though I stand for a further three minutes. I glance at my watch. It is ten minutes to eight. I am six hundred seconds from my appointment. I can't imagine it will make much difference if I am a few seconds early. I move towards the staircase.

Even on the first footfall it creaks alarmingly. I sense it swaying, though that could be my imagination. The treads are thick with dust but I notice that in the centre there is a clear set of shoeprints, pointing upwards. Someone has been here, though I cannot tell in the darkness whether the prints are recent. I can't see a smaller shoeprint, the kind that might be made by a small child.

I take the stairs one at a time, stepping up with my left foot then bringing my right up next to it. Kids' steps. I feel the narrow metal guard rail with my left hand and slide my palm upwards as I climb. It's difficult to tell if any steps have rusted away. I climb blind and trust. It takes much longer than I thought, maybe because of my staccato rhythm, or possibly because I have misjudged the building's height. I turn and turn and it seems I will never reach the summit, that I'm doomed to climb forever in a bubble of despair and rising panic. Eventually, though, I see a glimmer of light above. I stop then and listen, but all I hear is the beating of my own heart. I turn one last bend and the room is ahead of me.

It is empty and just as described. Featureless walls, dimly lit by a couple of gaping holes in the roof. It takes less than a second to be certain I am alone. There is nowhere to hide. I gag, but manage not to vomit. I realise that I had been holding my breath, with every muscle and nerve tensed against a confrontation and a reconciliation. Seeing Phoebe. Seeing the monster who had taken her from us. Now, the emptiness sucks away hope.

My head drops, and that is when I see it. Writing in the dust.

*Leave. Turn right. Building facing you. We will be there.*

My first thoughts had been right. He would never come to an enclosed space. This rendezvous was a test to determine whether I had indeed come alone. A test I had passed.

I take the stairs down much faster than I did coming up. She is within a few hundred metres and time now is a burden, something to rush through until I see her face. I nearly stumble halfway down. My foot slips and I thump down a tread or two before catching my balance. I hear parts of the staircase, spots of rust probably, chink against metal as they fall. Then I am moving again.

The ground arrives sooner than I anticipated. I turn a bend and there in front of me is the door, a blaze of white light against the darkness. I move towards it, but I do not get there.

I am not aware of pain. All I know is that my legs suddenly give way and then, an instant later, there is a supernova in my head. Lights blaze and flash in brilliant arcs. They flood from a central point and for a moment bathe the world in glory, before reversing on themselves. Tracers fly back to the centre. I am aware of one bizarre thought – that this is how the universe came to be and how it will one day end – before the light implodes into darkness.

# CHAPTER 27

**I awake to pain.**

It's still dark, but that's because I don't dare open my eyes. The pain is a fire, not just in my head but flowing throughout my body. It bathes me in agony. I don't know who I am. Nor do I care, because the pain admits no rival for my attention. I think I am groaning, but perhaps not. The blackness returns and this time I welcome it, pray for it to endure.

It doesn't, but I sense that time has passed when I next come to. There is a strange ringing in my ears and now the pain has become localised. A crashing thumping at the back of my skull, so intense I involuntarily retch. But even that is infinitely better than the other pain I remember. At least I have some part of my mind that can consider alternative things. I am aware, though I keep my eyes closed. I know that I'm lying on my side and that the ground is cold and hard. There is something tied around my wrists and it's biting into my flesh. I wait for a few minutes and the pain eases, though not by much. I try to move my hands, but they're bound tightly. I listen. There is nothing but the pulse of blood in my ears. I make a conscious effort to open my eyes. The lids are sticky, gummed, and they make a faint ripping sound as they part.

There is very little light, and I'm grateful. I see a wall a metre or so in front of my face and it is familiar somehow, a thing I have seen, a feature imprinted on my memory. The pattern of bricks strikes a chord. And then it comes back. The wall in Phoebe's video. The wall that formed the backdrop to her message and the self-conscious parading of the local newspaper. She was here. But she is not here now. I do not have the energy to roll over, but I don't need to. I know I am alone. I can feel it in the air. So I close my eyes again. This time I sleep, rather than pass out. I sense my body needs this to recover, so I don't fight it. Everything else must wait.

'Jamie? Are you with me?'

The voice comes from a long way away, but it is insistent. I try to ignore it for as long as possible, but it won't leave me alone. Fragments of memory return and it's as if I'm piecing myself together, establishing a sense of who I am and what the immediate past has revealed. Phoebe. The kidnapper. The rendezvous. The money. The gun. And urgency overwhelms pain, which has subsided anyway to a lump of fire at the base of my skull.

I open my eyes. My vision is blurred. There is light now. I feel tears run down my cheeks and they must help because I find a focus. I'm aware that I am sitting at a table and that there is a man sitting opposite. It takes a few seconds for his features to stop swimming.

For one absurd moment I am filled with elation. I see the salt-and-pepper moustache, the heavy jowls, and hear the hiss of air between teeth. He raises a hand and takes a drag on his cigarette. In that moment I feel safe. And then it all crashes down.

'Dixon,' I say.

He nods and takes another drag.

'How are you feeling, Jamie?'

I don't bother answering.

'You,' I finally croak. My throat feels like it's lined with sand-paper.

'Yes.'

I close my eyes again. I would shake my head to clear it, but I can't risk the pain. I listen to him sucking his teeth. Part of me is filled with surprise and horror. Another part isn't.

'I've brought you some water,' he says. 'And a couple of pain-killers. I imagine you could do with them.'

'Where's Phoebe?' I ask.

'Safe. I promised I would do her no harm and I keep my word.'

I open my eyes. In front of me, on the table, is a glass of water and two white lozenges. The glass is beaded with condensation. I do not want to take anything from him, but my throat is parched and the pain in my skull is insistent. Dixon pushes the glass towards me and I'm forced to use both hands to lift it. A black cable tie binds my wrist. I take a long drink and the water is cool. I don't think I have ever tasted anything so beautiful. I replace the glass and pick up both capsules, raise them to my lips. Then I take the glass again and wash them down. It's probably psychosomatic, but the pain in my head eases almost immediately. I place the glass down carefully on the table. Already I am thinking it might be useful as a weapon, but almost as soon as the idea crosses my mind I discard it. This isn't game theory. It's Game Over.

'I want to see her,' I say.

'Of course you do,' says Dixon. 'And I'll bring her to you very soon. But first, we need to talk, you and me.'

'Are you going to kill us?' I say.

Dixon raises an eyebrow, lifts his cigarette to his lips, takes a final drag and crushes the butt into an ashtray.

'Why would I do that?'

'You knocked me out, back there in the industrial site,' I say. 'Why would you do that, if you were just going to let me go? What's the point, when I had the money and all that needed to be done was to exchange? You must have been sure by then that I had come alone. The violence was unnecessary.'

Dixon leans back in his chair and examines me. He strokes his moustache very slowly.

'You brought the violence on yourself, Jamie,' he says. 'Since when was it part of our deal that you come along to our little meeting armed?' He smiles and takes out my gun from beneath the table, places it next to his ashtray. 'I must admit, I wasn't expecting that. In fact, throughout our game you have been full of little surprises. But the gun changed things fundamentally. Do you want to know how all this was *supposed* to pan out?'

I nod and it isn't too painful.

'It was never my intention to bring Phoebe along to our rendezvous. I needed her as insurance, in case things went pear-shaped. What was supposed to happen was that you handed over the money. In return, I tied you up, possibly to that metal staircase. Then I would drive to where I have transport arranged to get out of Australia. Just before I left – maybe just *after* I left; planes aren't part of my escape strategy – I was going to ring the authorities, give them two locations where they would find Jamie and Phoebe Delaware, both of them unharmed. You know game theory, Jamie. Was that a sensible plan?'

I watch Dixon. He is enjoying himself. I suspect he always anticipated this meeting, where he lays out his strategies, shows me how thoroughly he out-thought and out-manoeuvred me. He still wants my applause, my congratulations on a game well played. Two players chatting about how the checkmate was inevitable from move thirty-one. An amicable analysis. This might be of use, but I can't think how.

'It makes sense,' I say.

He nods as if pleased by my acknowledgement.

'But you threw me a curve ball,' he continues. 'The gun. Dangerous things, guns. Unpredictable.'

He smiles.

'I followed you from the moment you left home, Jamie,' he says. 'I had already secured the meeting point. No one ever goes there, except for the occasional drug addict. And, of course, I knew that you hadn't told Gardner about our conversation. In this situation it's very useful to be a police officer. You have access to all sorts of information.'

'Like the green Commodore and the children's clothing?'

'Exactly.' He smiles. 'It was almost like cheating. But a game player must use every advantage at his disposal, wouldn't you agree? And the gossip in police investigations is quite shocking. All you need to do is keep your ears open in the station, maybe ask the occasional pertinent question. Of course, the media coverage helped as well.'

'So how exactly did you know that I hadn't told Gardner about our meeting? That's not something that would come out in gossip.'

Dixon taps the table impatiently.

'Think, Jamie.' His tone is one adopted by a teacher impatient at an obtuse student. 'Gardner had everything in place. Special Forces were on standby. All of the arrangements, all of the paper-work...all done. The only thing missing was the command to go. To deploy to the location. Therefore, he was still waiting to find out where. But you knew somewhere around four o'clock when you got the last phone call. It isn't difficult to work out.'

'You were with me when I got that call.'

Dixon grins, immensely pleased with himself.

'I know. It was probably unnecessary, but I couldn't resist. You rang me asking for a meeting. I recorded a phone call, one that didn't require much in the way of response from you, set a timer on my computer to make the connection and then turned up at the park on time. Instant alibi. Admit it, Jamie. That was clever, wasn't it?'

'How did you know I had a gun?' I say.

Dixon is disappointed I don't acknowledge his cleverness. He waves a hand dismissively. 'Tucked into the back of your pants. You've watched too many Hollywood movies, Jamie. For someone following a couple of hundred metres behind, it stuck out like a sore thumb. Where did you get it, by the way?'

'Spider,' I reply. I cannot think why I should keep this information to myself.

'Ah,' says Dixon. 'The connection to the underworld. Yes. I should have foreseen that. But frankly, Jamie, I didn't think you had the balls.'

'I want to see Phoebe.'

'Soon. Let's just talk, shall we? How is your head, by the way?'

'It's been better.'

'I can imagine. But that's what I mean when I say you brought this on yourself. I couldn't take the risk of getting into some kind of fight with someone armed. Not that I imagine you would know what to do with a gun.'

'I've never fired it,' I admit. 'Well, only with blanks.'

'Yes. Best avoided, really. But so many things could go wrong. Maybe you'd get lucky. Maybe you'd already planned to kill me, regardless of what happened. So while you were whiling away the time watching the building site, I took the opportunity to go up to the tower and write that message. Then I stayed downstairs and waited.'

He spreads his arms. *The rest we know.* The pounding in my head has eased considerably, but that doesn't mean my thought processes are organised. I'm not sure what advantage I can hope to gain by continuing to talk, but I see no reason not to. *The man's ego is huge*, I think. And maybe, by feeding it, he will let me see Phoebe sooner.

'So why bring me here?' I ask. *Wherever here is.* 'You knock me out, but the situation hasn't fundamentally altered. Why not tie me up, as in the original plan, and get the hell out?'

'It occurred to me,' admits Dixon. 'But I also thought it would be fun to chat. So I bundled you into the back of my car – *not* a green Commodore, as you know – and brought you here. At least, when I do ring, the authorities will have only one location to find both of you.'

I shift in my seat. It is the first acknowledgement that Phoebe is close by, but I don't want to react too strongly. I resent any gratification I might give him. And anyway, why should I accept anything he says as the truth? Maybe Phoebe isn't here. Maybe she's . . . I can't think about that. Instead I focus on my body. Now my head has improved I am aware of other aches and pains.

My right leg hurts. I notice also that my ankles are bound with another cable tie. I glance at my watch. It is one-thirty: I have lost about five hours. I think about Mum and Dad and Summerlee. I wonder about their reaction when they discovered I was missing. Gardner would work out what I had done, especially if he checked the pack in the front room and found a collection of maths textbooks and a ream of printing paper. He might not be Sherlock, but he wouldn't have to be. How would Mum and Dad react to the news that two of their three children were now missing? I can't afford to think about this. Too much pain lies that way and there is nothing I can do. Give Dixon what he wants and maybe the nightmare will end. And what Dixon wants is the exultation of victory. But only after we have examined every facet of his triumph and I have applauded him for his genius. Talking might end this, bring the curtain down on his masterpiece.

'And the reason you've joined the Dark Side?' I ask. I suspect he wants to explore motivations. 'You're a police officer. Aren't you sworn to stop people like you?'

When Dixon grins again I know it is the right question. He wants to deliver a sermon.

'Did you know I was involved in your sister's arrest?' he asks. 'When she trashed that hotel room? Oh, I don't mean I was an arresting officer, but I was in the station when she was brought in. And it was like some kind of epiphany. You know the meaning of the word?'

'An insight into the profound through the contemplation of

the ordinary,' I reply. We had covered this in English class.

'Exactly,' says Dixon. 'And there was nothing more ordinary than Summerlee Delaware. A silly, stupid eighteen year old, pissed and stoned. The kind we put into the drunk tank every Friday and Saturday. Our bread and butter, really. Except, of course, this useless teenager was also a multi-millionaire. Seven and a half million dollars in the bank. Come on, Jamie. It must have occurred to you how unfair it was.'

'And that's your epiphany?' I ask. 'Someone gets lucky and you take it as a personal affront?'

Dixon's eyes narrow and he taps his fingers on the table. Then he takes out another cigarette from his pack and lights it.

'I've worked hard all my life,' he says. 'Protecting people like your sister from all the nastiness of the world. And she treats me like shit. And what has she done? Nothing, apart from having the good fortune to choose six numbers that came up in the lottery. At eighteen, she has her future assured, whereas I couldn't retire if I wanted to.'

'Yeah, well,' I reply. 'Nobody said life's fair. Most of us get over it.'

'I decided I didn't *want* to get over it,' says Dixon. 'So I also decided to do something. Redistribute the good fortune.'

'You're a regular fucking Robin Hood,' I say. I'm not sure if it's wise to antagonise him but I'm also not sure if I care anymore.

Dixon just smiles.

'You must be hungry, Jamie,' he says. 'How about I make you

a sandwich and we can continue this conversation? I'm having a good time.'

'I don't want a sandwich,' I say. 'I want Phoebe.'

But he doesn't pay any attention. He pushes back his chair and stands, tucks my gun into his waistband.

'Cheese and tomato?' he says. I don't answer. He shrugs and goes to the door off to my right. 'Back soon,' he says, and leaves.

I take the opportunity to look around. The room is bare apart from the table and chairs and a light bulb dangling from the ceiling. It's like something out of a movie – a bare room where suspects are interrogated. The only thing missing is the two-way mirror. I stand and attempt to shuffle a few steps. The cable tie around my ankle is tight and I almost fall. The only way I could move is by making short jumps. I know I will fall if I try, so I stand for a minute or two. The pain in my legs abates somewhat.

In the end I sit down again and wait.

# CHAPTER 28

When Dixon returns he is carrying the backpack, slung over his left shoulder. In his right hand is a plate of sandwiches. He drops the pack on the floor and places the plate on the table in front of me. I ignore it.

He opens the bag and takes out a block of green notes, puts it next to the plate. I ignore that as well. Then he takes his seat again.

'Do you know what surprised me, Jamie?' I decide this is a rhetorical question. He picks up the slab of cash and flicks through it. 'The counting of the money. And just how much fun it is. An appalling cliché, I know. Sitting there, counting up the blocks. Then counting all the notes in each block. Checking that the hundred dollar bills were all present and accounted for, that no one had substituted blank paper in the centres. Ensuring that the whole lot added up to two million. Which it does, by the way. God, I had fun.'

'I'm pleased for you,' I say. 'Now bring me Phoebe.'

'Be patient.'

'No,' I say. 'I can't be patient. I do not want to sit here replaying your brilliance. If you want my admiration you are welcome to it. You were amazing, Dixon. Well played. You outclassed me, okay? I was a beginner and you were the pro. You kicked my butt. You destroyed me. I give up. Now bring me Phoebe.'

Dixon picks up a sandwich and takes a bite. He chews for a moment and then grimaces, puts the rest back on the plate, wipes his mouth with the back of a hand.

'Probably wise of you not to eat,' he says. 'I'm not much good in the kitchen. Even a cheese and tomato sandwich is beyond me, it seems. The bread is stale. The cheese is processed. Like plastic. Even the tomatoes are tasteless.'

I close my eyes.

'I'll get your sister for you,' he says quietly and I open my eyes again, wondering if I've heard right. 'I know what you're thinking. That maybe she's dead and I *can't* bring her to you. But I told you, Jamie. She's fine. I just thought we might have a little chat without her, but maybe that's unfair. I understand. I'll get her.' He stands and leaves.

Suddenly my heart is racing. Now that the moment is almost here it's unbearable. Maybe unbelievable. Dixon was right. The thought that perhaps Phoebe isn't in this building, that possibly she is stiff and cold in some dark place, has never left my mind. It wriggles there still, like a pale maggot. I stare at the door, which he has left open. I long for that blank space to be filled with her. My mouth is dry and a bead of sweat drips into my right eye, blurring my vision for a moment.

When it clears, Phoebe is standing there. Dixon is behind her and has one hand on her shoulder.

She stands like a maths equation, perfect and indisputably true.

Something rises in my throat and I gag on it. And then everything blurs. I make no sound as I weep, but my body is trembling. I tilt my head and wipe my eyes on my shoulder. I resent anything hindering my vision. When I'm able to see again, she is still there, still true.

Phoebe runs to me and buries her face in my neck. I try to put my arms around her, but my hands are tied so I can't. She mumbles something into my ear. I think it is my name, repeated over and over. I feel her tears, damp on my skin. We stay like that for a long time, Phoebe clinging to me, arms wrapped tightly. I luxuriate in her warmth. Eventually, she moves her head away, plants a kiss on my cheek, hugs me again.

'I keep my word,' says Dixon, but I don't pay him any attention. 'Phoebe, love, come over here, there's a good girl. I know you've missed your brother but he and I need to chat for just a little while longer and then this will all be over. You'll go home to Mum and Dad and your sister and everything will return to normal. I promised you that and like I've said, I keep my word. So come and sit with your uncle Dixon.'

Phoebe immediately breaks contact with me and goes over to Dixon's side of the table. He has placed a chair next to his and she sits. Phoebe glances up at Dixon and gives him a small smile. Tears still run down her cheeks, but she smiles. I hated him before. I hate him even more now. He will *not* take a part of my sister with him, not even the smallest part of her mind or her affections. I will not lose any more of her. Not to him. Not to anyone. Dixon smiles back, pats her on the head. My hands tense.

'I tell you, Jamie,' he says. 'I've met a few kids in my time but none to match your sister here. I never had children myself, and that was a source of regret, you know? The job took up too much of my time, physically and emotionally. Cost me my marriage.'

'Are you asking for my sympathy?' I ask.

Dixon waves a hand dismissively. 'Of course not,' he says. 'But I suppose I want your understanding. I am not a bad guy, Jamie. Seriously, I'm not.'

I don't say anything. It's still too dangerous. But I'm stunned by the man's arrogance. He kidnapped my sister, put all of us through the worst kind of hell and he wants my understanding? For the first time, I think he might be mad. Clever, but mad. I have to be careful.

'Tell him, Phoebe,' he says. 'Tell your brother how you've been treated while you've been my guest.'

'It's been fun, Uncle Dixon,' says Phoebe. Her eyes are all round with sincerity. I notice she is still wearing that appalling dress, the green smock with the bright bow. She swings her legs to and fro in front of the chair. Her shoes are different as well. They are shiny and have big buckles. Her hair is scraped back into a ponytail. I have never seen her wear a ponytail before. Phoebe meets my eyes. 'Uncle Dixon lets me cook sometimes, Jamie. I've done spaghetti bolognese and I've put chips into the oven and everything.' There's something different about her voice as well. It's sing-songy and slightly too high in pitch. I feel as if my real sister is somewhere else and this girl is playing her part, an understudy only.

Dixon laughs.

'She's a much better cook than I am,' he says. 'Though that's not saying a lot. No, Phoebe has been a marvel. She's cooked and she's cleaned and dusted.'

The sense of unreality grows. Phoebe doesn't clean and dust. She doesn't cook. I don't say anything.

'And Uncle Dixon tells me stories at bedtimes,' Phoebe says breathlessly. 'Really, really good stories. About Red Riding Hood and Goldilocks and the Three Bears. And he tells them brilliantly.' She is staring earnestly at me and I can't help but think she's trying to tell me something, but that I'm too stupid to understand. Phoebe outgrew those fairy stories years ago.

'She's a credit to your family,' says Dixon. 'She really is.'

'Can I make myself a mug of Milo, Uncle Dixon?' says Phoebe. 'Can I, please? Pretty please?'

He pats her on the head. I wonder how many times we will have to wash her hair before the taint is gone.

'Of course, Phoebe,' he says. 'And help yourself to a biscuit. Be careful with that kettle, though.'

'I will, Uncle Dixon,' she replies. 'Thank you sooo much.'

'And then you should pack up your things. Your brother and I are nearly done here and then it will be time to go home. You'll like that, won't you, Phoebe?'

'Yeees,' she says, her mouth drawn down. 'But I will see you again, won't I, Uncle Dixon?'

'Maybe, Phoebe,' he replies. 'Whatever happens, I will write to you. That's a promise.'

'Back soon, Jamie,' says Phoebe, and she *skips* through the door. I watch her go and wonder if the blow to the back of my head has done more damage than I thought. Dixon sighs.

'I'll miss that kid,' he says. 'Still, with two million dollars, I should be able to set myself up nicely. There are plenty of countries where two million will keep you in considerable luxury for the rest of your days. Who knows? Maybe I'll meet some nice woman, have kids of my own. They say it's never too late.'

I don't say anything.

'Nearly time to go, Jamie,' says Dixon. 'I *will* keep my word. It will take me a couple of hours to get to where I need to be. Then I'll ring Gardner personally, tell him how to get here and release the two of you. There's no point shouting, by the way, once I'm gone, though feel free if you want. This place is very isolated. Belongs to a guy I put behind bars, actually. He used it to make crystal meth and you need isolation so no one picks up on the chemical fumes. Anyway, Gardner should get here within three hours.' Dixon glances at his watch. 'Another hour back to yours. You should be home by, oh, six-thirty at the latest. And then I really hope you can put all this behind you and get on with your lives. You're decent folks. Pity about your other sister, mind.'

I don't say anything.

'I've enjoyed our games, Jamie,' he says. 'You should know that. And thanks for the lesson on game theory. I'd never heard of it until you told me. All that stuff about being busy when I first rang – well, then it fell into place. A tactic to throw me off. Hats off to *you*, kid. It worked. I thought, *what the hell does he mean, "I'm too busy"?* That was good. Not good enough, of course. But then you had no way of knowing that you were confiding in the wrong person. Hey, Phoebe.'

My sister is back, a mug in her hand. She has a chocolate biscuit in her mouth and there are smudges around her lips. She sits next to Dixon, swings her legs again.

'No problem with the kettle then?' he asks.

'I used the microwave, Uncle Dixon,' she says. 'It heats things up much more than a kettle. In fact, it gets water up to way past boiling point if you leave it on long enough. We learned that at school.'

A flash of confusion runs across Dixon's face but it doesn't stay there long. Phoebe swivels in her chair and flings the contents of her mug into his face. It takes a second or two before he screams.

# CHAPTER 29

I'm too stunned to react. Seconds seem to slow. Dixon gets up from his chair and claws at his face. The scream, abrupt and high-pitched to start with, modulates into a low keening. He staggers to the side, drops a hand, reaches behind his back, fumbles for something. My mind processes the information sluggishly. Phoebe is shouting but I can't make out the words. I realise I am standing, though I can't remember moving. Dixon's hand fastens on something. The polished butt of the gun. *My* gun. He starts to pull it free of his waistband. For a brief moment, I remember his habit of hitching his trousers and it all seems so absurd, a farce. Then time starts to move properly again and I know I have to act.

I try to move but forget my feet are bound and lurch into the table. It crashes over onto Dixon's chair on the other side, but I remain standing. I see his hand withdrawing from his belt, the gun's barrel snaking out. I hop. Even now, I am aware of how fantastical this is. He is seconds from pointing a gun at me and

I'm doing an impersonation of a fucking kangaroo. It's likely that I won't get to him before he starts firing. True, with boiling liquid in his face it's doubtful he will be able to aim, but it's a small room and the odds are good he will hit one of us. Why did Phoebe do that? We were moments from being left alone. Why?

It takes three hops to get to him, and by some miracle, I do not fall. But I am on the point of falling when I hit him, so my head is lowered and I crash into his chest. Despite his large gut, the point of contact is bony and I feel a surge of pain run through my skull. We smash into the wall and slide to the floor. I notice that his grip on the gun has not been shaken. I try to get my hands on the weapon, but the cable ties dig into my flesh and my arms are wedged somewhere between our two bodies. Dixon is grunting, his face centimetres from mine. I see that his skin is inflamed and already starting to blister. But, despite his injuries, he is strong, and I only have my body weight to keep him pinned. It will not be enough.

I arch back and then head-butt him with all the force I can muster. I read somewhere that you should aim for the bridge of the nose with your forehead. But we are thrashing around and I can't be accurate so I go for brute force. Something cracks and I have to fight hard not to vomit or pass out from the pain. When I open my eyes it's difficult to focus but I see a wreck where Dixon's nose used to be. It is bent to the side and blood covers his mouth and cheeks. His eyes flutter back in their sockets and his strength, for the moment at least, has gone. He lies beneath me, inert. I struggle to move my head to one side and when I shout it sounds strange and tinny in my ears.

'Phoebe, get the gun. Be careful.'

She moves into my field of vision and I watch as she bends Dixon's fingers back, prises the gun from his hand.

'Now get me loose,' I say. 'Smash the glass that was on the table. Cut these ties.'

She doesn't say anything but I see her move. I desperately want to close my eyes and rest but already Dixon is starting to struggle again. There is a sound of smashing. 'Be careful,' I call out, but there is no reply. Then I see her, a shard of broken glass in her fingers, and she is trying to get my hands out from between our bodies.

'Do my feet first,' I say, and she disappears from sight. I hear a scraping sound and suddenly my feet are free. I kneel up on Dixon's chest, one knee across his throat, and hold my hands out to Phoebe. 'Quickly,' I say. She saws at the tie, but it's fastened very tightly and there is little room to work. I feel a sharp pain in my wrist and blood blossoms. Phoebe stops.

'Don't worry,' I say. 'Keep going.'

She obeys, her face twisted in concentration. More blood is spilled but so much of me is hurting that I barely notice. And then my hands are free. I can hardly work my fingers because they're so numb. Dixon is moving.

'Give me the gun, Phoebe,' I say, and she presses it into my hand. I almost drop it. The safety, I notice, is off. I get to my feet and my legs only just support me. I step back a couple of metres and watch Dixon twitch, one hand pushing against the floor as he tries to lift himself into a sitting position. I hold the gun in both hands and aim the barrel at his chest. I remember all the times I'd vowed I would kill the guy who had taken Phoebe. That I could empty the chamber then reload and do it all again. But I don't feel like that now. His face is a mess, red and ruined. But I also know he is not finished, and that if he is able to get to his feet, somehow get the gun back, then this time there would be no hope of salvation, no chance to wait for the cavalry to arrive. This time he would kill us.

So I shoot him in the foot.

I *try* to shoot him in the foot, but my aim is not good and I smash up his ankle instead. It dissolves into a mass of blood and bone splinters and the sound makes my head throb so much I can barely see. I think I hear Phoebe scream. Or it might have been Dixon.

'I need something to tie him up with, Phoebe,' I say. 'Can you find anything?'

I see her leave the room out of the corner of my eye, but I don't let my gaze move from Dixon. He's not struggling anymore. He is slumped and seems unconscious, but I can't trust my eyes. I have the feeling that if I was to stop concentrating, if I was to flick my gaze away for even an instant, he would rise up from the ground and have his hands around my throat, like in some bad thriller. So I watch and wait for Phoebe to return.

She comes back with a pack of cable ties. The pack has already been opened, presumably for my feet and wrists. I take a couple and move carefully over to Dixon's body. I put out a foot and nudge him, but he doesn't respond. I back away until I'm at Phoebe's side.

'I want you to take the gun, Phoebe,' I say. 'Hold it in both hands and move around to the side. Keep it aimed at his legs. I'm going to turn him over so I can tie up his hands behind his back. If he so much as moves, I want you to press the trigger, okay? Don't think, just fire. Can you do that?'

She nods, but her eyes are wide. I position the gun in her hands, which actually shake less than mine did. Then I squat beside Dixon's body and push him over. For a moment his arms get caught and I have to manhandle him to get both hands behind his back, but I manage. I use two ties and ratchet them as tight as I can.

'He has house keys in his pocket,' says Phoebe. It's the first time she's spoken since this began. 'We need them to get out.'

I put my hand into Dixon's trouser pocket, find the keys and pull them out. He doesn't move and I step back. Sweat drips from my forehead. I think about binding his feet but his shattered ankle makes it unnecessary. I take the gun from Phoebe's hand. For the first time I feel the beginnings of relaxation.

'Let's get out of here,' says Phoebe. 'Now, Jamie. Please. Before he wakes up.'

I nod, but I don't move my eyes away from Dixon's body.

Phoebe takes the keys from me and I pick up the backpack. We leave the room and I close the door. Phoebe locks it. And then, suddenly, we are running up stairs, through another door, down a brown, dank corridor and out into sunshine. It's like a blow between my eyes and I stop for a moment, blinking. There is nothing in front of me except trees and an over-arching sky. Phoebe grabs my arm.

'C'mon, Jamie,' she says. 'Let's go.'

I hitch the pack over my shoulder and we run away from the house. I turn back. The place is old, almost ruined. Some windows are missing and those that remain are cracked. Phoebe and I step out through a broken gate and onto a rutted track. It leads in one direction only. We walk. Only later do I realise that Dixon's car must be somewhere. But I don't see it and even if I had there's no way I'd go back into the shack to find car keys.

**We walk in silence for half an hour before we come out onto a small bitumen road.** It's extremely narrow and it seems unlikely we will encounter any traffic. There are no signs telling us whether we should turn right or left. Phoebe turns left and I follow. Up to this moment, I have not trusted myself to speak. And no words seem adequate for the situation, anyway. But the longer we say nothing the more unnerving I find it.

'We made it, Phoebe,' I say, as if to prove the inadequacy of words.

'Yes,' she says. She doesn't look at me.

'Why did you do that?' I splutter. I don't want recriminations, but I can't help myself. 'Don't get me wrong, Phoebe. You were brilliant back there. But why do that with the drink when he was about to leave? Was it to protect Summer's money? Because if it was, that was dumb and you know it.'

Phoebe says nothing for a few seconds. Then she stops and faces me.

'He was going to kill us, Jamie,' she says.

'How do you know that?' I reply. 'He said he was going to leave us while he got away. If he intended to kill us, why wait? He had you for days and he could have killed me easily back at the place where we met. He had the money, after all. No. I believed him.'

Phoebe looks at me for a moment and then starts walking again. I skip to catch up with her.

'Hold my hand,' I say.

'Not now,' she says.

I wonder if either of us will recover from this. We walk in silence for a couple more minutes. When Phoebe speaks again, she does so without looking at me, almost as if she's talking to herself.

'I spent days with him,' she says. 'And he was crazy. I know he was. You can't spend that amount of time with someone and not find that out. He wanted to be liked. No. He wanted to be *loved*, and admired. That's why he kept us alive, so we could be his audience, so he could keep playing games with you. But he was going to kill us. It was all a fairy story, Jamie. Leaving the country so we could go on with our lives and he would be safe overseas? Why leave if no one could identify him? And if he got rid of us, then he'd have nothing to worry about.'

I don't say anything. I wonder what happened to my sister. She is someone else now. She has grown up and it is reflected in the way she speaks. She is seven, going on thirty. I find this sad. I think also about what she has just said. It makes sense, but it's still only guesswork. How can a seven year old be so cynical?

'He bought two cans of petrol,' she says. 'Brought them into the house and put them in the front room. I saw them. I don't think he was planning on driving somewhere where there are no petrol stations. So what was he going to use them for?'

She isn't expecting an answer and I don't give one. I think about a house way out in the middle of nowhere. I think of petrol splashed around the place, a glowing cigarette end thrown onto the porch and the whoosh of flame, the house erupting. I think of the time it will take for anyone to even notice the fire, let alone get a fire engine out there. And when it does there would be nothing left except a pile of smouldering ash and, maybe, somewhere deep down in the cellar, a jumble of charred bones. It's warm with the sun on my back, but I shiver. I reach out my hand and this time Phoebe takes it.

'How did you survive, Phoebe?' I ask.

'Game theory,' she says. 'Think about what the other person wants and then use that to your advantage. Dixon wanted me to love him, so I did. Dixon wanted me to be a cute little girl, so

**311**

I was. Did you really think I would have chosen that dress, Jamie? He gave me choices, so I picked the one he wanted me to pick. And I was sweet and loving and I asked for fairy stories and he believed me. He trusted me. I think that was the only mistake he made.'

I keep walking and thinking. All this time I believed I was on a mission to save my little sister's life and all the time she was saving mine. And I think about loss of innocence and I wonder if I will ever get the old Phoebe back. But these are things to consider at another time.

For the moment I am happy to walk towards home, with the sunshine on my back and the weight of my sister's hand in mine.

# ABOUT THE AUTHOR

Barry Jonsberg's YA novels, *The Whole Business with Kiffo and the Pitbull* and *It's Not All About YOU, Calma!* were shortlisted for the CBCA awards. *It's Not All About YOU, Calma!* also won the Adelaide Festival Award for Children's Literature and *Dreamrider* was shortlisted in the NSW Premier's Awards. *Being Here* won the Queensland Premier's YA Book Award and was shortlisted for the Prime Minister's Award. *My Life as an Alphabet* won the Gold Inky, the Children's Peace Literature Award, the Territory Read, Children's Literature/YA Award and the Victorian Premier's Literary Award, and was shortlisted in the Prime Minister's Literary Awards, the CBCA awards, the West Australian Premier's Book Awards and the Adelaide Festival Awards.

Barry lives in Darwin. His books have been published in the USA, the UK, France, Poland, Germany, Hungary, Brazil, Turkey, China and Korea.